NIGHT MOVES

JULIE MULHERN

J & M PRESS

❀ Created with Vellum

For Matt

ACKNOWLEDGMENTS

Gretchen, Rachel, Sally, how could I do this without you? A million thanks.

Judy O., thank you for your eagle eye! You get a million thanks as well.

And a million more thanks to everyone who takes time to read Ellison's adventures. I am so grateful to you.

CHAPTER ONE

May 1975
Kansas City, Missouri

Aggie opened the back door and took the shopping bags (three of them—Harzfeld's, Swanson's, Woolf Brothers') from my right hand. "Busy morning?"

"Grace needed new shorts." Admittedly, one pair of new shorts hadn't required stops at five stores on the Country Club Plaza, but I wanted to be thorough. "And there are some darling things in for summer." So many and so darling that I still held four shopping bags in my left hand. I stepped over the dogs, Max and Pansy, and hefted the bags onto the kitchen island.

"Anarchy called a few minutes ago."

I glanced at my ring finger and felt my lips curl into a smile. Not yet accustomed to the weight of Anarchy's engagement diamond, I swiveled my hand and admired the sparkle. "Oh?"

"He cancelled lunch. He caught a body." My fiancé was a homicide detective, and Aggie, my housekeeper, had taken to using the lingo from her favorite shows (*Columbo*, *Adam-12*, *Hawaii Five-O*, *The Streets of San Francisco*, *Kojak*, and *Baretta*) to describe his work.

Anarchy investigating a murder where I hadn't stumbled over the victim made for a nice change. I had an unfortunate habit of finding bodies. Not entirely unfortunate. Finding a body was what brought Anarchy and me together. "That's too bad." Some poor soul lost their life; I could hardly complain about a missed lunch.

"If you'd like to eat here, we have chicken salad, roast beef for sandwiches, and there's quiche if you don't mind waiting while I warm it up."

"Chicken salad sounds delicious. With some fruit?"

"We have strawberries, grapes, and cantaloupe." Aggie gave the kitchen island, which I'd covered with shopping bags, a pointed look.

I got the hint. "I'll take these bags upstairs and give you room to work."

"Should I make coffee?"

I blew a tiny kiss at Mr. Coffee (he would never, ever cancel lunch plans). "No, thank you." Mr. Coffee would forgive me. "Tab with lime."

"Give me ten minutes."

Max, the Weimaraner with plans for world domination, lifted his head. Follow me or see if Aggie dropped any chicken? The choice was easy. Chicken. If Max stayed, so did Pansy. The latest addition to our family, a gorgeous, ill-mannered retriever, followed Max's lead in most things (when she didn't, things went badly).

I climbed the stairs alone, emptied the shopping bags on my bed, and divvied up the clothes between me (a wrap dress, a shift dress, blouses, and a pair of white kilties with hot pink trim), Grace (t-shirts, shorts, and new Dr. Scholl's sandals), and

Aggie (I'd spotted a light blue kaftan dotted with red geraniums that was just her style).

Brnng, brnng.

I picked up the phone. "Russell residence."

"Ellison? It's Jinx." Jinx was a dear friend and a wellspring of usually correct gossip. "Have you heard?"

I wedged the receiver between my ear and shoulder and held up a new blouse. "Heard what?"

"Clayton Morris dropped dead."

"Heart attack?"

"No one knows…" Jinx fell silent.

The silence had weight, and I pictured Jinx rubbing her hands together. I sat on the bed's edge, suddenly worried the weight was about to crush me.

"Anarchy's investigating."

"Was Clayton murdered?"

"They're not saying." They. The police. Anarchy. No wonder Jinx called me.

"Start over," I demanded. "What happened?"

"Clayton collapsed around ten o'clock this morning. They called an ambulance, but he died before he reached the hospital."

"Who is they?"

"How would I know? Someone at the office."

"Poor Karen. Are they sure it's murder?" If Anarchy was there, chances were good.

"Suspicious death," Jinx replied. "Last I heard, Anarchy and his partner were interviewing everyone at the company." Clayton worked as the Chief Financial Officer for Patriot Produce, a regional distributor of fruits and vegetables. "Have you talked to him?"

"He left a message with Aggie and cancelled our lunch date."

"Now you know why. It has to be murder."

I wrapped my fingers around the receiver and straightened

my neck. "Can you imagine Clayton making anyone mad enough to kill him? It must be a heart attack."

"I don't know," Jinx replied. "Remember when he audited Karen's market account?"

"I forgot about that." Like many of my married friends, Karen regularly wrote a check for a few dollars more than her grocery bill and pocketed the cash. Five dollars here. Ten dollars there. Mad money to be spent without explanations to nosy husbands. For a woman without a job or income of her own, those dollars felt like independence.

"Clayton worried she was overpaying for produce."

"I guess he'd know."

"The man was tight as a tick. Apparently there's produce the stores and restaurants won't take. Bruised apples. Wilted lettuce. Spotted bananas. He used to bring it home."

"Why did he stop?"

"Hubb started giving it to soup kitchens." Hubb Langford was the company president. "I think Karen was more grateful for the new policy than the soup kitchens. That reminds me, Mel Langford is subbing for Daisy at bridge tomorrow." Aha! Mel was Jinx's source.

"I'll ask Aggie to make a Bundt cake."

"For Karen? When will you take it?"

"Either tonight or tomorrow after cards."

"I need time to bake a ham. If you go tomorrow, I'll go with you."

Far better to suffer through a visit with company. "It's a date."

"If you hear anything about Clayton before I see you, call me."

I made a noncommittal sound in my throat.

"I mean it, Ellison. What's the point of marrying a homicide detective if you can't get the inside skinny?"

Getting the skinny and sharing the skinny were very different. "Talk soon."

"Wait!"

"What?"

"Your new neighbor. Have you heard anything?"

"A divorced man from Houston. He moves in tomorrow. Thanks for reminding me. I'll ask Aggie for two Bundt cakes."

"How old is he? Does he have children? Why Kansas City?"

"Good questions. I don't have the answers."

"Find out."

"Will do." Won't do. I dropped the receiver in the cradle, then hung up my new clothes.

As I walked down the stairs, the front door opened. My hand tightened on the railing as Mother blew into my house with the force of a March gale. Her hair was a perfect silver helmet. The pearls at her neck were the size of marbles. The handbag hooked over her elbow was crocodile.

She looked up at me—her steely gaze taking in my simple dress and flats, my hair pulled into a low ponytail, and my barely there makeup—and pursed her precisely painted lips. "What are you doing?"

I descended the last few steps. "Aggie fixed lunch. Would you like to join me?"

She waved aside my offer. "We need to talk."

I walked toward the kitchen. "About?"

She followed me. "You know good and well."

"We've already discussed this, Mother." She'd made her feelings abundantly clear. While she ceded that Anarchy wasn't the opportunist she'd feared, she didn't approve of her daughter marrying a cop.

"You're making a mistake."

"Think of us as *McMillan & Wife*."

"Anarchy's a cop, not a commissioner."

"True." Also true? Anarchy was better looking than Rock Hudson. I stepped into the kitchen.

Aggie wiped her hands on a tea towel. "Good afternoon, Mrs. Walford. May I fix you a plate?"

"No thank you, Aggie. I won't be staying."

Thank God for small miracles. I sat down at the kitchen island and picked up a fork. "This looks wonderful."

"No grapes." Aggie knew well my extreme dislike of grapes in chicken salad.

I took a bite. "Delicious."

"Aggie, please excuse us?" Mother wouldn't discuss my impending disastrous marriage in front of the help.

My housekeeper offered me an apologetic shrug and abandoned ship.

"Ellison, you're not taking this seriously."

I glanced at the ring on my left hand. "I am."

"What about Grace?"

"Grace adores Anarchy."

"And a few years from now, when she's presented to society? How will she feel about a cop standing next to her on the dais while she curtsies?"

"Only you would think of that."

"Someone has to."

Max stood and rubbed his face against my leg. He'd like some chicken, please. Now, please.

"Anarchy and I are getting married. End of story. Nothing you say will change my mind."

"If you were as head over heels as you claim, you'd have picked a date."

"I'm waiting till Henry's been gone a year."

"That's just an excuse."

"It's not." My first husband died—was murdered—eleven months ago. Out of respect for his role as Grace's father, I'd wait a year before making solid plans to replace him. I took another bite. "This really is delicious. Are you sure you won't have some?"

"Positive." Mother scowled at Pansy. "Your collection of oddities is unseemly."

I speared a strawberry. "Anarchy is not an oddity."

"He's a senator's grandson. He went to Stanford. He could do anything. Be anything. And he works as a cop."

"Some might find that admirable."

Mother's lips pinched.

Woof! Pansy didn't like Mother's expression.

"That dog—" she avoided looking into Pansy's liquid brown eyes "—is a menace."

I didn't argue. Not when she was right. I speared another strawberry. With force.

"Ellison." Mother's voice turned cajoling. "I want more for you than missed dinners, cancelled plans, lonely holidays, and nights spent wondering if your husband is safe."

Now was not the time to admit Anarchy broke our lunch date.

"Mark my words." Mother tapped on the island for emphasis. "This won't end well. I can only hope that when it comes crashing down, you'll still be young and attractive enough to attract a decent man."

"I appreciate your optimism, but stop."

Her brows lifted.

"Stop." I pushed off the stool. "Not another word about Anarchy, my marriage, or my dog."

She opened her mouth.

"I mean it, Mother. You want to be a part of my life, a part of Grace's life, you'll keep your opinions to yourself."

She huffed, turned on her heel, and marched out of the kitchen. No surprise. We'd had similar mutually unsatisfactory conversations every day for the past week. She'd be back tomorrow with a new argument.

I SAT at the kitchen island and sipped wine.

Aggie stirred a pot on the stove. "Thirty minutes till dinner."

"May I help?"

"No," she replied with insulting alacrity. Aggie's low opinion of my cooking skills was no secret. I was allowed to wash produce—and even then she checked my work.

The offer made, I took a larger sip of wine. "What are we having?"

"Roast pork loin, Brussel sprouts, and parmesan risotto." She adjusted the flame beneath the pot. "Will Anarchy be here?"

I swirled the wine in my glass. "I haven't heard from him."

"We have plenty."

Max's ears perked. Leftovers?

Ding, dong.

"I bet that's him." Aggie's encouraging smile told me I'd been moping. "I can't leave the stove."

I rose from the stool, and my stomach fluttered. Would Anarchy one day become old hat or did I have a lifetime of flutters ahead of me? I hurried to the front door.

Anarchy waited on the stoop. He grinned at me, and the flutter in my tummy spread through my limbs. I suspected he had that effect on most women. Tall. Lean. Warm coffee-brown eyes. And a smile that could melt a glacier.

"Hi," I croaked.

"Hi." He stepped forward and kissed me.

My across-the-street neighbor, Marian Dixon, was probably already dialing Mother to report our public display of affection. With our lips still fused together, I found Anarchy's hand, pulled him into the house, and closed the door.

The kiss deepened. Long, perfect seconds passed.

"Sorry about lunch," Anarchy murmured against my lips. "I missed you."

"Missed you too." I missed his lips on mine. "Can you join us for dinner?"

"If it's no trouble."

"No trouble. I'll tell Aggie to set another place." I nodded to the living room. "Help yourself to a drink."

I dashed into the kitchen, and my face cracked with an enormous smile. "He's here for dinner."

Aggie nodded, and I grabbed my wine glass.

When I entered the living room, Anarchy sat on the loveseat with his long legs stretched toward the cold fireplace. An old-fashioned glass with a finger of brown liquor rested in his hands.

I sat next to him and stole a quick bourbon-flavored kiss. "You're investigating Clayton Morris's death."

He chuckled. "Word gets around."

"It does."

"How well did you know him?"

"I know his wife. Karen is..." How to explain? "There are regular bake sales at Grace's school."

"Oh?"

I shuddered. "I sent store-bought cookies, and the PTA president called me. According to her, a bake sale meant actual baking."

He sipped his bourbon, trusting I'd get to the point eventually.

"I'm not much of a baker." I accepted the blame when Andy Clifford broke a tooth on one of my sugar cookies. Although I still maintained the Cliffords had weak teeth. "For years, Karen baked for me." Rice Krispies treats, Rocky Road fudge, cupcakes, brownies—I'd lost count of how many times she baked extra batches for Grace to take. Karen might have considered her baking for me as a public service, but I'd be forever grateful. "Now, if there's a bake sale, Aggie makes her chocolate chip cookies." According to Grace, Aggie's cookies were always an early sell-out.

"You like Karen Morris."

"I do."

"And Clayton?"

I waggled my hand. "Not so much. We chatted once or twice at parties. Clayton had no interest in women's opinions on current events. He didn't like art. And he was completely ignorant about his children's lives. It didn't leave us much to talk about." I'd met garden slugs with more personality.

Anarchy sipped his bourbon. "Anything else?

"He kept a close watch on his money."

Anarchy's eyes glinted. "He was cheap?"

"Not exactly." How to explain? "Every penny spent—he needed to know where it went. He didn't care if Karen spent fifty dollars on a dress or two hundred, as long as she showed him the receipt. He checked her grocery bills."

"I bet that got annoying."

"They recently added onto their house. I'm sure Clayton drove the contractor crazy." My late husband had many faults, but he hadn't questioned my spending. Not once. "What do you think killed him?"

"Don't share this."

"I won't." Sorry, Jinx.

"The medical examiner guessed poison."

"Jinx guessed murder." Had I just made Karen the prime suspect with my talk of grocery receipts? "What's your guess?"

"Hi." Grace hovered in the entrance to the living room with a tray in her hands. "Aggie thought you might like an hors d'oeuvre." She stepped inside and put the tray filled with various cheeses, salamis, olives, and crackers on the coffee table.

"Thanks, honey."

Anarchy leaned forward and helped himself. "Where are the dogs?" A fair question, since Max kept a close eye on all food consumption.

"Aggie just took a pork loin out of the oven. They're watching the meat." Grace grabbed a cracker and perched on the edge of a wingback chair. "I have a question."

"What is it?"

She nibbled on the cracker's scalloped edge. "When you get married, what will you do with McCallester?"

McCallester was the cat Grace rescued. His inability to live in the same house as Max meant I'd found him a new home. With Anarchy. "Maybe Max won't care about McCallester now that he has Pansy." Wishful thinking. More likely the problem would grow exponentially. I suppressed a shudder as I remembered McCallester swinging from a chandelier. "We'll figure it out." We had no choice.

Grace nodded and reached for a cube of smoked Gouda.

"How old are the Morris kids?"

She frowned. "Adam's a freshman at Princeton. Sarah's either a junior or senior at Mizzou. Why?"

I glanced at Anarchy. "Their dad passed away."

"That's awful." Grace closed her eyes, hiding their expression.

I worried how Grace dealt with her father's death. She adored Anarchy, but was she ready for her mother to remarry?

"Is that why Aggie's making Bundt cakes? To take to the Morrises'?"

"One for Karen. One for the new neighbor."

"New neighbor?" Anarchy's brows reached for his hairline. "I never saw a for sale sign."

"Apparently the buyer wanted a house in this neighborhood. He had his realtor reach out to homeowners. Marshall accepted his offer."

Aggie appeared in the doorway. "Dinner is served." She scowled over her shoulder. "Max, I'm watching you."

Max was an expert counter-surfer and fully capable of

clearing the counter and eating the entire dinner before we made it to the table.

I stood. "We're coming."

Aggie hurried back to the kitchen in a swirl of spring green kaftan.

The three of us took our seats around the dining room table.

"What happened?" asked Grace. "To Mr. Morris?"

"We're not sure," Anarchy replied.

"But you're investigating?" Grace insisted.

He nodded. "I am."

"He was murdered?"

"It's possible," he allowed.

Was Grace thinking about her dad? Missing him? Remembering his murder?

She frowned at me. "Mom, did you find him?"

"Clayton Morris? I did not."

Her expression cleared. "Does this mean your streak is over?"

I held up my crossed fingers. "We can hope." I had a terrible feeling about Clayton's death. "This could be the start of a whole new body-free chapter in my life."

No one said a word. We all knew I wasn't that lucky.

CHAPTER TWO

I breezed into the clubhouse, stopped briefly at the receptionist's desk for a lemon drop, and arrived in the card room five minutes early.

My favorite spot called, and I sat and enjoyed the golf-course view till Libba plopped into the chair across from me. She wore a gray dress, and a thundercloud followed her as if it were attached to her wrist with a piece of string.

"Good morning," I ventured.

"What's good about it?" she growled.

"The sun is shining. The birds are singing. I didn't find Clayton Morris's body."

She shook her head as if I were a hopeless case. "Jinx called me last night. She guesses it's murder."

I kept my expression neutral.

"She also told me Anarchy's investigating."

"Yes."

"Well—" she crossed her arms "—what did he say?"

"He didn't tell me anything."

She tilted her head and lowered her chin. Clearly she didn't believe me.

"If he did, I couldn't share it."

The hovering thundercloud threatened lightning, but rather than smite me, she stuck out her tongue. Ever the adult, that Libba.

We'd been best friends since preschool, and Libba's moods were as familiar to me as my own. The cloud above her head had "man trouble" written all over it. In neon. The only chance for a decent morning was to rip off the Band-Aid. I took a deep breath. "How's Jimmy?"

Libba grabbed a deck of cards, shuffled, and scowled at her hands. "He asked for a commitment."

Uh-oh. Most single women wanted their relationships to go somewhere. And by going somewhere, they meant to church. Libba wasn't most women. She didn't want marriage. She wanted independence and a man-friend available for dinner, dancing, and sex a few nights a week.

Jimmy, her latest, was a firefighter and achingly young.

"What did you tell him?"

"What choice did I have? I ended it."

"Just like that?"

"He's a sweet boy. He wants a wife, children, a dog, and a bungalow in Waldo. I'm not the right woman for him. Not even close."

"Does he want a cat?"

"What?" She frowned at me.

I changed course quickly. "So you're dating again?"

"Not ready. Not this week."

I reached across the table and squeezed her hand. "I'm here if you need me. I have a freezer full of ice cream and a refrigerator full of wine."

"Butter brickle?"

"If that's what you want, Aggie will add it to the grocery list."

"I need an Aggie."

Everyone needed an Aggie. Aside from Grace and now

Anarchy, Aggie was the best thing that ever happened to me. "There's only one Aggie, and you can't have her."

"Hmph."

Jinx, dressed in tennis whites, stepped into the card room. "Good morning."

My brows lifted. "Have you already played?"

"Doubles this afternoon."

"Did you forget our plans?"

Jinx pressed her palms to her cheeks. "Oh, Ellison. I'm so sorry. I did."

"What plans?" Libba demanded.

"Aggie made a Bundt cake for Karen Morris. I'm stopping by her house after bridge."

"I don't know what I was thinking," said Jinx. "Forgive me?"

"Forgiven." I'd walked Bundt cakes into far more awkward situations by myself.

Jinx settled into her chair. "Did you ask Anarchy? Was Clayton murdered?"

"She's not telling," sniped Libba.

"We had other things to talk about. We're planning a wedding."

"Did you decide on your maid of honor?" Libba demanded.

"We discussed what to do with his cat."

Libba's eyes narrowed.

"Anyone who takes the cat is definitely maid-of-honor material."

"That's extortion."

"You're giving away a cat?" Mel Langford stood in the cased entrance to the card room. She wore a wrap dress and had tied an Hermès scarf around her neck.

"I am. Are you interested?"

"Heavens, no." She hung her handbag over the back of the chair across from Jinx's and took her seat. "It's so nice of you to ask me to play. I hope I don't embarrass myself too badly. Do you table talk?"

"No," Jinx replied. "I play Stamen, Jacoby transfers, Gerber, and Blackwood. Oh, and weak twos."

Mel nodded. "I can handle that."

We drew for the deal, and Libba won with the Jack of spades. "How's Hubb?"

"The poor man. It's so upsetting for him."

Jinx leaned forward. "What happened to Clayton?" If I wouldn't confirm her suspicions, she'd use a different source.

"He collapsed. A heart attack."

I kept my face blank.

Jinx sat back in her seat. "They're sure?"

Libba dealt the last card. "If it were murder, Ellison would have found the body."

Mel gasped.

"Ellison finds murdered bodies like most people find spare change."

It was official, I needed a new best friend. Except she had a point.

I scowled at my ex-best friend and sorted my cards—four spades, four hearts, five diamonds, and twelve points, not counting the void. "Are you bidding?"

"One spade," Libba replied.

"Two clubs," said Mel.

I counted my hand a second time and included five points for the void. "Four no-trump."

Jinx tapped her cards closed against the table. "Pass."

Libba closed her eyes and scrunched her face.

"She's counting," I told Mel. "She may use her fingers."

Libba slitted her eyes. "Five hearts." That meant she had two aces.

I held the other two. Should I ask for Kings? "Six no-trump."

Mel passed, and Libba peered into her hand. "Six spades." She held three Kings.

"Seven spades."

Mel led the King of clubs, and I laid down the dummy hand.

Libba studied the cards, smiled, and trumped Mel's King.

"Ellison, can you tell me why the police sent a homicide detective to the office when Clayton died from a heart attack?" asked Mel.

"I'd like to know that too." Jinx lifted a doubting brow and threw the three of clubs.

"It might be standard procedure."

Mel frowned. "That can't be right. Every time someone dies, the police come? They'd be swamped."

"Clayton was young, and he dropped dead. I suppose the police are erring on the side of caution."

"My poor husband." Mel pursed her lips. "First Clayton dies, then the office is overrun by police."

"Shh." Libba took nine tricks without trying, but now her forehead creased.

"Sorry," Mel whispered.

Libba played a diamond from the board, won the trick in her hand, and played the ace of clubs. "The rest are mine."

"I believe you," said Jinx.

Mel eyed her cards. "Let's play it out."

Libba won the remaining tricks.

"Well done," I told her.

"The next time you bid slam, you're playing it." Libba cut the cards, and Mel dealt.

"May I get you ladies anything?" asked a waitress.

"Coffee, please," I replied.

"Ooh." Mel sent a card into Libba's stack. "That sounds good. Two coffees."

"Iced tea, please," said Libba.

"Perrier." Jinx gave the second deck a final shuffle and put it down near my left hand.

Mel dealt. "You all must think I'm a heartless ghoul talking about Hubb's troubles when Clayton is dead."

"Not at all," Jinx replied. "Clayton was a difficult man."

"My heart goes out to Karen," I replied. "She's such a nice woman."

Libba snorted. "You're just saying that because she covered your bake sale donations for years."

"Like I said, a nice woman."

"Ellison doesn't bake," Jinx explained to Mel.

"Ellison doesn't cook," said Libba.

"I wish I didn't." Mel sorted her cards. "If I hear 'what's for dinner' one more time, I may murder someone." She bit her lip as if she'd realized her comment might be in poor taste and shifted a card. "You're right, Ellison. Karen is nice." We could hear the *but* coming loud as a freight train. "Have you heard—"

"Here we are." The waitress arrived at the exact wrong moment. "Coffee for you, Mrs. Russell. And here's your cream." She set a cup, saucer, and small creamer on the table to my right.

"Thank you."

"You're welcome." She served Mel, Libba, and Jinx then disappeared into the hallway.

I considered asking Mel to finish her sentence, but Jinx wouldn't let a juicy tidbit go that easily. I sealed my lips and assessed my cards. Even distribution and seventeen points.

"I'll pass," said Mel.

My bid was easy. "One no-trump."

Jinx side-eyed me. "We know who's getting the cards today. Pass."

"Two clubs," my partner replied.

Mel passed.

"Two hearts," I replied.

Jinx waved at the table. "We're out. You two figure this out."

"Three hearts," said Libba.

I nodded, and when my bid came, I said, "Four hearts."

Jinx led a low spade. "You were saying, Mel? About Karen?"

Libba laid down the dummy hand, and we all looked at Mel.

Her cheeks pinked. "I shouldn't say."

I shifted my attention to the dummy hand (four good hearts and plenty of faces in clubs) and waited for Jinx.

She offered Mel an encouraging smile. "You can't leave us hanging."

"I don't like to tell tales," Mel demurred.

"But?" Jinx urged.

Mel leaned closer to the table. "Karen may not be too sad over Clayton's passing. They had problems."

Libba waved off Mel's comment. "Any marriage that included Clayton Morris would have problems."

Jinx, more attuned to gossip, tapped her lips with her fingertips. "Are you saying Karen was having an affair?"

"No!" Mel held up her free hand and spread her fingers wide. "I did not say that."

I pulled the Queen of spades from the board, and Mel played low.

The Queen took the trick.

"Then what are you saying?" asked Jinx.

"Nothing." Mel's cheeks had turned a deep shade of rose. "They weren't happy. I doubt she'll mourn. That's it."

"Karen is a good mother. Even if she doesn't miss Clayton, she'll grieve the loss of Adam and Sarah's father." I played the two of hearts from the board and realized I'd revealed too much.

Mel followed suit with the nine. "How long has Henry been gone?"

"Nearly a year." I played the King from my hand and gazed out the window at the verdant golf course. "When he died, the police trampled my hostas. It's odd to see them lush and green again."

Jinx played the four of hearts. "We're here if you need us."

"Thank you." I considered the ring on my finger. "The hostas recovered, and I have too."

We'd played for two hours when Jinx, who was dummy, looked at her watch. "This is it for me, girls. I'm due courtside."

Mel took the last few tricks. "Thanks for letting me play with you."

"Would you play again?" Jinx stood and gathered her belongings. "Daisy's kids are about to get out of school for the summer." Experience told us Daisy's adult life would soon implode—wrecked by tennis, golf, and swim lessons at the club, art lessons at the gallery, drama and singing lessons, preparations for sleepaway camp, and managing a house filled with munchkins with mayhem on their minds.

"Absolutely. I'll walk out with you."

When Jinx and Mel were gone, Libba asked, "Is that wine offer still good?"

"Always."

"Tonight?"

"Whenever you need me."

"Can we substitute martinis for wine?"

"Bring an overnight bag." I glanced at the side table where my coffee cup rested. "Uh-oh."

"What?"

"Mel forgot her glasses." I picked up a pair of readers.

"Leave them with the lost and found."

I shook my head and dropped the glasses in my handbag. "I'll return them to her. What time tonight?"

"Five?"

"I'll have a pitcher ready."

~

I STOPPED AT HOME, picked up a chocolate Bundt cake drizzled with chocolate icing, and drove to Karen's.

The Morrises' house was ten blocks south of mine. A well-manicured lawn sloped gently to a curb packed with cars. I swallowed a sigh, found a parking spot, and drifted up the front walk. My recent engagement to a homicide detective was as interesting to the ladies who lunched as Clayton's death, and I was in no hurry to face a barrage of questions.

Too soon I stood on the stoop. I balanced the cake and pressed the doorbell.

Karen opened the door. Her skin was pale and her eyes drooped, but she smiled warmly. "Ellison, how kind of you to come."

"I'm so sorry for your loss." I held out the Bundt cake. "Don't worry, I didn't bake it."

Her answering laughter caught the edge of a sob. She took the cake from my hands. "Please, come in."

I followed her inside. "I really am sorry. Please let me know if there's anything I can do for you or the kids."

Her smile quivered. "Let's take this to the dining room. We have coffee. Would you like some?"

"Please."

A Battenberg lace cloth covered the table. Pink Minton cockatrice cups and saucers surrounded a silver coffee urn. Trays of finger sandwiches sat next to a bread bowl filled with dill dip (probably from Elise Chandler; she always brought dill dip). There were bowls of pimento-filled olives, plates of cookies, and a country ham surrounded by egg rolls.

"Everyone's been so generous." Karen nodded at the table. "I don't know what we'll do with all this food. There are five casseroles in the fridge." Casseroles and Bundt cakes were the culinary equivalent of a hug.

"We want you to know we care."

Karen pressed her palm against her lips. "I can't believe this happened. The kids are destroyed."

"What can I do? I found a counselor for Grace when Henry died." She'd refused to go. "I can share her name and number with you."

"Thank you, Ellison." She took the cover off the Bundt cake, put it on the table, and frowned. "Should I get a cake plate?"

"Absolutely not. You should sit down. What can I get you?"

Karen glanced through the dining room's cased entrance into the living room. "A Valium? They're whispering Clayton was murdered." Hope dawned on her tired face. "The detective —he's your fiancé. Oh my stars—" she pressed her palms to her cheeks "—I should have called and offered best wishes. I'm so happy for you. You deserve someone who adores you."

"Thank you." Celebrating my happiness when she'd lost her husband felt hollow.

"Can you tell everyone Clayton died from a heart attack? They'll believe you."

I reached for her thin hand. "I don't know anything about Clayton's death, and I shouldn't discuss Anarchy's cases."

Her face fell. "I understand. It's just so ridiculous. No one would kill Clayton." She pulled her hand free, filled a cup with coffee, and handed it to me. "If I were you, I'd head to the family room. Prudence Davies is in the living room."

Avoiding Prudence, a horse-toothed woman with whom my late husband played hide-the-pickle, was a constant goal. "Thank you." I added a jot of cream to my cup. "I'll do that. The next week will be horribly busy for you, but when you get past it, I'll take you to lunch. Better yet, dinner."

"I'd like that."

The doorbell rang, and her shoulders slumped lower.

"Let me answer that. You go sit."

"You don't mind?"

"Not in the least. Go."

Karen disappeared into the living room and I opened the front door to Elise Chandler. She held a pumpernickel bread bowl and a Tupperware container filled with dill dip.

I welcomed her, told her Karen was in the living room, and watched her scowl when she realized someone had stolen her bread-bowl thunder. She quickly rearranged the table so the country ham hid the rival pumpernickel.

I stepped into the foyer.

The house had a center hall plan. The living room and screened porch to the left. The dining room and breakfast area to the right. The kitchen lay behind the dining room. Karen and Clayton had added to the back of the house.

I strolled into an enormous room filled with light. The wall across from where I entered had two enormous picture windows with a view of the large backyard. Between them, a simple mantel and a Frank Stella lithograph floated above a limestone fireplace. The wall that was originally the back of the house now held bookcases, a wet bar, and an entrance to the living room. The other two walls had plenty of windows and French doors that opened to patios. The decorator had used earth tones and pops of orange.

Just my luck, Prudence entered from the living room as I entered from the hall. She wrinkled her nose as if she smelled rotten eggs.

I offered up a bland smile.

"I heard you're getting married."

I nodded.

"Aren't you worried?"

"Worried?"

"That he'll get bored with you like Henry did."

I'd asked for that. Engaging with Prudence was always a mistake. Maybe she was right and Henry grew bored, but I chose to believe his infidelity was due to my making more money than he did. His attitude about my artistic career began with *what a cute hobby*, morphed into *your first priority should be your family* (it was), and ended with snide *you're a flash in the pan* disdain.

"Tell me, do you wake up in the morning and decide to be hateful, or does it come naturally?"

Prudence choked on her wine, her cheeks colored an unattractive red, and her mouth opened and shut as she composed a retort.

"Prudence, what a lovely scarf. Is it new?" asked Lisa Markham.

Prudence touched the Vera scarf at her neck. "No." Her eyes narrowed to a hateful glare, which she shared with me. "Henry gave it to me."

Lisa ignored Prudence's grenade. "Well, it's very becoming."

Prudence turned her glare on Lisa as if she suspected mockery.

Lisa had a kind heart. It wasn't in her to be cruel—not even to Prudence. She'd simply headed off an argument. "Have you eaten?" Lisa asked. "There's a chocolate Bundt cake on the dining table that looks divine." She winked at me, linked arms with Prudence, and led her away.

I mouthed *thank you* and felt small. Karen had lost her husband and I'd nearly started a fight with Prudence.

"Didn't they do a fabulous job?" Jane Addison stood next to me. Her well-schooled gaze tallied the room's square footage.

Wasn't it a bit early for her to be angling for the listing? Jane sold most of the houses in our neighborhood. She knew almost as much gossip as Jinx—but Jane's focused on who was considering divorce, who was seriously ill, and who might be relocating to a nursing home.

"Gorgeous." My voice was desert dry. How long till Jane asked to sell it?

"Karen's a dear friend. I'm here to support her." It was almost as if Jane could read my mind.

We both watched her lie stretch out on the shag area rug till our silence became uncomfortable.

I forced a smile. "What have you heard about my new neighbor?"

She frowned. "Not much. The buyer used Jim Holden, and the seller didn't use an agent." Her tone made clear her low opinion of those who eschewed realtors. "The house needed work. Plus...well, you know."

I did know. Whoever moved next door had me as a neighbor. I found bodies. Sirens split the night. And the dogs—they caused their own brand of mayhem.

Jane's gaze shifted to my left hand, and the calculating expression in her eyes had me stepping backward till I hit the bookcase. "What about you, Ellison? Will you be staying put? Does your fiancé want to live in the house you shared with Henry?"

"It's also the house where Grace grew up. I'm not selling."

"Too bad." She shifted her attention to the Morrises' addition. "This house, I could get top dollar."

"Too soon, Jane."

"Pfft. Karen's having an affair with the architect. This house was coming on the market even if Clayton didn't conveniently drop dead."

CHAPTER THREE

Libba arrived carrying her handbag, an alligator overnight case, and a vodka bottle. "In case you run out." She wore no makeup, she'd scraped her hair into a messy ponytail, and red rimmed her eyes. Ten miles of bad road looked better.

I set the case on the stairs and led her to the patio. "It's too nice to sit inside."

"Hmph." She stirred the waiting pitcher of martinis, poured herself a to-the-rim glass, sank onto the nearest chair, and rested her feet on the ottoman.

I poured a scant glass, settled into a chair near hers, and sipped.

The sky was lavender velvet. The air was mild. The dogs were happy to patrol the perimeter for daring squirrels and foolish rabbits.

"The French call this time of night 'l'heure bleu.'"

Libba lifted a single brow.

"Neither daylight nor darkness. The light is special. Blue."

"We're not all artists."

Cranky, cranky. If Libba was in a mood, we might as well discuss the reason. "You did the right thing."

She drank. Deeply. "There are lights on next door. Has your new neighbor arrived?"

Or we could ignore the Jimmy situation for trivia. "Someone would have told me about a moving van. They've been working on the interior. Maybe the house painters forgot to flip the switch."

"Hmph." Libba dug in her handbag till she found cigarettes and a lighter. "Do you mind?"

"Not if it's outside. There's an ashtray on the table next to you."

She lit a cigarette and sent a plume of smoke into the darkening sky. "I did the right thing."

"I agree."

"The right thing sucks eggs."

Libba wouldn't get any argument from me. "What can I do?"

She held out her half-empty glass, and I stood, picked up the pitcher, and refilled.

"I don't want to talk about Jimmy. Tell me about the wedding plans."

My turn for an extra-large sip of martini. "You know Mother."

"Undermining you every chance she gets?"

"And then some. But she has a contingency plan."

"Oh?"

"If we insist on proceeding with this—her words—ill-advised alliance, she'll wear me down with wedding details. Seated or buffet? White tie, black tie, or cocktail attire?" My free hand squeezed into a fist. "White tie? No one wore tails the first time."

"You mean the time when your sister was the matron of honor, and your best friend was a mere bridesmaid?"

"That's the one."

She crushed out her cigarette. "It's your wedding. What do you want?"

"Small. Low key. Family and a few close friends."

"Are you sure? Imagine Celeste Jones at a black-tie affair at the club." My future mother-in-law had strong opinions about vaginas and wasn't afraid to share them (the opinions, not the vaginas).

"Mother would have a coronary." I smiled at the thought.

"An aneurism." Libba's smile was wider than mine. "That, or she might kill someone."

Most likely me.

"What does Anarchy want?"

"I asked him, and he says he doesn't care as long as I'm his wife when it's over."

Woof! Pansy barked at an oak.

"It's a good thing that dog is pretty," said Libba. "Cause she's not bright."

Woof!

Hoo, hoo.

"She's barking at an owl, not the tree."

"She's still the dimmest bulb in the box." Libba sipped. "How was Karen's?"

"Awful."

She nodded. "Those things always are."

"Prudence was there."

Libba stood and refilled both our glasses. "That woman is a menace."

"She's in a snit because I'm marrying Anarchy. It's as if she thinks I'm being untrue to Henry's memory." My late husband cheated with reckless abandon, belittled my career, and was a mostly horrible human. I didn't owe his memory a moment's thought.

"Untrue? To Henry? That's rich."

"That's Prudence."

Libba collapsed into her chair. "Who else did you see?"

"Jane Addison. She claims Karen is having an affair with her architect."

"Whose architect?"

"The one who designed the addition on Karen and Clayton's house. The room is fabulous."

Libba, an apartment dweller, wrinkled her nose. She had no interest in home projects. "Do you suppose Jane's right?"

"It can't have been easy being married to Clayton."

"Wait!"

"What?"

She lifted her martini glass. "A toast."

"To what?"

"To your not finding the body."

Hoo, hoo.

Woof!

We clinked glasses and drank.

"Pretty night." Libba crossed her ankles and gazed at the stars. The darkness around us was as soft as cashmere, and a gentle breeze carried the scent of lilacs.

"Gorgeous," I agreed.

"If Jimmy and I were together, we'd have dinner on my balcony." She pressed the back of her hand against her mouth. "Why can't I find what I'm looking for?"

"Refill?"

She held up her glass. "You didn't answer the question."

"Most women want marriage." I poured. "You don't. Finding the right man for you is a challenge. It's like looking for a couture gown at Sear's. You can look and look, but you won't find what you want."

"Your point?"

"Change what you're looking for or change where you look."

"Any ideas? I've been through most of the eligible men in

Kansas City. Unless I move to St. Louis or Chicago, I'm out of luck."

"You can't move to St. Louis."

"I know. It's impossible to fit in unless you went to high school there." She swirled her martini. "So, where do I look?"

"Your own backyard."

"I live in an apartment. I don't have a backyard."

"Are there any single men in your building?

"I've never noticed."

"Notice."

"Do you think it's true? Karen and the architect?"

"Maybe. I heard it from Jane, not Jinx." Jinx was one hundred percent reliable. Jane made mistakes.

Libba frowned. "Marriage is a bad bet."

"Thanks for that sentiment as I head to the altar."

She shook her head harder. "Not you and Anarchy—"

Woof! Woof! Woof! Pansy spun in tight circles as the owl took flight. The night bird soared toward us, almost as if we were the prey.

"Duck!"

"What?"

The owl swooped and its talons clutched Libba's bouncing ponytail.

"Aieeee!" Libba levitated off the chair and waved her arms like a crazy woman.

"Let go!" I yelled.

The owl ignored me, and Pansy barreled toward us.

"Get it out of my hair!"

The owl spread its wings—flapped its wings—but it didn't rise. Its talons had tangled in Libba's hair. The bird was stuck.

"Aieeee!" Libba staggered toward the back door.

"Stop!" I cried. "Where are you going?"

"Get. It. Off."

"Fine. But do not enter my house with an owl on your head."

It would be wrong—very, very wrong—to laugh. I covered my mouth with both hands.

"Do something!"

The owl flapped its wings harder.

Woof!

"Pansy! No!"

Pansy ignored me and leapt at the owl. Her blonde body thunked into Libba.

Libba windmilled her arms and went down hard. She thudded to the bricks with a squirming Retriever in her lap and an owl still attached to her head.

Undeterred by the fall, Pansy leapt to her feet, lifted her paws to Libba's shoulders, and snapped at the owl.

The owl shrieked. And flapped. And shrieked some more.

I grabbed Pansy's collar and hauled her off Libba. "Bad dog."

She struggled against me, determined to catch the owl even if it meant flattening Libba.

Woof! Woof! Woof!

"Do you need help?"

"Yes." I didn't question where the strange man in my backyard came from. "Please."

"Do you have a broom?"

"A broom?" Libba shrieked as loud as the owl. "What will you do with a broom? You know what? I don't care. Get it off."

I dragged Pansy toward the back door.

"You're leaving me?"

"Broom."

"Hurry!"

It took five seconds to find a broom and a full minute to lock an unwilling Pansy in the laundry room. By the time I returned to the patio with the broom in my hand, the stranger had liberated the owl.

"Are you hurt?" I demanded. "Did the owl scratch you?" I mentally readied myself for a trip to the emergency room.

"It stole part of my hair." Libba pressed her fingertips to her scalp.

"If we go inside, I can take a look. I'm a doctor."

Libba shook her head, remembered her swinging ponytail had attracted the owl, and froze. "I'm fine."

"If it scratched you, you need medical attention. Those talons aren't clean."

A mulish expression settled on Libba's face. "I'm fine."

I filled a fresh martini glass, handed it to her, then turned to the stranger. "Thanks for your help."

"Are evenings in this neighborhood always so exciting?" he asked.

"This was nothing," Libba muttered. "They're usually murder."

"Ha." Now that the owl had flown away, I sized up the stranger in the light cast from the kitchen windows. He was around my age, had a good tan, sported a jaunty grin, and looked familiar. "Have we met before?"

"Once or twice." The smile widened.

"I'm sorry, I don't..."

He held out his hand. "Charlie Ardmore."

Libba choked on her drink. Her splutter covered the squeaky noise that escaped my lips.

"Did Frances send you?" Libba demanded. Mother wasn't above dropping an old boyfriend—especially an old boyfriend who was a doctor—in my path in hopes I'd forget Anarchy.

The first boy I ever loved frowned. "Pardon?"

"Never mind." Libba peered at us over the rim of her glass. "What are you doing here?"

"I moved back to Kansas City and bought the house next door."

Libba's answering smile was pure evil. "This is gonna be good."

Charlie's fingers still hovered in the space between us.

I swallowed a sigh and let his hand envelop mine. "Welcome home."

I WOKE up far too early, tiptoed downstairs, and pushed Mr. Coffee's button.

You look tired. Concern laced his voice.

"Nothing you can't fix." Not that I'd ever tell him, but some mornings he took an eternity to fill his pot. This was an eternity morning. I plunked onto a stool, crossed my arms on the counter, and lay my head on them.

Libba kept you up? he asked.

Max nudged me.

"Hold on. Let me put the dogs out." I opened the back door and Pansy raced into the still-dark yard. Max ambled.

A mug waited on the counter, and as soon as Mr. Coffee finished, I poured and added cream. My eyes closed for the first sip and I moaned. "I needed this. Badly."

Libba? he prompted.

"Nope. The new neighbor."

Oh?

"Charlie Ardmore."

Mr. Coffee waited patiently for my explanation while I revisited high school.

Charlie and I fell for each other in the way of teenagers. Hopelessly. Mother raised her brows at the intensity of our feelings, but she showered Charlie with benign smiles. Charlie's grandmother and mine were dear friends, and Mother basked in her mother's rare approval.

We graduated from high school, certain we could make a long-distance relationship work. I left for art school, and Charlie went to Rice in Houston where he met an oil heiress.

There was a tearful breakup over Thanksgiving break, and we hadn't seen each other since.

"I didn't recognize him," I told Mr. Coffee.

"Recognize who?" Aggie floated into the kitchen wearing a kaftan covered with leaves. Six shades of green—mint, olive, jade, spring, moss, and Kelly—fought for supremacy and complimented her red hair.

"Our new neighbor and I dated in high school." Dated was an anemic word for spent-every-waking-minute-together. "He rescued Libba last night. I can't believe I didn't recognize him."

"How long has it been since you saw him?"

I did the math and winced. "A while."

"Were you expecting him?"

"Heavens, no."

"He's older. Less hair?"

I nodded.

"Heavier?"

"I last saw him when we were nineteen. We're both heavier."

"That's why you didn't recognize him. He was out of context."

"You're probably right." At a reunion, I would have known him immediately.

Aggie held Mr. Coffee's pot aloft. "More coffee?"

I slid my empty mug toward her. "Please."

"Why did Libba need rescuing?"

"An owl attacked her ponytail."

Aggie's lips twitched.

"And Pansy attacked the owl."

Aggie's gaze shifted to the backyard. "Have you noticed there's trouble in paradise?"

"Max and Pansy?"

She nodded. "Pansy annoys him."

"Max is fickle?"

"Max wised up." Aggie was not a member of Pansy's fan club.

A scratch on the door had me rising from my stool. "I'll let them in."

I opened the door to Max. "Where's Pansy?"

Max trotted inside, collected a biscuit from Aggie, and settled on his mat. Maybe Aggie was right about Max and his doggy heart. He'd discovered that falling in love was easy, but staying in love was hard.

"Pansy?" I called.

No dog.

I wrapped my robe tighter and stepped outside where birds sang, a gentle breeze tugged my hair, and the pink-tinged sky had me itching for my paints. I took a bracing sip of coffee. "Pansy!"

No dog.

"She's gone," I called to the house.

Aggie appeared in the door behind me and scowled.

I mirrored her expression. Without regular, exhaustive exercise, Pansy dug. Her goal was China. Her preferred digging sites were the neighbors' flower beds.

"I'll check Margaret's yard if you'll check Charlie's." My neighbor Margaret Hamilton was a rides-her-broom-at-midnight hex-casting witch. If Pansy was in Margaret's yard—

I shuddered.

"Is this one yours?" The voice belonged to a man.

I adjusted my robe till it covered me to my neck and stepped into the dewy grass. "Pretty, blonde, not too bright?" Much like the girl Charlie dumped me for.

"She's definitely pretty." Charlie emerged from behind a row of blue spruce and beamed at me as if he weren't referring to the dog.

I swallowed. "I'm sorry about Pansy. Did she jump or dig?"

"Neither. I forgot to close the gate last night."

"I hope she didn't damage anything."

"This sweet girl?"

Pansy's entire body wagged.

I clutched my robe tighter.

"May I ask a favor?"

"A favor?"

Charlie nodded. "My coffee maker hasn't arrived. May I have a cup?"

No. Go away. Shoo. It wasn't in me to withhold coffee. "Come in."

Charlie followed me into the kitchen, spotted Aggie, blinked at all that green, then extended his hand. "Hi. I'm Charlie Ardmore, the new neighbor."

"Aggie DeLucci."

Charlie upped the wattage on his smile, and it was Aggie's turn to blink.

"Charlie's coffee maker hasn't arrived," I explained.

Aggie poured him a mug. "Cream or sugar?"

"A dash of cream."

Aggie added cream and handed him the mug.

Rather than taking his coffee to go, Charlie settled onto a stool. Pansy flopped at his feet and stared at him with adoring eyes. He bent and scratched behind her ears. "Nice dog."

"You want her?"

"You serious?" His eyes twinkled, and again I got the sense he wasn't talking about the dog.

Ding, dong.

"I'll get that." Aggie high-tailed it into the front hall.

I shifted my gaze to the comforting contents of my mug.

"I heard about your husband. I'm sorry for your loss."

"Thank you." I glanced at my left hand, where Anarchy's ring sparkled. "I'm getting married again." So stop with the compliments and the charming smile.

"Who's the lucky guy?"

"That would be me." Anarchy stood in the doorway. His coffee-brown eyes were cold and hard.

The two men stared at each other.

I went to Anarchy's side. "This is my new neighbor, Charlie Ardmore. Charlie, this is my fiancé, Anarchy Jones."

The staring continued.

Woof. Max rose from his mat and sat next to me.

Pansy remained at Charlie's feet.

"Anarchy's an unusual name."

"I have unusual parents."

The understatement of the decade.

"Are you from Kansas City?" Charlie asked.

"San Francisco. You?"

"A native, but I lived in Houston for a few decades." He shifted his gaze to me. "It's good to be home."

Next to me, Anarchy stiffened. "You bought the house next door?"

Charlie's smile was as bright as the morning sun. "I did." He held up his empty mug. "Thanks for the coffee, Ellison."

"You're welcome."

"Let's do this again soon." He strolled out the back door, and only Pansy was sorry to see him go.

"Looks as if I've got some competition."

"What? No."

"Seems as if you know each other."

I crossed to Mr. Coffee and held up his pot. "Coffee?"

"Thanks."

I poured Anarchy a mug and refilled my own.

"How do you know him?"

"We dated in high school."

His lips thinned.

"I haven't seen Charlie since Thanksgiving break of my freshman year in college."

"That's specific."

"He broke up with me." Broke my heart.

"And now he lives next door."

"Let's not talk about Charlie." I put down my coffee and kissed Anarchy's cheek. "How are you? How's the investigation?"

His expression softened, and he pulled me close. "Sorry. It's not your fault he wants you back." He kissed the tip of my nose. "The medical examiner guessed right. Someone poisoned Clayton Morris."

"Oh, no." I liked Karen, but I would not—could not—keep secrets from Anarchy. "I heard a rumor that Karen Morris is having an affair with the architect who designed the addition to her house."

Anarchy's brows lifted. "A rumor?"

"Might or might not be true."

"Can you find out?"

"I can try."

CHAPTER FOUR

I settled behind my desk in the family room and called Jinx. "How was your tennis game?"

"We won in straight sets. How's Karen?"

"She seemed okay—worried about her kids."

"Losing a parent is awful. When my father died, I cried for a week. And his death wasn't a surprise."

"Grace had a hard time with Henry's death. She mourned."

"And you didn't."

Henry's and my problems, both large and small, had eroded whatever affection we once possessed. "I mourned for her." I shifted in my chair. "That was my first time seeing Karen's room addition. It's fabulous. Do you know which architect they used?"

"Pat Gallagher."

Jinx's answer was definitive, but I sensed there was something she hadn't told me. "And?"

"What is it you're asking, Ellison?"

I'd hoped to avoid putting my cards on the table. I stalled with a sip of coffee.

"Well?"

"I heard that Karen and her architect..."

Jinx sighed. "I've heard that too."

"You don't know for sure?"

"I do not. Why are you interested?"

"Just curious," I lied. I couldn't tell Jinx that someone murdered Clayton Morris, not before the police made an announcement.

"I heard about Karen and Pat a few months ago, but no one has a shred of proof." And Jinx didn't repeat idle gossip. Hers was verified. "Are you asking because Clayton was murdered?"

"Clayton was murdered?" I stretched my pitiable acting skills. "Do you know that for sure?"

"Do you?"

We needed a change in topic. Quickly. "How did you like playing with Mel?"

"She's sharp. I love Daisy, but she makes at least three stupid mistakes whenever we play." Jinx exhaled, and I imagined her in a fog of cigarette smoke. "Mel didn't make a single error. And I don't think we saw her at her best."

"Oh?"

"She's worried."

"About?"

"The company. It belonged to her grandfather. Apparently the margins are tight. The traits that made Clayton a bad husband made him a good Chief Financial Officer. His death leaves a hole."

"She seemed more worried about Hubb than the company."

Jinx snorted. "You haven't been widowed long enough to forget that husbands bring their work home. Things go poorly at the office, and the man sharing your bed is a bear."

"Fair point."

"I meant to ask you yesterday, have you talked to the club about Daisy's birthday?"

"Her party's not till—" I glanced at the open calendar on my desk, and my stomach lurched "—sweet nine-pound baby Jesus."

"That's a no?"

"I'll call them as soon as we hang up."

"It's not like you to forget."

"I blame getting engaged. It knocked everything else clean out of my head." I downed the rest of my coffee. "How many did we invite?"

"Eighty. Libba has the replies."

Libba was sleeping off a pitcher of martinis upstairs in the blue room. I'd get the count from her before I left for the club.

I wrapped the phone cord around my finger. "I met my new neighbor." Jinx would hear about Charlie; better she get the details from me.

"The man from Texas? What did you think?"

"It's Charlie Ardmore."

"Oh, Ellison." Jinx knew our history. "Wait, he's married to an oil heiress."

"Not anymore."

"What's he doing in Kansas City?"

"I assume he'll practice medicine."

"I mean, why did he come back? Why not stay in Texas?" The sharp tap of Jinx's fingernails on a hard surface carried through the phone line. "A single doctor. Every divorcée in town will be camped on your block."

Jinx wasn't wrong.

"We'll ask him to Daisy's party," she declared.

"What?" I sounded as if I'd sucked helium.

"Is he still handsome? I bet he is. He'll do for Libba, you can re-introduce—"

"Jinx—"

"What? He's perfect for her—a single man with a pulse."

I lowered my forehead to my free hand. Libba and Charlie?

"Also, a pulse reminds me. Did Karen tell you when she scheduled the funeral?"

"She did not."

"If Clayton died of a heart attack, there'd be no reason for a delay. Is there anything you want to tell me?"

We'd been down this road already, and I couldn't confirm Clayton's murder. Not without Anarchy's say so. "Nope."

"Is Karen a suspect?"

I took a quick tell-Jinx-nothing breath. "Not that I know of. Listen, I should get over to the club and arrange the food for this party."

"Be that way. Will I see you at the Westbrooks' Saturday night?"

"Yes."

"Are you bringing Anarchy?"

"Yes. Listen, I should call the clu—"

"Wait. Before you go, did you see Elise Chandler at Karen's?"

"She brought dill dip."

"It's her signature dish."

"Why do you ask?"

"I can't say. Not yet."

Did Jinx have something juicy or was she playing tit for tat? I couldn't play that game—couldn't talk about Anarchy's investigation. "I'll call you later."

When I pulled into the club parking lot, it nearly overflowed with cars—golfers taking advantage of a perfect day. Soon heat and humidity would settle in for the summer, but today? Resort weather.

I stopped at the receptionist's desk and claimed a lemon drop. "Good afternoon. Deanna is expecting me."

"Of course, Mrs. Russell."

I waited while the receptionist pushed a clear plastic button at the bottom of the phone and spoke into the receiver. She smiled at me. "She'll be with you in a moment."

"Thank you."

I perched on a settee and sucked on my lemon drop.

"Ellison!" Elise Chandler stood in front of me dressed for tennis. "I'm so glad to see you. That cake you brought to Karen's was delicious. Did you make it?"

Elise and I were acquaintances (she was six years older), not friends. My friends and anyone with kids near Grace's age knew about my baking challenges. "No."

"You bought it?" Enthusiasm made her squeak. "Where?"

"My housekeeper made the cake."

"Oh." Her face fell, then she clasped her hands together. "Does she share her recipes?"

"I'll ask her."

"Would you? Please? Does she use sour cream or buttermilk? See? I'm still thinking about the cake." She frowned. "And Karen. I'm still thinking about Karen. Such a loss. I'm sure having you as a friend will be a comfort."

Because my husband had also been murdered? Elise couldn't know about Clayton. I frowned.

"Losing your husbands while you're still young, I mean. You must miss him." Her gaze traveled to my left hand, and she blushed. "Scads of people will miss Clayton."

I produced a polite smile. If the rumors were true, Elise was very wrong. "Karen mentioned the kids were having a hard time."

"The kids?" Elise blinked. "Oh. Right."

"Who did you mean?"

"Hubb." Elise sounded secretly pleased, as if she took delight in his misfortune. Why would Elise be pleased that Hubb Langford's Chief Financial Officer died? What did Jinx know but wasn't telling?

"Mrs. Russell?" Deanna offered her hand. "Sorry to keep you waiting."

I stood and shook her hand. "Elise, will you please excuse me?"

"Of course. Don't forget the recipe."

"I'll ask Aggie."

"If you'll come with me, Chef has suggestions." As the event planner, Deanna had a large, well-furnished office (because club members visited her). I once tracked down the bookkeeper (we were charged for four bottles of wine rather than four glasses). That woman worked in a closet (not really) (almost) at a metal desk constructed in 1952.

I sat in a comfortable wingback chair across from Deanna's desk and watched her open a file folder. "Chef came up with this buffet dinner menu especially for you."

And there was a bridge in Brooklyn for sale. I smiled and read. The menu included snails in garlic butter, an opened-face sandwich tray, lobster tails with dilled mustard sauce, roast chicken in aspic with olives, and raspberry ice cream torte.

"Is this set in stone?"

"What would you like to change?"

"No snails. Daisy hates them."

Deanna made a note.

"Roast chicken is fine, but no aspic." Ever since my former neighbor brought a Jell-O salad to my house, I shuddered at the sight of food trapped in gelatin.

"What would you prefer?"

"A chilled soup. Cucumber and mint?"

She nodded and made a note.

"Perhaps we could add a vegetable?"

"Asparagus?"

"Perfect. Also, it's a birthday party. We'll want chocolate cake and ice cream, not the raspberry torte."

Deanna made another note. "How many guests?"

When I asked a still-sleeping Libba about replies, she

responded with a rude hand gesture. "We invited eighty. When do you need a final count?"

She consulted her calendar. "Next Tuesday."

"No problem." Libba would be lucid by then. "We'll need an open bar."

"House liquor?"

"Top shelf."

Deanna made yet another note.

"What are we forgetting?"

"What color for the linens?"

"Spring green and white." Jinx had ordered bouquets of daisies for the tables and the buffet. "We'll need a table for gifts."

"Place cards?"

"No. But we'd like a reserved table for Daisy."

Yet another note. "Of course."

"I think that's everything." I stood. "Thank you for your help."

Deanna rose from her chair. "My pleasure."

I stepped out of Deanna's office and heard raised voices. Well, one raised voice. "That can't be right. With a bar bill like that, we could buy drinks for every member."

Someone else had found the bookkeeper's closet.

As I walked down the hallway, the closet door flew open and Nat Clifford emerged.

Nat was pretty, with a strong chin and a stronger personality, and she'd never really forgiven me for her son's chipped tooth. "Oh. Ellison. Hello."

"Hello, Nat."

She glanced over her shoulder at the bookkeeper's closet. "You heard that?"

"A mistake with your bill?"

"Exactly." She nodded emphatically. "I nearly died when I opened it."

"I know how you feel."

She raised a brow.

"When the June bill arrives, I need a glass of wine handy before I slit the envelope." June was swim team month when Grace spent long days at the club, eating club sandwiches or cheeseburgers, sucking down Tab with lime, and snarfing French fries. Not to mention the swim meets. Those required substantial lubrication (I happily claimed that expense). Then there were the post-meet banquets, tennis and golf lessons, the racquet that needed new strings, and always a new putter.

"In June, we rack up charges. This?" She scowled at the bookkeeper's door. "If we drank this much, there wouldn't be any bourbon left in the state. This is a mistake."

"I hope you get it worked out."

"You can bet I will." She straightened her handbag's strap over her shoulder and marched away.

When I stepped out of the clubhouse, I spotted my father stashing something in his trunk. "Dad!"

He looked up, grinned and hurried toward me. "Sugar!" He dropped a kiss on my cheek. "What a nice surprise. We're having drinks on the patio. Join us."

"Who is us?"

"Byron Clifford,"—Nat Clifford's father-in-law—"Bill Chandler," —Elise Chandler's father-in-law —"and Tom Horton."

"I'll be in the way."

"Not at all." He tugged my arm. "I insist."

"One drink." We walked toward the patio with its view of the putting clock. "How was your round?"

"One under par."

"Congratulations. You keep this up, you'll have a scratch handicap." Amateur golfers had handicaps. The lower the handicap, the better the golfer.

Dad shrugged. And smiled. "I don't care about handicaps or other golfers. I play against past performance."

That was so patently untrue I didn't bother with a reply.

When we reached the table, Daddy's cronies stood.

"Please." I pressed my palms down. "Sit."

"Ellison agreed to join us for a drink."

"That's what this group needs," said Byron. "A pretty girl."

I answered with a weak smile.

"Your father brags about you all the time," said Bill. "You broke the ladies' club record."

I could have paintings hanging in the Metropolitan and the Guggenheim, and my father would still tell his friends about one fluke round of golf. "I had a good day."

"Pretty and humble." Byron sipped his Old Fashioned. "I hear you're getting married."

"I am."

"To a cop."

"A homicide detective."

Byron's gaze slid toward Daddy.

"Anarchy adores Ellison. Since she finds bodies on a weekly basis, I'm glad she found a man who can keep her safe."

"No bodies this week," I protested.

"The week's not over, sugar."

Daddy's cronies chuckled.

"How's the painting coming?" asked Bill.

"I'll be showing in a gallery in Chicago later this year."

"Not New York?" Tom tapped his fingertips together.

"I may do that too." If I wanted to work myself to exhaustion.

"What may I get you, Mrs. Russell?" A waiter placed a martini in front of Daddy.

"A spritzer, please."

"My ticket," Daddy told the waiter.

"Thank you."

Tom stared at me. "I guess this means we'll have a homicide detective as a member. Does your fiancé play golf?"

"I don't know."

"Tennis?"

"I'm not sure."

"Cards?"

I couldn't imagine him spending long afternoons playing bridge or gin for a nickel a point. I shrugged.

"Does the man drink?"

"Bourbon."

Tom nodded his approval.

"Beautiful day for golf," I murmured.

"Too nice to be in the office," said Bill.

"When was the last time you spent a full day in the office?" Byron asked.

The two men, both of whom had their sons running their companies, shared a smile and clinked glasses.

"I hear your fiancé is investigating Clayton Morris's death," said Tom. "Was it murder?"

Four sets of eyes fixed on me.

"I couldn't say."

"You can tell us, sugar."

"Anarchy doesn't discuss his cases." Such a lie.

Tom's brow furrowed. "What kind of name is Anarchy?"

"Give her a break, Tom." Daddy leaned back in his chair and crossed his arms. "She didn't name him."

"Can't help but wonder how Morris's death will affect the company," said Bill.

I stayed very still. If they forgot I was there, they might say something worth hearing.

Byron shook his head. "They'll hire another CFO."

"I heard Patriot has problems. Entire loads written off due to poor refrigeration in their trucks, late deliveries, that sort of thing. They need an eagle-eyed financial officer," said Tom.

Bill rubbed his chin. "When Martin ran that company, it was like a license to print money."

"I'm sure Ellison would rather talk about her wedding than business," said Byron.

He was dead wrong.

"Maybe Martin should have put Mel in charge," I suggested. And why not? Mel was personable and smart and capable.

Four gazes fixed on me. Daddy patted my hand, and Bill offered me an indulgent, isn't-she-cute smile. "The grocery business is tough."

And women weren't tough enough.

"It's not just juicy grapes and ripe bananas. There's transport, warehousing, unions, and spoilage." Bill's patronizing tone tightened my shoulders. "When you girls go to the market, you expect to find every item on your list, but you never consider what it takes to get those items on the shelves."

"Melanie—Mel—is incredibly capable."

"Most women are. I couldn't make it through a day without Beth," said Tom.

"Imagine Harrington without Frances." Bill smirked, and Tom and Byron chuckled.

"Men and women are good at different things," Byron explained. "I'm useless in the kitchen."

"I am too," I replied.

"Does your detective know that?" Byron's voice was teasing, but his faded blue eyes were hard.

"He does." Arguing with men of Daddy's generation about women's roles was pointless. Their opinions had calcified over the years. Rigid. Set. Not subject to change just because their friend's daughter poked a time or two.

The waiter served my spritzer.

"Thank you."

"May I get anything for you, gentlemen?"

Byron twirled his index fingers. "Another round for the table." Maybe Nat was getting Byron's bar tab.

Bill leaned back in his chair and steepled his fingers. "I heard Dean Ardmore's son moved back to Kansas City."

Daddy's brows lifted. "Charlie?"

I swallowed. "He bought the house next to mine."

Concern wrinkled Daddy's brow. "Does your mother know?"

"I haven't told her." I'd rather ram shims under my fingernails. The instant Mother discovered Charlie was back, she'd begin a *replace Anarchy* campaign.

"She'll find out," Daddy warned.

"Undoubtedly." I took a restorative sip of spritzer.

"Ellison and Charlie dated in high school," Daddy explained.

I made myself smile. A light, isn't-this-amusing smile. "Half a lifetime ago."

"What does your fiancé think of your high-school sweetheart moving in next door?" asked Tom.

It was official. Men gossiped as much as women. Maybe more.

"He didn't seem bothered when I introduced them." That hard expression in Anarchy's eyes was none of Tom Horton's business.

Tom steepled his fingers. "Good man. It would bother the hell out of me."

CHAPTER FIVE

"I'm home." I dropped my handbag on the bombé chest in the front hall where a stack of mail awaited my attention. I flipped through the envelopes. Invitations. Bills. A letter from Aunt Sis. That I opened. She'd enclosed a Polaroid of her and her new husband (high-school sweethearts who'd rediscovered their love). Posed in front of swaying palm trees, they looked ridiculously happy.

Max trotted in from the kitchen and greeted me by rubbing his head on my hip.

I scratched behind his ears. "Where is everybody?"

He wasn't telling.

I scratched till he hummed with contentment and leaned most of his weight against my legs.

"Love you too."

Together we walked to the kitchen. Two notes sat on the counter. "Aggie's at the market." I picked up the second note. "Grace is looking for Pansy? How long has she been gone?"

Max regarded me with unreadable amber eyes.

"Where did she go?" From the back door, I scanned the back

yard. Pointless. Pigs would fly before Pansy returned on her own. I opened the screen, and Max trotted outside.

"Where is she?" Pansy loose in the neighborhood was an expensive proposition.

Max stared at me for long seconds then ambled toward the fence line I now shared with Charlie.

Oh, dear Lord.

"Pansy," I called.

Max looked over his shoulder and rolled his doggy eyes. By now I should know Pansy didn't come when called.

"She's your girlfriend."

Woof.

We slipped through a break in the blue spruces' boughs, and I stared at the open gate.

Max trotted through.

I followed at a slower pace and stopped just inside Charlie's property line. "Pansy?" Softly, so the dog could hear me, but the homeowner could not.

Woof.

Swallowing a giant tangled lump of annoyance and trepidation, I stepped fully into Charlie's yard.

Pansy had spent a busy afternoon. She'd dug up at least four feet of boxwood hedge.

"Bad dog!"

She looked up from her digging.

"Bad. Dog." I shook a finger at her and advanced.

Unfazed by my censure, her head and shoulders disappeared into the freshly dug trench. Soil flew.

"Pansy!"

The soil's arc reached for the trees' limbs.

I hurried toward her.

"Ellison?"

I tripped over a stick and fell.

A half-second later, gentle hands lifted me from the grass. "Are you all right?"

"Fine." I avoided looking at Charlie. I brushed stray blades of green from my skirt and scowled at the still-digging dog. "I'm terribly sorry. I'll pay to replace your boxwoods."

"My what?"

I pointed. "Pansy destroyed your hedge."

Pansy lifted her head from her tunnel to China, spotted Charlie, and bounded toward us.

"Bad dog."

She ignored me, and her body wriggled with joy at Charlie's knees.

"Who's a pretty girl?" he asked.

Pansy took his question as an invitation. She stood on her hind legs, planted her muddy paws on Charlie's shoulders, and licked his face with a none-too-clean tongue.

Charlie fell backward.

Pansy fell with him.

They landed in a heap on the grass.

I grabbed her collar and hauled her off Charlie's chest. "I am so very sorry."

Charlie shook.

"Did she hurt you?"

He shook harder.

"What's wrong?"

His laugh rousted birds from the trees. "Never fails." He wiped his eyes. "I was going for suave and sophisticated, and instead I land on my butt."

"Suave and sophisticated?"

"How else can I compete with your Steve McQueen lookalike?"

"Compete?" My voice was faint.

Charlie pushed onto his elbows and smirked at me. "Are you going to repeat everything I say?"

"No." I held out my left hand. "I'm engaged."

He waved a hand as if Anarchy were nothing but an inconvenience.

"I love him."

Charlie frowned and held out his hand. "Help me up?"

He didn't need help, but my dog had knocked him flat. I extended a hand.

His fingers closed around mine and he stared into my eyes. Charlie was older—his waist was thicker, his chest broader, his hair thinner—but his eyes hadn't changed. They were a soft blue and twinkled with intelligence and humor.

I pulled him off the ground, freed my hand, and dropped my gaze to the unrepentant dog. Her tongue, dotted with bits of earth and boxwood leaves, lolled from her mouth. "You're in big trouble, sister."

"Dogs will be dogs."

"Her first owner didn't teach her any manners. I sent her away to school, but the lessons didn't take. I'm afraid it's too late."

"Old dog, no new tricks?"

"Something like that."

"She's gorgeous. My kids will be visiting soon. They'll love her."

Max, whose paws were pristine, gave me a time-to-go nudge.

"I'm so sorry about this." I waved at the shredded hedge that used to edge his empty patio. "Let me know how much it is, and I'll replace everything."

"Who do I call?"

"Pardon?"

"To replace the bush. Who do I call?"

"Rosebluff Nursery."

"Anyone in particular?"

"Talk to Ash."

"Should I use your name?"

I nodded. "Tell him it was Pansy and ask him to send me the bill." Ash had received so many it-was-Pansy calls he should give me a volume discount.

"You've done this before." He glanced at his watch. "It's almost five o'clock."

I jerked my finger toward the fence. Max took a few steps, but Pansy ignored me.

"Have a drink with me."

"I can't—"

"It's the least you can do. Your dog destroyed my bushes and mauled me." His hands brushed bits of mud off his shirt. "For old time's sake."

There was a time I would have given anything to sit down with Charlie and ask what changed between the tearful our-love-will-last-forever goodbye in late August and the Thanksgiving breakup. Closure. I'd wanted answers, an explanation, an apology. Desperately. Till I didn't. We'd been too young, crazy in love, and blind to each other's faults. Our story wasn't new, original, or even interesting. "One drink."

"I'd invite you to sit outside, but Caroline got the patio furniture." He opened the back door and waited for me to enter.

"What about the dogs?" If I left Pansy outside, she'd destroy the rest of the hedge.

"They can come inside."

"Pansy's filthy."

He waved aside my objection, and Pansy darted into the house.

Charlie's kitchen held three untouched packing boxes, a brand-new Mr. Coffee, and a score of empty coffee mugs.

He frowned as if he'd just realized his kitchen was (except for Mr. Coffee's sunny presence) barren. "Let's sit in the living room."

"Lead the way." I followed through the front hall and into a room where two hideous plaid club chairs flanked a collapsible card table and faced a new television. The card table held a stack of ruffled newspapers, bourbon, scotch and gin bottles, a pair of readers, a copy of *Centennial* by Michener, and a telephone.

Charlie frowned again. "I need a decorator. Anyone you'd recommend?"

"I haven't had much luck with decorators." They kept dying.

"Could you go shopping with me? I need a couch."

"You need more than a couch. When do your kids arrive?"

"After Memorial Day."

"Do you have a place for them to sleep?"

"They like camping."

Maybe for a day or two. "I bet they like beds too."

"So you'll go shopping with me?" He hit me with a beseeching expression. "If you don't, my children will be reduced to sleeping on the floor."

I held up my left hand and waved it so the light caught the diamond on my ring finger. "It's a bad idea."

"He won't let you have male friends?"

Friends? That's not what Charlie hinted at on the lawn.

With balls of damp earth stubbornly clinging to her fur, Pansy leapt into one of the empty club chairs.

"Pansy! Bad dog."

She ignored me and made eyes at Charlie.

"Don't worry about it, Ellison. Those chairs are uglier than sin. That's why Caroline let them go. What'll you have?"

"Scotch." I scowled at the dog and pointed to the floor.

She pretended she didn't hear or see me.

Charlie poured two generous fingers of McCallan.

"Trying to get me drunk?" I accepted the glass.

"Nope. You said one drink. I figured I'd make it last." He poured bourbon into his glass, waved me toward the empty chair, and convinced Pansy to vacate.

Max settled at my feet.

Pansy trotted into the front hall and disappeared.

I pushed out of my chair.

He stopped me with a raised hand. "Let her explore."

"She's destructive." A tornado was destructive. Pansy was something else—something worse.

"There's nothing to destroy." He brushed the dirt off the chair, sat, and stretched out his legs.

I glanced around the unfurnished living room. "How long has it been?"

Charlie knew what I meant. We'd always read each other as easy as primers. "We signed the papers two weeks ago."

"And you're already moved?"

"Such as it is." He sipped his bourbon. "Things were bad for years."

"What happened?"

"The usual. I worked too much. She was lonely." He took another sip of bourbon. "He's a good guy, and I don't blame Caroline. What about you?"

"Henry and I stayed together for Grace. If he hadn't died, we'd be divorced."

"And the fiancé?"

"He investigated Henry's murder."

"What does Frances think of you marrying a cop?"

"Need you ask?" My turn to sip. "What brought you home?" I could never move away from Grace.

"A job."

"And the kids?" Didn't he miss them? Surely they missed him.

"They're happy at their school."

Kids needed a father, but Charlie hadn't asked for my parenting advice. I sealed my lips and studied the chair's burnt umber and avocado green plaid.

"It's better this way," he said.

For him. Maybe for his ex-wife. For the kids? I remained unconvinced.

"Caroline is marrying him." Pain decorated the edges of his voice like lace on a Valentine.

"I'm sorry."

"I'm not. Like I said, it's been a long time coming. The kids like him." He shrugged off the lingering ache of a failed marriage. "Meg and Davie will spend the summers with me, and we'll alternate Thanksgiving, Christmas, and spring breaks." He sipped again and surveyed the mostly empty room. "About that couch—"

Crash!

I leapt from my chair. Even in an empty house, the destructive force that was Pansy had found something to break.

MUTTERING DIRE (LARGELY IGNORED) THREATS, I dragged Pansy home. Thanks to her, Charlie had one less box of plates to unpack.

"You are a bad, bad dog." I pushed open the back door and three gazes settled on me.

"You found her!" Grace fell to her knees and wrapped her arms around Pansy's neck. "Where was she?"

"Next door at Charlie's."

Anarchy's eyes narrowed.

"She's a bad dog."

Immune to my censure, Pansy's tail wagged wildly. She licked Grace's face and grinned.

Aggie crossed her arms. "How did she escape?"

"The gate was open."

"The gate?" asked Anarchy.

"It's hidden behind the spruce trees."

"I'll get a lock."

If I didn't know better, I'd suspect he believed Charlie left the gate open on purpose. "Thank you."

"Did you see Dr. Ardmore?" asked Grace.

"I did. We had a drink."

Anarchy stiffened.

"Pansy destroyed his boxwood hedge."

"A whole hedge?" Aggie didn't seem that surprised.

"At least three feet of a mature hedge."

She tsked—a reminder that she'd opposed adding Pansy to our family.

"What happened to your skirt?" asked Grace.

I glanced down at the grass stain. "I fell."

"Quite an afternoon." Anarchy didn't just look stiff; he sounded stiff.

"I'm glad it's over." I shook a finger at Pansy. "Don't do that again."

She wagged her tail.

I swiped a piece of cheese from the platter Aggie was preparing. "How was everyone else's day?"

"School was a drag."

"Oh?"

"Mrs. Simms caught Peggy and Kim passing notes, so we have a pop test tomorrow." She scowled. "It's totally unfair that we all have to suffer."

"You've never passed notes?"

"That's not the point, Mom." Her tone was the equivalent of an eyeroll.

"Maybe you should study." The suggestion (and my lack of outrage) earned me an actual eyeroll.

Grace hefted her backpack over her left shoulder and stomped up the stairs.

I reached for a second piece of cheese.

Now Aggie rolled her eyes. "If you'd like to sit in the living room, I'll bring this when I've finished." Her cheese trays were edible works of art.

"Thank you." I offered Anarchy a nothing-happened-at-Charlie's smile. "Would you like a drink?"

"Please."

"Go." Aggie shooed us out of her kitchen.

Anarchy and I left, but the dogs stayed and supervised salami placement.

Anarchy paused in the hallway. "You had a drink with him?"

"We're old friends."

"I suspect he's interested in more than friendship."

"He's been divorced for two weeks. I doubt he's looking for a relationship. And even if he was—" I held up my left hand "—I'm not available."

Anarchy's expression cleared and he pulled me close." You're sure?"

"Positive."

"I bet your mother liked him."

"She did. But that was two decades ago."

"Does she know he's back?"

"Not yet."

"When she finds out, she'll push him at you." No flies on Anarchy.

"Probably," I admitted. "I'm sure Celeste has a Birkenstock-wearing free spirit picked out for you."

His lips brushed my forehead. "Undoubtedly."

"We're united in disappointing our mothers."

"Seems that way." I lifted on my toes and kissed him. "Missed you today."

Anarchy smiled, and his lean, serious face transformed. "Missed you too."

I claimed his hand and led him toward the living room. "Let's have a drink and you can tell me about the investigation."

We entered the living room, and Anarchy crossed to the bar cart. "What'll you have?"

"Scotch." Best not mix liquors.

He poured two glasses, and I kicked off my shoes and curled up in the corner of the couch with my feet tucked beneath me.

"Thank you." I accepted a glass.

"You're welcome." He sat next to me.

"Your day?" I asked.

He sipped. "Rough. Did you find out if Karen Morris was having an affair?"

"I did not. Do you have any other suspects?"

Anarchy shook his head.

"How was he poisoned?"

"We're not sure."

"So someone at his office might have killed him?"

"It's possible."

"Anyone with a motive?"

"By all accounts, he ran his department well. He wasn't liked, but he was respected. His employees claim he had almost mythic abilities when it came to spreadsheets."

"Mythic abilities?"

He nodded. "That's what they say."

"If I had a mythic ability, I'd want something better than spreadsheets."

"Such as?"

"Finding good parking spots."

Anarchy's eyes sparkled.

"Don't laugh. You know the trouble I get into in parking lots."

"Fair enough."

"What about you? What mythic ability do you want?"

He rolled his shoulders. "Solving crimes."

"You do that already."

"But not at a mythic level."

"If Karen didn't kill Clayton, and he was respected at work, who did it?"

"Do you know anyone who wanted him dead?"

"Some people, they make it through a day without being murdered and it's a miracle. But Clayton? He didn't evoke enough emotion." I sipped my scotch. "Maybe he discovered the contractor or architect stole."

"Even if he did, how would they poison him?"

"We're back to Karen?"

"Afraid so."

"I don't think she did it." I crossed my fingers.

"Find me another suspect."

I leaned forward and kissed him. "I will."

"Hors d'oeuvres?" Aggie stood in the living room entrance holding a cheese tray.

"Please," I replied.

She positioned the tray on the coffee table. Brie, Edam, sharp cheddar, goat cheese, and smoked gouda shared space with sliced salamis, crackers, and grapes.

"That looks marvelous. Thank you."

"You're welcome. Dinner will be ready at half-past."

I glanced at my watch. We had thirty minutes.

Anarchy leaned forward and helped himself to a piece of cheese and a cracker. "It's almost too pretty to eat."

Aggie flushed at the compliment.

"Can you join us for a few minutes?" I asked her.

"I'm behind in the kitchen."

"You?"

She nodded hard enough to make her hair bounce. "I witnessed a terrible accident."

"Was anyone hurt?" I asked.

"I'm afraid so. It was awful. A car ran a red light, and a pickup truck t-boned the passenger side. I had to stop. Had to. I gave my name and number to the patrolman in case they need a witness."

"Ellison, what's wrong?" asked Anarchy.

I looked up from my clasped hands.

"All the color drained from your face." Anarchy brushed a warm finger against my suddenly cold cheek.

"Clayton Morris was in a similar accident."

Both Anarchy and Aggie gaped at me.

"It was years ago."

"Someone was hurt?" Anarchy asked.

"Someone died."

His warm palm covered my chilly left hand. "Who?"

With my right hand, I raised the scotch to my lips and drank. "David Ardmore."

"Any relation to your new neighbor?"

I drew air deep in my lungs and reminded myself of my loyalties. "Charlie's older brother."

"That sounds like a motive," said Aggie.

"Not really," I argued. "It happened ten years ago. And it was an accident." A terrible accident.

"You don't think the timing's interesting?" asked Anarchy. "Ardmore moves back to Kansas City and the man responsible for his brother's death dies."

"Why wait ten years?"

"Revenge is a dish best served cold. Speaking of cold, unless you want a cold dinner, I need to get back to the kitchen." Aggie left us.

"Charlie didn't kill Clayton. He wouldn't."

"How do you know?"

"I know. I know Charlie." Did I? He'd fallen for another girl while we were still together. That had been out of character.

"If you don't think it's a possibility, why mention it?"

"Because I don't want to keep secrets from you." I stared into my scotch. "The idea is nonsensical."

If Anarchy's crossed arms and lowered chin was an indication, I'd failed to convince him.

"Charlie's a successful doctor. Why would he commit murder?"

"Clayton Morris ran a red light and Charlie's brother died."

"It was a horrible accident. Charlie wouldn't kill Clayton."

Anarchy shook his head as if I'd disappointed him. "You should keep an open mind; follow the evidence."

"Evidence? There isn't any."

"We haven't looked for it." He patted my hand. "But we will."

I swallowed. "Do you really think Charlie could be a killer, or is this because..."

"Because he wants you back?"

"You noticed?"

"It's painfully obvious."

"You didn't answer my question."

"Charlie has a motive. I'd be remiss if I didn't investigate."

CHAPTER SIX

I stepped away from the canvas and let my inner critic take over. The lake's turquoise hues were too bright. The water needed more shadow, more depth.

"I'm sorry to interrupt." Aggie's voice floated up the stairs to my third-floor studio. "Your mother is on the phone." Usually Aggie put her off—whatever Mother wanted couldn't be good.

"Did she say what she wanted?" I replied.

"You and Grace are invited for dinner." Aggie made the invitation sound like a demand.

"Not Anarchy?"

"She didn't mention him."

"Please tell her we're otherwise engaged."

Aggie's answering silence told me she had no intention of fighting my battles—especially when those battles featured Frances Walford.

"Fine." I put down my brush and plugged the phone into the jack. "I'll talk to her." My fingers closed around the receiver. "Hello."

Mother ignored the coolness of my greeting. "Dinner's at seven. Come for drinks at six."

"Is Anarchy included in this invitation?"

"Not tonight."

"We have plans."

"Change them. There are things we need to discuss, Ellison. Wedding things. Anarchy would be bored."

Or mortally offended. Possibly grateful. I'd be grateful if I could skip this dinner. "As I mentioned, tonight is not convenient."

"Why not?"

I searched for a reason.

"Please, Ellison?" Now she cajoled. "I promise I won't mention Anarchy's mother or his job."

She promised that now, but after her second martini, all bets were off.

"If you intend to go through with this—" she made marrying Anarchy sound less appealing than a root canal "—we need to plan."

"We want a small wedding. There isn't much to plan."

"There's still the menu, flowers, the cake, your dress, the photographer, and—"

None of which were her concern. She'd planned my first wedding. This time I'd taken charge. That considered, I could argue or I could paint. "Fine. We'll be there at six o'clock."

"We'll eat in the dining room."

That meant scraping the turquoise paint from under my fingernails. That meant dressing for dinner. I wore paint clothes —faded jeans and one of Henry's old shirts with a frayed collar —and I didn't want to change. My shoulders sagged.

"I expect Grace to look like a young lady, not a chippy."

"Grace always looks nice."

"You can't mean that. She wears denim to school."

"All the kids wear jeans."

"*All the kids are doing it* has never been or will ever be a valid reason."

Paint or argue? I swallowed an annoyed sigh. "Mother, I'm painting. If there's nothing else, we'll see you at six."

"Don't be late."

"We'll be there." The words slipped through gritted teeth. I hung up and reclaimed my paintbrush.

The lake needed more shadow, and I lost myself in the mix of color and light and dark. For as long as I could remember, painting had been my way to channel emotion. Frustration with Mother's demands? I deepened the waves' indigo. Frustration with Anarchy? A new emotion, but he'd refused to listen when I insisted Charlie couldn't be a killer. I added midnight streaks to the water.

I took a step back.

Too much shadow. The lake's waves hid ominous secrets—maybe a kraken.

I added lighter shades to my pallet, dipped the brush, and lost myself for three glorious hours. Because my next gallery showing was in Chicago, I'd created a series of lake scenes. This, the most recent, had a summer's-gone-the-carnival's-closed feeling. The regret that imbued the painting came as a surprise. Some paintings refused to comply, their hidden message more important than my intent.

I stood ten feet away from the easel and nodded. The painting wasn't what I'd planned, but it was striking, the kraken had retreated to the depths, and I was pleased with the wistful shadows in the water. I'd done enough for today. I washed my brushes, scrubbed the paint from my hands, and descended the stairs.

Grace's backpack rested on the kitchen counter. The kitchen clock read half-past three. The day had slipped away from me.

"Grace?"

"Outside." Her voice drifted through the screen door.

I stepped onto the sunny patio where Grace watched Pansy

chase a tennis ball. Max was too regal to chase inanimate objects. "We're having dinner at your grandparents'."

She frowned. "Seriously?"

"What's wrong?"

"I have a test tomorrow."

"You had a test today."

"That was history, and the test was easy."

"And tomorrow?"

"Chemistry. It won't be easy. I totally need to study."

I spent half my life caught between pleasing my mother and my daughter. "We'll take two cars, and you can leave after we eat." A compromise. Mother lingered over after-dinner coffee, and I'd be there for at least an hour after the last bite of fruit tart disappeared.

Worry creased Grace's brow. "Granna won't approve."

"Your grandmother's disapproval is nothing new. We should be used to it by now."

Pansy dropped a slobbery yellow ball at Grace's feet and wagged her tail.

Grace picked up the ball and hurled it to the far reaches of the yard. Pansy took off running.

Max yawned.

"Is Anarchy going?" His presence dampened Mother's enthusiasm for criticism.

"He wasn't invited. Your grandmother has something to discuss." I added air quotes. No doubt the discussion would center on the mess I'd made of my life when I accepted his proposal—that or appropriate wedding dresses for middle-aged widows.

"You could say 'no.'"

"I could." I indulged in a three-second fantasy—one that included me, jeans, a couch, and a good book. "She's my mother. No matter how pushy she is, I love her. We may not agree, but in her mind, she's looking out for me."

"She pushes you around."

"Not as much as she used to." Standing up to Mother was new since Henry's death.

"You two are so different. How did that happen?"

"I have a theory."

Pansy returned with the ball, Grace threw it, and the golden streak zipped across the lawn. "What's the theory?"

"Daughters study their mothers and pick the things they like least."

She nodded. "With you so far."

What did Grace like least about me? "Those are the things we avoid as mothers."

"So you avoided controlling me?"

"I tried."

"What did Granna avoid?"

"My grandmother was a slave to fashion."

"Granna always looks nice."

"True, but over the years Mother has made comments—I think she found her mother frivolous. Your grandmother identified a personal style and sticks with it no matter what *Vogue* tells her." Mother wore Chanel suits, solid colors, and pearls. Always pearls.

Grace wiped her hands on her jeans. "Granna does have a distinctive look."

"We pass more to our children than our genes—whether we mean to or not." I touched my throat, where a gold chain usually hung.

Pansy returned with the ball. Rather than drop the slobbery thing in a wet puddle at Grace's feet, Pansy collapsed on the floor. Her tongue lolled from her mouth. She panted. And she grinned.

"You're a terrible dog," I told her.

Her doggy grin widened.

"She's a handful," Grace agreed. "I think she's even getting on Max's nerves."

"Aggie said the same thing." I eyed Max. "You better get used to her. She's ours now."

He sighed and settled his chin on his paws.

Grace bent, petted both dogs, and produced a Granna's-dinner-makes-my-life-harder sigh. "I'd better get some homework done." She left me.

I turned my face toward the afternoon sun and stretched. I felt better. Painting and a few mostly drama-free minutes with Grace gave me a fresh outlook. Charlie Ardmore wasn't my problem. He hadn't killed Clayton, and Anarchy wouldn't find evidence to suggest he had. As for Mother, I'd listen to her then do as I pleased.

GRACE and I arrived at Mother and Daddy's at precisely six o'clock (arriving fashionably late did not apply to daughters).

Daddy opened the door, pulled me into a hug, and whispered, "Sorry about this, sugar."

Mother probably had a long list prepared.

"Grace, you sure look pretty."

Grace, who wore a Lilly Pulitzer shift and sandals, kissed her grandfather's cheek. "Thank you."

"Frances will be down in a minute. What can I get you girls to drink?"

"White wine," I replied.

"Tab, please. With lime if you have it."

We followed Daddy into the living room where a mushroom-stuffed Brie *en croute* sat in the center of the coffee table and small sterling silver bowls filled with mixed nuts dotted the side tables.

Unease rubbed my spine. "Daddy?"

"Yes, sugar?" He wouldn't meet my eye.

"Who else is coming to dinner?"

"What makes you think someone else is coming?"

I pointed to the Brie. Mother didn't serve Brie *en croute* for family. Puff pastry was strictly for company.

Ding, dong.

"I'll get it." Mother's voice carried from the front hall.

Daddy handed me a generously filled wineglass, and I caught his eye. "She found out?"

He nodded, an apology in his eyes. The man was a traitor.

"How could you?" I held out my hands as if begging hard enough could somehow make him take it back. "She asked him to dinner?" How could she? And why was I surprised?

"If I didn't tell your mother, and she discovered I knew..." He grimaced. "Don't shoot the messenger."

Could I shoot the man who spilled the Charlie beans?

"Who's joining us?" asked Grace.

Before I could answer her, Charlie and Mother appeared in the entrance to the living room.

"Harrington, you remember Charlie Ardmore? Grace, this is your new neighbor." Mother wore a navy skirt, a creamy silk blouse, pearls, and Cheshire cat smile.

Charlie took the room's temperature (frigid) and jammed his hands in his pockets—a gesture that reminded me of the boy he'd once been.

Long awkward seconds passed before Charlie pulled his right hand from his pocket and shook. "Nice to see you again, sir." He smiled at me, then turned his attention to Grace. "You're just as pretty as your mother."

Grace snorted. Then, with her grandmother glaring a be-polite-or-else hole into her chest, she extended a hand. "Nice to meet you."

"I have a daughter about your age. Maybe when she comes to Kansas City, you can show her around."

"Sure," Grace replied with zero enthusiasm.

"Maybe the pool one afternoon?"

Mother pursed her lips—Grace and I teaming up to disappoint her. "Harrington, get Charlie a drink."

"What's your poison?"

"Bourbon."

Daddy splashed two fingers of Wild Turkey into an old fashioned. "Ice?"

"Please."

Daddy added ice to the glass and handed it to Mother's guest. "Frannie, what'll you have?"

Mother glanced my way, weighed the likelihood of me stomping out (somewhere around sixty percent), and said, "A martini. Extra dry."

Grace perched on the edge of the couch and watched the adults as if we were characters on *As the World Turns*.

"Here you are, my dear." Daddy offered Mother a glass of gin.

She smiled her thanks. "Charlie, it's such a treat to have you with us." She raised her glass. "To old friends."

Everyone with alcohol drank. Deeply.

"It's kind of you to ask me to dinner, Mrs. Walford."

"Frances," she corrected. "Please call me Frances."

I swallowed half my wine in one sip.

"Charlie and your mother were high-school sweethearts," Mother told Grace.

"You're the one who went off to college and cheated on her?"

Mother choked on her gin.

"Are you all right, Mother?" Sweeter than pure sugar cane, that was me.

"Fine," she snapped.

"Boys do stupid things." Charlie answered Grace's question, but he stared at me. "Breaking up with your mother counts among the stupidest things I've ever done."

"Why'd you do it?"

"Grace!" Mother used her scandalized voice and shot me a death glare as if I were responsible for Grace's questions. I wasn't. But I was enjoying them.

Charlie pulled at his collar. "I was too young and stupid to know better." He offered me a smile. "I'm older and wiser now."

Mother beamed as if he'd presented me with the Hope diamond. "Charlie, you must try some of the Brie."

Charlie ate Brie, and I held my empty wine glass out to Daddy.

"Anyone else need a refill?"

Mother gave me a don't-drink-like-a-lush look.

I gave her a don't-you-dare-judge-me look. If I downed the entire bottle, she had only herself to blame.

"I wouldn't say no to another," said Charlie.

Mother's expression softened. She couldn't chasten me for a second glass of wine when Charlie was putting away bourbon like Libba downed martinis. Recklessly.

"I'm terribly upset with you, Charlie." Mother didn't sound upset. She sounded like a spider delighted with the new fly in her web.

"What have I done?"

"I'm on the board at St. Mark's, and you took a job at a different hospital."

"What kind of medicine?" asked Daddy.

Charlie helped himself to a cracker, covered it with double-cream Brie baked in puff pastry, and said, "Cardiologist."

"Well, we're thrilled you're home. Aren't we, Ellison?"

"Thrilled."

Charlie's eyes crinkled in amusement.

"How are your parents enjoying Santa Fe?" Mother asked.

Charlie's parents had retired and bought a home off Canyon Road in Santa Fe.

"They still love it."

"Ellison enjoys Santa Fe."

Oh, dear Lord. With my wedding to Anarchy looming, Mother had dispensed with subtlety.

"What do you like about Santa Fe?" Charlie asked.

"Gorgeous scenery. Wonderful artists."

Mother wrinkled her nose. Adobe buildings, turquoise jewelry, and Pueblo art didn't figure on her list of favorite things. "Who's that woman? The one who paints flowers."

"Georgia O'Keefe?" I replied.

"That's the one."

"What about her?" Daddy asked.

"She has a studio in Santa Fe," Mother replied.

With conversation like this, Charlie would need a third bourbon before dinner.

"Do you have family in Kansas City?" asked Grace.

"No. My parents are in Santa Fe, and my niece and nephew are in Denver."

"Denver?" Mother's brows rose.

"After David died, Marilyn moved back to Colorado." The bleakness in Charlie's voice made me think he still mourned his brother.

"How long has it been since..." Mother's voice trailed to a silent question.

"Ten years. The ten-year anniversary passed a few days ago."

"Such a tragedy," she murmured. "You heard Clayton Morris passed away?"

"I heard." A jeweler could cut diamonds with the edge of Charlie's voice.

"Does Anarchy know what killed him?" asked Daddy.

Mother gave Daddy a do-not-mention-Ellison's-poorly-chosen-fiancé-in-front-of-Charlie look.

I closed my lids and saw the quirk of Anarchy's smile (Mother's machinations might amuse him) and the warmth of his coffee-brown eyes. "He's still investigating."

"Ellison has been dating a detective," Mother explained.

I held up my left hand. "We're not dating. We're engaged. And Charlie met Anarchy."

Mother's eyes narrowed. "Oh?"

Charlie nodded and his fingers drifted toward his collar as if they sensed we covered dangerous ground. "How's Libba?"

I sent him a silent, heartfelt thank you. We needed a change in topic. "She's fine."

"What happened to her?" Daddy asked.

Charlie returned his hand to his lap. "An owl attacked her ponytail."

Daddy smiled into his drink. "Sounds dreadful."

If she'd made it into my house with an owl attached to her head, it might have been. "Just another day at the funhouse." I turned to Charlie. "Did you talk to Ash?"

"Not yet."

"Ash?" Mother tilted her head. Why did Charlie need a nursery?

"Pansy damaged Charlie's hedge."

She shook her head—not remotely surprised. "That dog is a menace."

"But she's gorgeous." Charlie smiled at me. It was the same smile that sent my teenage heart racing.

Another large swig of wine. "Pansy has a thing for Charlie."

Mother's answering smile said she approved Pansy's preferences.

"If you decide you want a dog, let me know."

"Mom!" Grace leapt from her seat on the couch and planted her fisted hands on her hips.

"She'd be next door, sweetie."

"You'd give me your dog?" Charlie asked.

"She adores you and can visit Max whenever she likes."

Mother smiled her approval. "You can share her." And then combine households.

"It's a genuine offer," I told Charlie. "But think about it. She'll cost you a small fortune in landscaping."

"The house is lonely at night, and the kids would love her. Could she play with Max during the day? I'd hate for her to be alone when I'm at work."

"Mom!"

I'd spoken too soon. "Grace and I need to discuss this before we make any decisions."

Charlie nodded.

"Well, I think it's a splendid idea," said Mother. Splendid because Charlie and I would see each other every day if we shared a dog. She stood and smoothed her skirt. "I'll check on dinner. May I get anyone anything while I'm up?"

Grace and I knew better than to answer. The question was for Charlie.

"Do you cook, Mrs. Walford?"

Mother forced a smile. "No. But my housekeeper is almost as talented as Aggie." Her meaning was clear: Aggie was an extra incentive for pursuing me. "Ellison will invite you for dinner soon. Aggie's roast beef is simply divine."

"She also makes a mean Bundt." I stood. "May I help you in the kitchen?"

Mother's mouth opened, but no words came out. She'd rather not point out that her daughter was a kitchen disaster—not in front of a single doctor who still carried a torch. "I have everything covered."

"You're sure?" I had things to say to her. Many things. None of them suitable for guests.

"I can manage. You keep Charlie company."

CHAPTER SEVEN

"I can't decide." I preferred the candlesticks, but Anne Driscoll and her fiancé Jay Gilstrap had registered for the God-awful tureen. Presumably that meant they actually liked it. "Which do you prefer?"

Carmen, a sales associate at Hall's Plaza's china department, eyed the soup tureen and the candlesticks and tapped her lips. "The tureen is stunning."

Was she serious? The tureen was a giant cabbage, probably made to hold cabbage soup. And who in their right mind willingly ate cabbage soup?

"The candlesticks have a certain presence." Carmen was no help.

"I'll take the candlesticks. I only use my soup tureen three or four times a year. We light candles almost every night." Flickering tapers could make grilled cheese and tomato soup feel elegant.

"We'll have them wrapped and sent."

"Thank you. I also need a shower gift for Genevieve Farchmin and her fiancé." Wedding season was upon us, and my Saturday nights had filled with nuptials and showers.

"The fiancé's name?"

"August Westbrook. Gus."

"Of course. There's a kitchen shower this weekend." Carmen flipped through a forest-green three-ring binder. "Here they are." She scanned the page. "They're registered for a French press."

Foolish children. Why would they want a French press when Mr. Coffee was a million times easier to clean? "Fine. What about everyday china? Are they registered for mugs?"

"They picked the new Portmeirion pattern. It's called Botanic Garden." Carmen pointed to the place setting on the wall of china.

Most likely Genevieve had selected the pattern. Hard to imagine Gus Westbrook chose the delicate flowers.

"Pretty," I murmured. Infinitely preferable to a giant cabbage.

Carmen ran her finger down Genevieve and Gus's registry. "They still need eight."

"The press and eight mugs. I'll need to take this gift with me."

"Gift wrap?"

"Please."

Carmen pursed her lips. "It may take a few minutes."

"Not a problem. I'll swing by the makeup counter while I wait." I handed her my charge plate.

"I'll be just a moment." Carmen disappeared behind a partition, and I studied a wall of fine china.

When Henry and I married, we spent an afternoon registering for china, silver, table linens, kitchen gadgets I didn't know how to use, bed linens, candelabra, crystal, and everyday dishes. Henry, already bored with the process, hadn't noticed or cared when I picked a Spode pattern with pink tulips and a pink scalloped edge. Hopeful and excited, my younger self might have harbored a doubt or two (or twenty) about her upcoming marriage, but she'd never voiced them. Instead she'd selected

Reed and Barton's Francis First sterling and smiled adoringly at the man holding her hand.

Carmen returned with the sales receipt and a chit to claim the wrapped gift.

I signed. "Fifteen minutes?"

She frowned. "It might be thirty."

"Not a problem. Thank you for your help."

"My pleasure, Mrs. Russell."

I crossed the store (resisting the Steuben gallery's siren call) and stopped at the Estée Lauder counter.

"Good morning, Mrs. Russell."

"How are you, Esme?"

"Fine. Thank you for asking."

"I need to replace a lipstick."

"Your usual shade?"

"Please."

She closed her eyes and tapped her forehead. "Cinema Pink?"

"I don't know how you remember."

Esme merely smiled. "What else today?"

"That's it. Just the lipstick."

"Ellison?" Mel Langford joined me at the counter. Dark half-moons hung beneath her eyes and her skin sagged. "How nice to see you."

"You too. Are you feeling okay?" If I looked like Mel, I'd be home in my bed with a cup of hot tea. I could only stomach hot tea when I was ill.

"I'm just tired." She eyed Esme. "You girls always look so perfect. It's intimidating for us mere mortals." Mel wasn't wrong. Like most of the women who worked at Hall's, Esme looked like a fashion model and followed a strict dress code. The sales associates were walking advertisements for the store's wares.

Esme offered us a smile and turned to the storage tower behind her.

Mel picked up a bottle of Private Collection and sniffed. "I came down to pick up a gift for Genevieve Farchmin's shower."

"I just left Carmen. I bet she still has their registry handy."

Mel eyed the new summer lipstick shades and frowned.

"How's Hubb? Is he feeling better?"

"No," she breathed. "Not at all." She lowered her voice. "They're saying Clayton was murdered." Mel glanced at Esme's back. "How do you do it?"

"Do what?"

"Deal with murder. I'm terrified Hubb and I will be slaughtered while we sleep."

"Do you think Hubb might be a target?"

Mel pressed her hands to her chest. "I can't imagine that. But someone killed Clayton." She cut her gaze to Esme who still searched a drawer for my lipstick.

"Do you know something?" I asked.

"I shouldn't say—"

"Here's your lipstick, Mrs. Russell."

Drat. I handed Esme my charge. "Thank you."

Mel retreated a step as if she'd said too much. (She hadn't said enough.) "I have errands to run, Ellison. It was lovely to see you."

"Wait."

Her brows rose.

I dug in my handbag. "I have your glasses. You left them at bridge."

"I wondered where I'd lost them."

I reached the bottom of the bag and found no glasses. "I changed bags. They must be in the purse I carried to bridge. May I drop them off later?" We could talk without interruption.

"That's very kind, but it's out of your way." Mel and Hubb lived in Leawood in a sprawling ranch on a couple of acres—out

South and not convenient. "I misplace them all the time, so I have five or six pairs. Bring them to the party." She squinted at her watch. "Lands! Is that the time? I must run. Talk soon."

Mel dashed off to buy a shower gift, and Esme presented me with a tissue-stuffed bag and a sales receipt.

I signed my name at the bottom of the slip and claimed my lipstick. "Thank you."

"You're welcome." Esme glanced out the glass double doors at the sunny sidewalk. "Enjoy your day."

"I will. I'm meeting my fiancé for lunch."

Her gaze strayed to my ring. "When's the big day?"

"We haven't decided."

An unexpected expression flashed in her eyes. Pity. She thought Anarchy had cold feet.

Did Anarchy worry I had doubts? We'd discussed setting a date, and he'd understood my hesitancy. Or maybe he hadn't. Maybe he'd hidden his hurt feelings.

I forced a smile. "Have a nice day, Esme."

Grace and I needed to talk. Did she even care if Anarchy and I picked a date? That conversation might be difficult since Grace wasn't speaking to me. Me offering to give Pansy to our new neighbor was a silent-treatment offense.

I wandered toward the gift-wrap counter—at least I meant to. My feet took me to the escalator, which carried me to the ladies' sportswear department. A peasant blouse with a round neckline, embroidered poppies, and a scalloped hem finished with the same thread used for the bright flowers caught my eye.

"May I help you?"

"Do you have this in a four?"

"I'll check." The sales clerk searched the rack and pulled the blouse. "We do."

"I'll take it." Grace would love it. She might even forgive me. I wasn't above bribery.

The clerk swaddled the blouse in tissue paper and slipped it into one of Hall's signature green-and-gold-striped bags, and I signed another sales slip.

With the peace offering (bribe) hanging from my wrist, I stopped by the gift-wrap counter, claimed the shower gift, and headed home.

Max met me at the front door.

I unloaded my purchases onto the bombé chest and stroked his silky ears. "Where's Pansy?"

He wasn't telling.

"Aggie?" I found her in the kitchen. "Where's Pansy?"

She looked up from measuring flour. "Sunning on the patio."

I peeked out the window and breathed a relieved sigh. "Did Grace tell you?"

"It's a fine idea." She frowned. "Too bad you sprung it on her."

"Not my finest parenting moment. What are you making?"

"Chocolate chip cookies. Are you home for lunch?"

"No. I'm meeting Anarchy at a restaurant on the boulevard."

"Where?"

"Ponak's."

The woman wearing a blue kaftan splashed with red geraniums and an orange apron eyed my dress. "You might want to change clothes."

"Oh?"

"Mac took me there. Whatever you wear will smell like Mexican food when you leave."

I wore a silk blouse. "Thanks for the tip. I'll change."

I hurried upstairs, threw on khakis and a linen camp shirt, fastened several gold chains around my neck, and switched handbags.

When I descended the back stairs, Aggie nodded her approval. "Much better. I can wash that."

I checked my watch. "I should go."

"Will you be back this afternoon?"

"I plan on it. I need to paint." I scratched behind Max's ears, grabbed my new lipstick on the way out the door, and drove north.

ANARCHY STOOD when I approached the table. The warm expression in his eyes soothed my fears—maybe my reticence in picking a date hadn't hurt him.

He kissed my cheek and pulled out my chair.

We sat and stared into each other's eyes for long seconds.

"May I get you a drink?"

I dragged my gaze from Anarchy and glanced at the waitress. "Iced tea, please?"

"Coming right up."

"Thanks for meeting me here. I spent my morning at Patriot Produce."

"Is it nearby?"

"A couple blocks west. What do you think of Ponak's?"

I took in the restaurant's knotty pine paneling, wood floors, and bar constructed with bricks. "It has character."

"So diplomatic. Wait till you try the food."

"I tried making tacos once."

"And?"

"It didn't go well." The experience had put Grace off Mexican food for years.

"I asked around. Mexican immigrants came to Kansas City for jobs with the railroads and meat-packing plants. They stayed, and the good cooks opened restaurants."

"You've eaten here before?"

Anarchy nodded.

I picked up the menu from the table. "What should I order?"

"The tacos are odd, but they're delicious."

"Odd?"

"They're topped with parmesan."

"I'll try them." I returned the menu to the table and smiled at the man sitting across from me. I couldn't help it. He had that effect on me. "Did you learn anything useful at Patriot Produce?"

He frowned. "No one saw anything, nor can anyone imagine why Morris was murdered."

"I saw Mel Langford at Hall's this morning."

"Mel?"

"Hubb's wife. Patriot is her family's company."

"Go on."

"She mentioned being terrified someone would target Hubb."

"You think he was the target?"

"I don't know what to think. Daddy's cronies say the produce business is tough." Temptation defeated willpower, and I selected a tortilla chip from the basket on the table and dipped it into a bowl of salsa. "Mmm. Delicious. Is there a competitor who might buy the company if it were in trouble?"

Anarchy rubbed his chin. "I don't—"

The waitress put my tea on the table. "Are we ready?"

"Tacos, please."

"Chicken or beef?"

I looked to Anarchy for guidance.

"Beef," he replied. "Two orders."

The waitress made a note on her pad. "We'll have that out soon."

I folded my hands in my lap. Folded hands couldn't grab chips. "You were saying?"

Anarchy munched a chip. "How did the killer poison Morris? If a competitor did it, how did they get access?"

I frowned. "Karen's still a suspect?" And Charlie?

"Murderers believe what they do is justified. Doesn't matter if it's heat of the moment or cold and calculating."

I helped myself to a chip (impossible to eat only one—I never should have tried the first one) and waited for his point.

"Killers don't necessarily look like monsters. They look and act like everyone else."

"I'm aware." The dryness in my voice was Mother-worthy. I sipped my iced tea. "Perfectly lovely people commit murder."

"I wouldn't go that far." His voice was equally dry.

Charlie was definitely still a suspect. I scowled at the innocent basket of chips.

"Let's talk about something else," he suggested. "What were you doing at Hall's?"

"Wedding and shower gifts. Are you still planning to escort me to the Westbrooks' party?"

"Saturday night?"

"Yes."

"I'll be there. What did you get them?"

"A coffee press and mugs."

"A press? What would Mr. Coffee say?"

"He'd applaud the idea but tell me the press will soon gather dust on a shelf while Genevieve and Gus push his buttons."

"You've given this some thought."

"Not really. I just know him well."

Anarchy's brows drew together.

"Mr. Coffee and I have a special relationship," I explained. I wasn't making this better. We needed a different topic. "Do you want to set a date?"

"A date?"

"For the wedding."

Anarchy froze with a chip halfway to his mouth. "I thought you wanted to wait till Henry had been gone a year."

"I did. I do. But what do you want?" It was our wedding. We should both have a say.

"If I could, I'd marry you tomorrow. As far as I'm concerned, we need a license, a justice of the peace, and Grace."

"What about your family?"

"You met my mother."

I reached for the chips. "Yes." Celeste didn't approve of me. I was too staid, too boring, for her brilliant son.

"She's the easiest member of my family."

"Oh."

"Imagine it now." Anarchy waved his hand across the table. "My father quoting Che Guevara at the country club. My sister would be barefoot. She won't wear shoes. My brother will hit on every married woman there."

"Not the single ones?"

"He doesn't do commitment."

"Maybe I should introduce him to Libba."

"Libba wants a commitment. She doesn't want marriage."

He was absolutely right. "I never—"

"Here you go." The waitress put plates filled with parmesan-dusted crispy tacos, rice, and refried beans in front of us. "You need a refill?"

My tea was half-empty. "Please."

Anarchy tilted his head and bit into a taco.

I pushed rice around my plate with my fork. "So, if Grace doesn't mind, shall we set a date?"

"Are you kidding?" He beamed at me. "I can't wait to call you my wife."

My cheeks warmed and I tilted my head and bit into a taco.

"Would your mother hate me if we did what Sis and Gordon did?"

My aunt and her new husband had a surprise wedding. Their engagement lasted only a few days.

"She won't hate you, but she might not speak to me till Christmas."

His face fell.

"That's not necessarily a bad thing." Considering last night's dinner, her silence might be a boon.

"You say that now." He took another bite of taco.

The waitress returned with my tea. "How's everything tasting?"

"Delicious." I could be eating sawdust and wouldn't notice the flavor. "Thank you."

"What's the bare minimum you can invite?" Anarchy asked.

"Ten."

"That's it?"

"Mother, Daddy, Grace, Libba, Marjorie and Greg, Karma, Sis and Gordon, and my cousin David. I guess that's nine—wait, it's ten. Oh! Aggie and Mac. I'm up to twelve."

"For me it's five."

"Less than twenty guests? We can serve lobster and Dom Perignon."

"That might not go over well with my family."

"What if we got married at the house?" I liked this idea. "On the patio? I could have lunch or dinner catered."

"You don't want a fancy wedding?"

"I had a fancy wedding. I don't need another. You're the one who'd miss out. Do you want an elaborate affair?"

"Lord, no." His eyes sparkled. "How soon can we do this?"

"As soon as Grace gives her blessing." Hopefully that blouse made up for offering Pansy to Charlie. "After that, you can get a license, I'll call a caterer, and we can invite our families."

He grinned. "We're doing this?"

"With Grace's blessing, but she may not be in the mood to make me happy."

"Why not?"

"She's mad at me. I told Charlie he could have Pansy."

"Why?"

"He's lonely, and Pansy adores him."

"When did this happen?"

"Last night at dinner."

"You invited Ardmore to dinner."

"No! Mother did. She surprised me." Mother had never asked Anarchy to dinner. Not once.

"I don't like that guy."

What could I say that wouldn't make this worse?

"His marriage failed, and he decided to come home and pick up where you left off."

My jaw dropped, but I didn't argue his point.

"The man's an idiot for letting you go, but he's smart enough to want you back."

"Wow."

Anarchy scowled. "His brother who died? I looked it up. David Ardmore died on the same date as Clayton Morris."

"If Charlie wanted revenge, why would he wait ten years?"

"I don't know. Yet."

"You're not being objective."

He winced. "Doesn't mean I'm wrong,"

"Can't you take my word for it? Charlie's not a killer."

"Let me guess. He's one of those perfectly lovely people. There are rules, Ellison. If you break up with a woman, you don't get to waltz back into her life and steal her back."

This wasn't about me. "Who was she?"

"What?"

"You know my entire history, and I know next to nothing about your past."

"I'm an open book."

"Really? Who was she?"

"Summer Brixton."

I put my fork on the plate and waited for more.

"We met when I worked in San Francisco."

"How long were you together?"

"Five years."

"Five years!" That was longer than some marriages. I lowered my voice. "What happened?"

"Her first love turned up and swept her off her feet."

"A, she was an idiot. B, that won't happen again."

"Oh?"

"I am utterly, hopelessly in love with you."

His expression softened. "I don't doubt you." He stared into his glass. "After Summer left, I came to Kansas City. I didn't realize till I met you how wrong Summer was for me."

"I bet your mother loved her."

"A little bit."

I tilted my chin and waited for honesty.

"Fine. Mother went into mourning when we broke up. She's convinced Summer left me because I'm a cop."

"That's ridiculous."

"To you."

"You put this ring on my finger. You're stuck with me. I don't care if you're a cop or a lawyer or a ditch digger." Mother would have a coronary.

He gazed at my hand. "I'm the luckiest man on earth, and I'll try to keep an open mind about Ardmore."

"Just so you know, I mourned when Charlie broke up with me, but I would never give him another chance. Fool me once, shame on you. Fool me twice, shame on me. I've had enough with the men I can't count on."

"I'll never let you down."

"I know that."

"When does Grace get home from school?"

"Around three thirty. Why?"

"We could both talk to her."

"Don't you have a murderer to catch?"

"I do. But this is more important."

We finished our meals, and Anarchy walked me to my car. I dug through my purse for the keys and found Mel's glasses. "Are you going back to Patriot?"

"No. Why?"

"These are Mel's glasses. If I drop them off with Hubb, he

can return them and I won't have to drive out to where Jesus left his sandals."

He frowned. "I'm sorry, I'm due at the station."

"In that case, I'll drop them off."

Anarchy pulled me close and kissed the tip of my nose. "Be careful."

"I always am. Besides, what could happen?" Famous last words.

CHAPTER EIGHT

Lumber companies, hulking warehouses, the husks of warehouses, and hole-in-the-wall restaurants lined Southwest Boulevard. Less than twenty feet from the street, a freight train rumbled.

I drove west and spotted the building. It squatted near the street and a faded flag decorated its bricks. Patriot Produce's home had probably started as an icehouse. It had definitely seen better days.

I parked next to a Mercedes in the postage-stamp-sized lot. In and out. Five minutes—then I'd go home, paint, and plan the conversation with Grace. I found Mel's glasses, got out of the car, and pushed through the front door.

I entered a small waiting room. Curling posters of apples, grapes, pears, and tomatoes covered the faded walls and an empty dented metal desk took up most of the space. I rang the silvered bell on the desk's corner—*ding*—and waited.

A full minute passed, and I rang the bell a second time. *Ding, ding, ding.*

Again I waited. In vain.

I could leave, but that had to be Hubb's Mercedes in the lot.

A single door led out of the reception area. I pushed through it.

The dim warehouse was cavernous and chilly. Slatted crates reached for the twenty-foot ceiling, created a rat-in-a-trap maze, and hugged the brick walls. Their absence in the center of the warehouse created a wide aisle. The air carried hints of strawberry, lettuce, and rot.

A man driving a forklift spotted me, and his jaw dropped in surprise.

I took a step toward him but stopped. I didn't trust those teetering crates.

I watched the man maneuver a crate from the top of a stack and carry it to a truck parked at the open loading bay at the warehouse's rear. The man shifted the load to the truck, parked the vehicle, and strode toward me. "What do you want?"

"I'm dropping something off for Hubb—Mr. Langford." Your boss. We're friends. You should wipe the forbidding scowl off your face.

He grunted and pointed to a staircase on the far wall. "Offices are upstairs."

"Thank you." I climbed the steep open iron-work stairs with my hand clasped tightly around the rail. A second-floor balcony overlooked the warehouse floor.

This was not what I expected. If someone asked me to describe an office for Hubb Langford, I'd have conjured sleek furniture and a skyline view, not the scent of fruit and veg, not could-collapse-at-any-moment stairs, not the chill of three-feet thick windowless brick walls.

I ventured along the balcony and tapped on the first door I encountered.

No one replied, and I cracked the door and peeked inside. An ancient desk held an electric typewriter, metal filing cabinets crowded the exterior wall, and an overhead light—the kind with those ghastly tubes—buzzed.

I closed the door and continued.

The next door stood open. The office was larger. It held four desks. None of them occupied.

I sighed my frustration. Who knew returning Mel's readers would be such a challenge?

I reached the next door. I tapped. I opened. "Hello?"

Was that a foot? A shoe? My heart relocated to the base of my throat. I looked over my shoulder. Where was the forklift driver? Another human, even a grumpy one, would be a comfort. The crates blocked my view. "Hello? Are you down there?"

No one answered. I tiptoed inside.

Two people were behind the desk. The woman whose foot caught my attention sprawled across the carpet and stared sightlessly at the rust-hued shag. Hubb Langford slumped halfway out of his chair.

"Hubb?" My voice squeaked.

He groaned.

Thank God. I reached for the phone, knocked over a coffee mug filled with pens, snatched the receiver, and dialed the operator. "I'm calling from Patriot Produce. We need an ambulance right away."

"I'll connect you."

Click, click, click, ringtone. She'd disconnected me.

I scowled at the dead phone, swallowed my frustration and rising panic, and dialed Anarchy's office.

"Homicide."

Hearing Anarchy's partner's voice felt like a blessing. Things were bad when Detective Peters' voice was a blessing. "It's Ellison Russell—"

"He's not here."

"I'm at Patriot Produce—"

"What are you doing there?" I heard his glare, heard his face tighten, heard his mustache bristle. "You'd better not be meddling."

I'd explain the glasses later. "Please send an ambulance." I glanced at the woman. "You and Anarchy should come."

"Body?"

"Yes."

"Who?"

"I don't know." I rubbed my eyes. "A woman."

"How?"

"I don't know. There's no blood."

"Don't touch anything."

"Hubb's not dead." Yet. "What should I do?"

"Ambulance is on its way. Don't contaminate my crime scene."

I hung up the phone and crouched next to Hubb. "Can you hear me? How can I help?" It looked as if Hubb had got tangled as he slid from his chair. His left elbow was caught in the chair's arm.

"Hubb?"

He groaned.

I freed his arm, and he drifted onto the carpet. "Help is on the way. I'll meet them at the door." I paused on the balcony and searched the warehouse floor for the man who'd driven the forklift. If he waited for the ambulance, I could stay with Hubb.

The man had disappeared.

Unease dragged a cold finger down my nape, and I shuddered. I was alone in a deserted warehouse. Presumably someone had poisoned Hubb and the woman. I glanced at my watch. How long till the ambulance arrived?

With dread tightening my spine, I tiptoed down the stairs.

Somewhere in the warehouse, an apple or pear or Brussel sprout fell—the soft noise was impossibly loud in the unnatural quiet. "Hello?" My voice didn't quaver. Much.

I stepped onto the warehouse floor. The door to the reception area was less than twenty feet away. All I had to do was pass through that door. A sunny sidewalk and passing cars waited on the other side.

Easy.

But a visceral fear kept me rooted.

"Hello?" I sounded like a five-year-old child who'd heard her first ghost story.

I peered into the depths of the warehouse—darker now that the loading bay had closed.

Nothing. I was alone. And I was behaving like a fool. I inched forward.

A bouquet of too-sweet smells accosted my nose. I breathed through my mouth and ignored the way the stacked crates loomed. And teetered. I scurried forward. I refused to die beneath a ton of bananas.

My heart thudded so hard it hurt.

Fifteen feet.

What was wrong with me? I wasn't a nervous Nelly. I was strong. I was confident. I was woman. Hear me roar.

Crash!

I leapt four feet straight into the air.

Behind me, where I'd stood seconds ago, a crate lay in ruins. Cabbages rolled across the floor like disembodied heads.

"Eeep!" I ran, yanked open the door, blasted through the front room, and exploded onto the sidewalk. Was I safe?

I could run to my car. Lock the doors. Not that locked doors made much difference in a convertible. I clenched my shaking hands and took a deep breath. Where was that ambulance?

I glanced over my shoulder at the door. What could I do if the person who'd pushed the crate followed me onto the sidewalk? Despite the afternoon sun, I shivered.

A siren pierced the air, and I collapsed against the building. Only force of will kept me from sliding to the sidewalk. I held my breath and let the building's sun-warmed bricks ease the chill that had settled into my bones.

Seconds later an ambulance parked at the curb, and I straightened.

"You called for help, ma'am?"

I nodded at the young man. "This way." Re-enter that creepy warehouse? Not. A. Coward. "Follow me."

I led two EMTs through the empty waiting room and the crates, up the stairs, and to the office.

They pushed past me, took the woman's pulse, and shifted their attention to Hubb.

The rational part of my brain told me to return to the sidewalk and wait for Anarchy. The five-year-old child refused to cross the dark warehouse by herself. Not again.

"Ellison?" Anarchy's voice came from amongst the stacked crates.

I stepped onto the balcony. "Up here."

He bounded up the steps two at a time and ran to me. "Are you all right? Are you hurt?" He searched my face.

I fell into his arms. "I'm fine."

"What happened?" Detective Peters had followed Anarchy, and his mustache stood on end with disapproval. Of me. Of hugging at crime scenes.

I nodded to the office where the EMTs worked to save Hubb's life. "There's a dead woman. And Hubb..." Mel was right. Hubb was a target.

Anarchy's arms tightened around me.

"This place—" Now that I was safe, a golf ball lodged in my throat, and my jaw ached.

"What about it?" His voice was gentle.

I swallowed the golf ball. "When I arrived, a man on a forklift was loading crates onto a truck. He sent me up here."

"Where is he now?"

"Gone. He tried to squash me."

"Squash you?" Peters sneered.

"With a crate of cabbages." So glad I hadn't bought that tureen.

Peters snorted.

Anarchy stiffened. "Peters, why don't you check the crime scene?"

When Peters stepped into the office, Anarchy led me toward the stairs. "Tell me exactly what happened."

I told him.

"What did this guy look like?"

"Mean. Rude."

His lips quirked. "A description?"

"Oh. Five ten. Stocky. Square face. Close-set eyes. And a scar." I touched my face. "On his cheek. If you get me a piece of paper, I can draw him."

"That's great. Would you feel better downstairs?"

I imagined sitting alone in one of the windowless offices and nodded.

We descended the stairs, entered the waiting room, and I claimed the empty chair behind the receptionist's desk.

"I'll find paper. Don't move."

Not a chance. I sat at the desk and stared at the tomato poster.

"Who are you?" A woman stood in the outside doorway and stared at me. "What happened?"

"I—" How to explain? "I'm a friend of Mel's. I stopped by to drop off her glasses." I'd lost her glasses. I'd lost my purse. I lowered my head to my hands.

"Why are the police here?"

I looked up. "The body."

"The body? Where?" The woman clutched the door frame. She was young and pretty and wore too much eye makeup. Someone should tell her she'd look much better without blue shadow.

I kept my makeup tips to myself. "Upstairs."

"Mr. Langford?"

"Yes. No."

"Which is it?"

"The EMTs are working on him. He's not dead."

"You said there was a body."

"There is."

"Who?"

"A woman."

"Denise?"

"I don't know."

"Auburn hair. Blue eyes."

I pictured the sightless eyes. They'd been blue. "I don't know."

"I found paper—" Anarchy stopped short when he saw the woman in the doorway.

"You're back." She didn't sound happy. Usually women were thrilled to have Anarchy around. Maybe she didn't like cops. "She said someone died." She pointed an accusing finger at me. "Who?"

"We haven't identified the victim."

"What happened?" she demanded.

Anarchy handed me the paper. "Ellison, would you like to do this at home?"

"I can't leave."

His brows rose.

"I lost my purse."

"I'll find it." He speared the eyeshadow woman with a piercing gaze. "We'll have questions."

"I already answered your questions."

"We have new ones."

"I wasn't here."

"Where were you?"

"Lunch hour. We close every day from twelve thirty to one thirty."

"The entire company goes to lunch at the same time?" That seemed odd. Who answered the phones?

She shrugged. "Most days."

"The front door was unlocked."

"Sometimes I forget." Her gaze traveled the sad little reception area. "It's not as if there's anything worth stealing."

"If everyone went to lunch, who was the guy in the warehouse?"

"What guy?"

I smoothed the paper on the desk, selected a pencil from a cup, and drew. First the shape of his face, then the mix of features—the slash of his mouth, the squinty eyes, the scar. I took my time and ignored (mostly) the eyes watching me.

Anarchy crossed his arms and leaned against the wall.

The woman lit a cigarette and sent plumes of smoke toward the already stained acoustical tile ceiling.

"There." I finished. "That's him."

Anarchy studied the face, frowned, then shifted his gaze to Eyeshadow Woman. "Have you seen him before?"

She glanced at the drawing. Barely. "Nope. Never seen him before." She was lying. I was sure of it.

"He was in the warehouse. He operated a forklift. He loaded a truck."

She avoided meeting my gaze. "He doesn't work here." The EMTs wheeled Hubb through, and the woman paled. "Will he be okay?"

No one answered.

"What's your name?" I asked her.

"Why do you care?"

"Her name's Amber Leader," said Anarchy.

I forced a smile. "Nice to meet you, Amber. I'm Ellison Russell."

She blew smoke at me.

Anarchy picked up the drawing and helped me from the chair. "Come on, let's find your purse."

It wasn't as if Amber had told us anything—and from the stubborn tilt to her chin, she intended to keep her own counsel. So why did I feel as if I were abandoning her? She couldn't be much older than twenty. Only a few years older than Grace. "Are you okay?"

She blinked as if my concern surprised her. "Ducky."

Okay then.

I followed Anarchy into the warehouse. "This isn't what I expected."

"What do you mean?"

"This." I waggled my fingers at a crate of red onions.

"It's a warehouse."

"If you knew Mel and Hubb..." The couple I knew didn't fit with a rundown warehouse. "This is the headquarters for a regional distributorship, and it looks like a business hanging onto a cliff's edge by the tips of its fingers."

"There are other warehouses in Des Moines, Omaha, Wichita, Oklahoma City, Little Rock, and St. Louis."

Hopefully nicer—cleaner—than this one.

"According to Langford, his wife's grandfather started the company out of this place. They keep it for sentimental reasons."

"Hubb's never struck me as sentimental."

"Maybe his wife wanted to keep it."

"Maybe." I wasn't convinced. How long had it been since Mel visited this place?

"There." Anarchy pointed to a leather strap half-buried by cabbages. He bent and retrieved my bag.

"Thank you." I brushed grit from the floor and a cabbage ruffle off the bag and hung it over my shoulder.

"Are you okay to drive home?"

Was I? "Yes."

"Is Aggie home?"

"I'm fine."

"I worry."

"This isn't my first body."

He winced. "I know."

"I'll let you get to work." I didn't move.

He glanced at the balcony. "Thanks for the drawing."

"I hope it helps."

His hand, warm and comforting, closed around my arm. "I'll walk you to your car."

We passed through the empty waiting room, and I asked, "Where did Amber go?"

Anarchy huffed his displeasure. "We have her phone number and address. We can find her."

After the dark warehouse, the sun was too bright. I dug for my sunglasses and slipped them on my face. "I can make it to the car from here. I'm fine."

"I know you are. I still want to see you safely on the road."

"Where did they take Hubb?"

"Ellison." Anarchy's voice was a plea. "Please go home."

Mel might need me. "But Mel—"

"We haven't yet notified his wife."

"Surely the hospital will call her when Hubb arrives."

"I can't do my job and worry about you."

How could I argue with that? "Fine. I'll go home."

"I'll swing by as soon as we're done here."

We walked to my car, and he opened the driver's door.

"Don't get crushed by any cabbages," I directed.

"Promise."

"Or any other vegetables."

"What about fruits?"

"Those are forbidden too." Forbidden fruits?

He kissed me—a glad-you're-okay-but-I-still-worry, way-too-quick kiss. "I love you."

The words still had the power to make my heart skip a beat. "I love you too." I slid behind the wheel, started the ignition, and pulled into traffic.

Anarchy stood in the parking lot and watched me drive away.

I shifted to third gear and touched my lips where the press of his still lingered. Bodies aside, I was a lucky woman.

CHAPTER NINE

When I arrived home, a red Corvette convertible sat in my circle drive. I parked behind it and ventured into the house. "Hello?"

"We're in the kitchen," Libba called.

My feet dragged. I loved Libba. I did. But I'd found a body and nearly been flattened by killer cabbages. I didn't need more drama. Not this afternoon. Not when I needed bonding time with Mr. Coffee and a paintbrush in my hand.

I tamped down a sigh, pushed open the kitchen door, and stopped in my tracks. "Your hair?"

Libba fluffed her much-shorter hair. "Do you like it?"

"You look fabulous." The shaggy style was young and hip and suited her.

"This covers the bald spot." She touched her scalp and winced. "Also, I needed a change."

"Change? Does that explain the Corvette?"

"It's a pick-me-up."

"That's quite a pick-me-up." If she were a man, I'd call it a mid-life-crisis car.

She wrinkled her nose at me and waved a chocolate chip cookie in the air. "Have you tried these?"

"Not this batch."

"Aggie's cookies could solve the world's problems. Who knew?"

Aggie swept in with a laundry basket in her arms. "Chocolate chip cookies can't end a war or achieve equal rights." She stashed the basket on the back stairs. "For day-to-day problems, they can make a world of difference."

"I'll take two."

Libba pushed the plate filled with cookies toward me. "What's wrong with your day?"

I settled onto a stool and claimed a cookie. "I found a body."

"You did not."

"Did too."

"Where?" She glanced around the kitchen as if I kept corpses stashed in the kitchen cabinets.

I bit into the cookie and moaned. Crisp and perfectly browned on the outside, soft and gooey on the inside, and over-the-top chocolaty. "Aggie," I spoke around my full mouth. "This is the best cookie I've ever tasted."

Aggie nodded, taking credit where credit was due. "Did you really find a body?"

"I did."

"Where?" Libba demanded.

"Patriot Produce."

Her brow wrinkled. "Where?"

"It's a fruit and vegetable supplier," said Aggie. "Mac bought from them." Aggie's Mac owned an Italian deli and catered parties. "Their quality became a problem, and he switched suppliers."

"What were you doing at a produce company?" Libba demanded.

"Dropping off Mel's glasses."

A light bulb appeared above Libba's freshly shorn head. "The Langfords' company."

"Exactly."

She pressed a hand to her heart. "Not Hubb!"

"No. A woman."

"How?"

I took a bracing bite of cookie. "Poison? There was no blood."

Libba pursed her lips in a Mother-like expression (less sour pickles, more concern). "When it comes to bodies, you're the unluckiest woman in the world."

"No argument."

"Did you talk to Hubb?"

"No." I gave her a severe look. "If I tell you, you can't say a word."

She crossed her heart and leaned forward.

"Hubb was poisoned too. The last I saw him, he was being loaded into an ambulance."

Libba jerked back and grabbed the counter to correct her balance. "Does Mel know?"

"The police will notify her."

A deep frown brought her brows together. "Will the police tell her you were there?"

"I don't know. Why?"

"If you found my husband with a dead woman and you didn't tell me, I'd be furious."

"You don't have a husband."

"If I did."

I rolled my eyes. But she had a point. "Anarchy asked me to keep quiet." I eyed the cookie plate—this was definitely a two-cookie day. "One good thing—Karen won't be a suspect. She has no reason to kill Hubb." The same was true for Charlie.

"Maybe the woman was the target." Aggie opened the fridge,

took out a bottle of cold milk, and asked, "Would you like some?"

"Please."

She poured. "Who was she?"

"I think she worked there."

"And?" asked Libba.

"And nothing. I've told you everything." I'd left out the killer cabbages. I frowned. "Aggie, where are the dogs?"

"Next door. Dr. Ardmore offered to play fetch with Pansy. Max is supervising."

"Did you bribe him with cookies?"

Aggie grabbed a tea towel and wiped stray crumbs into the cup of her hand. "The man needs a dog."

"Wait!"

Aggie and I stared at Libba.

Libba pointed an accusing finger at me. "You tripped over another body."

Strictly speaking, I hadn't tripped. "Yes."

"And you're talking about Charlie needing a dog?"

I was also eating cookies and drinking milk. I wiped my mouth with the back of my hand. "He also needs a girlfriend."

Libba scowled at me.

"When the sky falls, it's comforting to discuss small problems." It was called avoidance, and she knew it well. I (also not a stranger to avoidance) bit into my second cookie. "What are your plans for the next month? Are you in town?"

"Yes. Why?"

I turned to Aggie. "What about you? No pregnant nieces?" Aggie came from a large Italian family. She was the aunt tapped for babysitting when her nieces went into labor.

She smiled. "Not a one."

"What's going on?" Libba's suspicious gaze was almost comical.

"Will you please be my maid of honor?"

She leapt from her stool and wrapped me in a bone-crunching hug. "Yes!"

"I should have asked you the first time I did this."

Libba loosened her hold. "What about Grace?"

"I'm hoping she'll give me away."

"Frances will have a stroke." She grinned as if she couldn't wait for Mother's reaction.

"My wedding. Aggie, I want you and Mac there as guests, but would you please make my cake?"

Aggie ducked her head. "I'd be honored."

"This is really happening?" Libba bounced on the balls of her feet. "Where?"

"Here."

She went still. "Here?"

"Back yard. Twenty guests."

Again with the I-love-trouble grin. "Frances will have a coronary."

"You already said that."

"I said 'stroke' the first time."

"She did," Aggie agreed.

I held up my index finger. Waved it. "No stroke, no coronary, no wedding—not without Grace's blessing."

"Pish. Grace adores Anarchy."

"True. But I'm not sure she likes me right now."

Aggie shook her head, and her red curls sproinged like mad. "Give her the blouse. I'll feed her chocolate chip cookies. She'll be in such a good mood, she'll say yes to anything."

"If she wants me to wait till her dad's been gone a year, I will."

"This year thing." Libba still grinned as if she'd downed an entire bottle of happy pills. "Your idea or Grace's?"

"Mine."

Libba and Aggie exchanged a loaded glance.

"Does she know you're postponing your wedding for her?"

"No."

"I figured. Talk to her. She'll tell you how stupid you are."

Brnng, brnng.

"I'll get it." Aggie picked up the receiver. "Russell residence." She listened. "One moment, Mrs. Walford. I'll see if she's available."

I shook my head and pressed my hands together in a please-don't-make-me-talk-to-her plea.

Aggie mouthed, "She knows."

"The body?" I whispered.

Aggie nodded.

Oh dear Lord. How had she found out so quickly? I rubbed the back of my neck, rolled my shoulders, took a deep cleansing breath, and accepted the receiver. "Hello."

"Another body, Ellison?"

"Yes."

"How?"

"I walked into an office, and there she was."

"What were you doing on the Boulevard?" Mother was well informed.

"I met Anarchy for lunch."

"You ate lunch down there? It's a wonder you haven't died of food poisoning." Mother favored restaurants with white linen tablecloths.

"Lunch was marvelous."

"Ellison—"

"Just because you don't eat on the Boulevard doesn't mean the restaurants aren't good."

"They're ethnic."

"Yes."

"Ethnic food gives your father indigestion."

Such a lie.

"Why were you at Patriot Produce?"

I explained Mel's glasses.

Mother couldn't fault my reasoning. "This wouldn't have happened if they didn't live so far away."

"I'm fairly certain—" one hundred percent positive "—the murder had nothing to do with their address."

"I'm not talking about the murder. I'm talking about you finding yet another body."

That. "How did you find out?"

"The ambulance brought Hubb to St. Mark's. Mel ran in as I left a committee meeting. She told me you'd found Hubb and his secretary."

"Who told her?"

"Detective Peters."

Of course he had.

"Mother, where are you now?"

"I'm still at the hospital."

"Should I drive down there?"

"Hubb's in ICU, and Mel's with him. The doctors won't let you in."

Relief washed through me. Not nice. Not kind. But I was almost as tired of hospitals as I was of finding bodies.

"What does Anarchy say about this?"

"What do you mean?"

"He doesn't care that you find corpses at an alarming rate?"

"He cares, but he doesn't blame me."

Mother's affronted hiss was a snake slithering through the phone line. "You're saying I do?"

If the shoe fit. "Mother, Libba is here with me. I'll call you later."

"Have you seen Charlie today?"

"No."

"You were good together." Her voice softened from strident to sweet. "He made you happy. You wrote *Ellison Ardmore* in your diary."

"You read my diary?"

"The point is you loved him."

"Twenty years ago."

"You could love him again. As often as you get hurt, marrying a doctor is a smart idea."

"I'm hanging up, Mother. If you talk to Mel, tell her I'm keeping Hubb in my prayers."

"Ellison—"

"Goodbye, Mother." I eased the receiver into the cradle.

"Did you hang up on your mother?" Libba's eyes were as big as Aggie's cookies. Enormous.

"In the nicest possible way." I warned her before I did it.

She snorted. "As if that makes a difference."

Grace stomped through the back door, dropped her backpack to the floor, and glared at me. Her gaze caught on Libba's new 'do, and her expression flickered. "Nice hair."

Libba fluffed. "You like it?"

Grace offered a grudging nod and spotted the cookies. The charcoal cloud above her head lightened to slate gray, and she helped herself.

"Would you like milk?" I asked.

With her mouth full of cookie, Grace scowled her answer. She wanted nothing from me, she'd pour her own milk, thank you very little. "Aggie, these are awesome."

"Cookies were your mother's idea."

Grace looked as if she might spit the cookie into the nearest napkin. She didn't. They were too delicious.

"I should go." Libba adored happy Grace. But moody Grace? Not so much.

"Who does the Corvette belong to?" Grace asked.

"Me," Libba replied. "I bought it today. What do you think?"

"It's amazing. Will you take me for a ride? Please?"

"Absolutely."

"Cool." Grace gobbled the rest of her cookie and chugged her milk. "Let's go."

"Now? Don't you want to tell your mom about your day?"

"No."

Libba winced for me.

It might take more than a new blouse and a plate of cookies to earn Grace's forgiveness.

Libba fished her keys from her handbag. "Where would you like to go?"

"Wherever." *Whatever*'s less angst-ridden second cousin.

Grace and Libba pushed through the kitchen door to the front hall, and I groaned. "This requires the big guns."

"Oh?" Aggie cleaned up Grace's crumbs.

"Dinner at Winstead's."

The frown on Aggie's face gave me pause. "What?"

"I defrosted a chicken."

I had bigger problems than an uneaten chicken. "Can we eat it tomorrow?"

"Of course. You're sure Winstead's will work?"

"It hasn't failed me yet."

GRACE and I waited just inside Winstead's door. Hungry customers filled the diner's booths.

"How many tonight?" asked the hostess.

"Two, please. Ruby's section."

She glanced over her shoulder. "It'll be five to ten minutes. I can seat you now if—"

"We'll wait for Ruby." I was taking no chances when it came to sweetening Grace's mood. Ruby was her favorite waitress—we'd happily wait.

Happily was a subjective term. Grace stood next to me with her arms crossed, her upper lip curled, and thunder on her brow.

"How was your ride with Libba?"

"Fine."

"Did she trade in her Mercedes?"

"She didn't say."

I stepped to the side and allowed a hand-holding couple access to the door. "Where did you go?"

"Around."

"Grace, I know you're upset with me, but—"

"It's not always about you, Mom." Teenage ennui threatened to drown me.

I blinked and swallowed a sharp retort. *It.* Grace's emotions. They weren't about me, but I'd do as a punching bag. I was tasked with pleasing her. And Mother. And Daddy. And the dogs. It was my job to keep everyone happy. My friends were in similar boats, but they added pleasing a husband to the list. *It's not always about you*. It was never about middle-aged women, but we were tasked with fixing *it*—whatever *it* was.

"Your table is ready." The hostess pointed to an empty table in Ruby's section.

That was quick. "Thank you."

Grace and I claimed our table, and Ruby appeared with short glasses filled with water and crushed ice. She smiled at Grace. "Hey, sugar."

Grace's dour expression softened. "Hi, Ruby."

"What may I get you to drink?"

"A cherry limeade, please."

Ruby turned her attention to me.

"The same."

"Coming right up." She made a note on her pad and moved on to the next table where a family of four polished off steak-burgers. "Did you save room for dessert?"

I switched my focus to Grace. She crossed her arms tightly and leaned her head on the seatback so she stared at the ceiling instead of me.

"About Pansy—"

"I don't want to talk about it."

"You're obviously upset."

She didn't bother responding.

"I make mistakes, Grace. I'm not perfect. I should have talked to you first. Pansy is our dog—not mine. I was wrong and I'm sorry."

Was that a tear glimmering on her lower lid?

"It's not Pansy." She wiped the tear away. "It is Pansy. And other stuff."

"What other stuff?" I braced myself for an it's-none-of-your-business eyeroll. "What's bothering you?"

"Ellison!" Elise Chandler stood next to our table. "I'm so glad to see you. Have you sent that Bundt recipe yet?"

I made myself smile. "I'm sorry, Elise. I forgot."

"I suspected as much."

"I'll ask Aggie in the morning."

"Thank you." She glanced at Grace and frowned. "Sorry to interrupt."

Years of good manners drilled into her overrode Grace's black mood. "It's nice to see you, Mrs. Chandler."

Elise's face cleared. "Are you a sophomore this year?"

"Yes, ma'am. I'll be a junior in the fall."

"That's right. Only a few more weeks of school."

"Twelve school days till exams."

"Counting the days, are you?"

"Till summer? You bet."

Her faith in the politeness of well-bred children restored, Elise returned her attention to me. "I checked on Karen this morning."

"How is she?"

"A wreck. She scheduled the funeral for Monday."

I made a sympathetic sound in my throat.

"She's dealing with so much."

"It's a difficult time."

"She has so much on her plate." Elise frowned. "I offered to pick up Clayton's things, but she insisted on going herself."

"Clayton's things?"

"Yes. From his office."

"Karen went to Patriot Produce this morning?"

"You'd think Hubb would drop them off, but some woman called and told Karen to pick them up."

The diners' chatter, the rustle from the wax papers wrapped around the steakburgers, and the clink of spoons in sundae glasses faded to white noise. "Karen went this morning?"

"I arrived at her house at ten thirty. She left around eleven."

I'd found Hubb and his secretary at twenty past one.

"Ellison, are you okay?"

"Fine."

"You went pale, Mom."

"Did I? I'm fine." I took a sip of water, and the crushed ice in the glass hit me in the nose.

"I won't keep you," said Elise. "Don't forget that recipe." She wagged her fingers and walked away.

I grabbed a handful of paper napkins and wiped my face. Karen had visited Patriot Produce, and someone else was dead.

Ruby interrupted my thoughts with two cherry limeades. And straws.

"Have you decided?"

"A steakburger with cheese and rings, please," said Grace.

"A steakburger with cheese and fries. Extra crispy."

Ruby made a note on her pad and bustled away.

Grace stared into her cherry limeade.

"What's bothering you?"

"Jared and I broke up."

Jared? Who was Jared? "I'm sorry, honey. What happened?"

"He cheated on me." She swirled the straw in her drink. "With Peggy."

Peggy counted among Grace's closest friends.

"I liked him." She looked up from shredding the straw's paper wrapper. "How could she? I feel like such an idiot."

"You trusted them, and they betrayed you. That's on them, not you."

"Is this how it felt with Dad?"

A toxic cocktail of shame, insecurity, and anger? "Yes."

"I miss him."

I assumed she meant her father. "Of course you do. Your dad adored you."

"Sometimes it seems as if I'm the only one who misses him."

Quite possibly. I searched for a suitable response and couldn't find one. I jammed the straw into my cherry limeade. "Your dad was well-liked. He's missed."

"Not by you?"

Not a bit. "We had so many problems, but he was a good father. I miss having him there for you." Had I said the right thing?

"He hurt you."

"He did."

"I wish things had been different." Tears filled her eyes.

I reached across the table and squeezed her hand. "Me too. I'll always be here for you."

"I love you, Mom."

"Love you too." I smiled at her. "How many fries for a ring?" The going rate varied from two to three.

"Four."

"That's extortion!"

"Three."

"Deal." Tonight was not the night to discuss my wedding, not when it might bring fresh tears to her eyes. I'd figure out the date later. Grace's feelings came first.

CHAPTER TEN

Mr. Coffee greeted me with a gingham-bright smile. *How did it go last night?*

"Don't ask." I took a mug from the cabinet, checked Mr. Coffee's reservoir and brew basket (both full—thank you, Aggie), and pushed his button.

How can I help?

"You do enough. I run on coffee."

His pot flushed with pleasure—or possibly steam. *What's on your agenda for the day?*

"I thought I'd run this morning." Yesterday's Mexican food, two chocolate chip cookies, and dinner at Winstead's made burning calories essential.

Are you taking the dogs?

Max lifted his head from his paws and gave me a don't-you-dare-go-without-me look.

My shoulders sagged. Running with both dogs meant constant vigilance—not at all the relaxing run I'd hoped for. "Yes."

Almost ready. Mr. Coffee was a tease.

I fetched the cream from the refrigerator.

Mr. Coffee finished dripping, and I poured the nectar of the gods into a World's Greatest Dad mug. I lifted the cup to my lips, breathed the heavenly aroma deep into my lungs, and savored my first sip. Hot. Slightly bitter. Creamy. "You're man's greatest invention since the wheel."

There's the internal combustion engine. Mr. Coffee was being modest.

"I'd rather drink coffee than drive."

But without the engine, the coffee beans might still be in Brazil. You need boats and trucks for transport.

"Fair point. You're number three."

He answered with a satisfied smile.

I shuffled to the front door and picked up the morning paper.

Pansy, who'd followed me, regarded the paper with hope in her eyes. Would I throw it for her?

"We're going on a run, and you will behave."

She wagged her tail but made no promises.

I took the paper to the kitchen, spread its pages on the island, sipped my coffee, and read.

The dead woman I'd found was Denise Bryce. She'd worked at Patriot Produce for sixteen years and was survived by two sisters.

With a few words, the reporter brought Denise to life for me. I gazed into my half-empty mug and the contents blurred behind a veil of tears.

Mother treated my finding bodies as an embarrassing inconvenience. Mother was wrong.

This summer, Denise wouldn't shoot fireworks with her nieces and nephews on Independence Day. Did she have nieces and nephews? In my mind, she did. Denise wouldn't spend a lazy Sunday afternoon in a shady hammock with a book she couldn't put down. She wouldn't plan a vacation, fix Thanksgiving dinners with her sisters, shop for Christmas presents, or enjoy the perfect cup of coffee.

My heart ached for a woman I didn't know.

You okay? asked Mr. Coffee.

I sniffled. "I'm fine."

"Who are you talking to?" A barefoot Grace had snuck down the back stairs.

"Myself."

"An affirmation?"

"Something like that. Are you feeling better today?"

"I am." She held her arms wide and spun. "Thanks for the blouse. I love it."

"It suits you."

Grace opened the fridge and selected a container of Dannon yogurt—strawberries on the bottom, her favorite.

"I should have asked last night—how did the chemistry test go?"

She rolled her eyes. "Let's not talk about it."

"That sounds ominous."

"It'll be fine." She plucked a spoon from the cutlery drawer and swirled her yogurt. "I passed, but it won't be pretty." She lifted the spoon, eyed the yogurt coating its bowl, and continued stirring. "I'm sorry I took my bad mood out on you."

"That's what mothers are for."

"You think?" The yogurt now perfectly stirred, she ate quickly.

"I do. Mothers are a safe place. A daughter can rage or cry or roll her eyes and know she'll always have her mother's love."

"How's that working with Granna?"

"It's not a perfect system."

She chuckled then licked the spoon.

"And I'm not saying I enjoy your rage, but I'm always in your corner."

"Always?" She hugged me.

I held her tight. "Always."

Too soon, Grace pulled away. She threw her empty yogurt container in the trash and took a sip of my coffee. "I should go. I told Debbie I'd meet her before school."

"Are you home for dinner tonight?"

"I'm going to a movie with Donna."

That meant Anarchy and I would have dinner alone, and I'd have to tell him I'd lacked the courage to discuss wedding dates with Grace. I'd also have to tell him about Karen's visit to Patriot. I'd rather have a root canal. "What are you seeing?"

"We haven't decided." She stopped by the door and slipped Dr. Scholl's sandals onto her feet.

"Love you, honey."

"Love you too. And thanks."

"For what?"

"Being my safe place."

She slipped through the door before I could respond. I sat and basked in the warm feeling she'd left behind. Teenagers were mercurial. Tomorrow she might rage, but today? Today she was near perfect. With a smile on my face, I refilled my coffee mug and climbed the stairs to change my clothes.

Ten minutes later I clutched two leashes.

When it came to squirrels, Max fancied himself an apex predator. Pansy wasn't so picky. She was willing to chase squirrels, rabbits, kids on skateboards, or little old ladies.

I tightened my hold on their leashes and jogged to Loose Park, where the squirrels were hosting a convention. The dogs' pull against my hold was constant.

"Stop pulling. No."

The tension on Max's leash eased. Pansy pulled harder.

"No," I repeated.

She grinned as if my feeble admonishments amused her.

Despite their best efforts, we fell into a steady rhythm—the slap of my sneakers, the click of their nails, the rasp of our breathing.

We rounded the corner on 51st Street and headed south toward the pond. With its arched bridge, weeping willows, and gliding water fowl, the pond seemed serene and beautiful.

I knew better. Those fowl meant the water was foul. It was also cold.

Max spotted a fat squirrel—one he might beat in a race to the nearest tree. I tightened my grip on his leash.

Pansy spotted the ducks and jerked against my hold.

With the dogs heading in opposite directions, I lost my grasp on Pansy's leash. She ran faster than Secretariat at the Belmont, a golden blur streaking toward the unsuspecting ducks. She leapt and launched over the water.

The splash was epic.

The ducks quacked their displeasure, and Pansy snapped her teeth at them as if she were the shark in the movie Grace wanted to see.

Max and I watched from the pond's edge. Max grinned (he was always game for chaos). I didn't grin. I yelled. "Pansy!"

She ignored me.

At least the park wasn't busy. No one witnessed my dog's utter disdain for commands. No one was there to see me beg. "Pansy, come here, sweetie. I'll give you a treat." My pockets were empty, but she didn't know that. I switched to angry. "Pansy!"

Not so much as a glance in my direction.

I wrapped Max's leash more tightly around my hand and scolded, "Pansy, you're a bad dog."

She didn't care. Not when she could chase ducks through the water. She paddled like mad. When she got too close, the ducks took flight. They flapped. They quacked. Pansy watched their progress and swam toward them as soon as their webbed feet touched the water.

"Pansy!"

Max snickered.

"It's not funny. How am I supposed to get her out of the pond?"

He favored me with a she'll-get-tired-eventually glance.

Bang.

Three things happened quickly. The ducks took flight. I looked over my shoulder for the car with engine problems. And Max jumped three feet. Forward. We didn't have three feet. He pulled me into the pond.

The water was every bit as nasty as I remembered. Cold. Brown. Noxious. I spluttered to the surface. The only thing quieting a string of curses was my reluctance to open my mouth.

A man stood at the pond's edge. He wore shorts, a shapeless t-shirt, and running shoes. His face cleared as I swam toward him. What was Charlie doing here?

"Let me help." He leaned forward, clasped my hand, and hauled me from the fetid water.

Soaked and ready to kill two dogs, I ground out my thanks.

Charlie ran his hands over his cheeks. "You're lucky."

"Lucky?" Me landing in the pond—again—was unequivocally bad luck.

"Lucky you weren't hit."

I frowned. "By what?"

He tilted his head. "You didn't see him?"

"Who?" Brown water ran down my legs. Was that duck poop on my calf? My lips drew back in disgust.

"You heard it, right?"

"Heard what?"

"The gunshot. A man driving a pickup truck pulled to the side of Wornall Road and took a shot at you. You're lucky Max pulled you out of harm's way."

My hero and his lady love were busy chasing the ducks who'd returned to the pond.

Charlie squeezed his eyes shut and grimaced. "We need to call the police."

I held up a hand. "Give me a minute to think." Not a car backfiring? I sighed. Deeply. Who wanted me dead? "I'd like to go home."

"Ellison, someone shot at you."

He'd already told me that. "I need a shower. I'm not waiting here for the police." I glared at the rank water. "Would you please call Pansy? She might come to you."

Charlie's forehead creased deeply. "Pansy. Come here, pretty girl."

Pansy, the hussy, swam toward us. Max followed. The ducks quacked good riddance.

~

CHARLIE WALKED ME HOME. The short trip took forever because Charlie stopped every few feet and looked over his shoulder. No pickup truck. No shooter. Thank God. Only the dogs, who realized they were in disgrace.

"Do you mind using the back door?" I asked. Tracking stinky water through the house would make more work for Aggie.

"Sure."

We entered the back yard, and Charlie unhooked the dogs' leashes. Max trotted to the door. Pansy licked Charlie's hand.

"She adores you."

Charlie ignored her. "Can we call the police now?"

"Anarchy will fuss."

"I expect so. Someone shot at you. Why?" Charlie opened the storm door, and I angled my body to prevent Max, who needed a bath, from slipping inside.

I stepped into the kitchen. "No idea."

He followed me inside.

Max, annoyed at being left outside, pressed his nose against the glass.

Charlie crossed to the telephone, picked up the receiver, and thrust it at me. "Call him."

"Call who?" Aggie's brows rose as she took in my soaked clothing. "What happened?"

"The pond at Loose Park happened," I replied. "And he wants me to call Anarchy."

"Someone tried to kill Ellison." Charlie's voice was too loud, too high.

Aggie blinked. Once.

"You aren't even upset." Charlie scowled at me as if my calm demeanor affronted him.

He was upset enough for both of us.

"Why aren't you hysterical?" he demanded.

"It's not the first time someone's shot at me."

"Or the second," Aggie added.

"Not even the third." Was it the fourth? How had I lost count of the attempts on my life?

"Gallows humor?" Charlie raked his fingers through his hair. "Seriously?"

Aggie and I smiled at each other, and I said, "I need a shower, and the dogs need baths."

That wiped the grin from Aggie's face.

I took the receiver from Charlie's hand and returned it to the cradle.

"This is not what we agreed on," said Charlie. "Call Jones."

His plan, not mine. My plan included gallons of hot clean water, shampoo, soap, and a loofah.

"Call him," he insisted.

"I will."

"Now."

"You're bossy."

"Ex-boyfriend prerogative."

"That's not a thing."

"You might be accustomed to attempted murder, but I'm not. Call him."

"Fine." I picked up the receiver and dialed.

"Jones."

"Hi. It's me." I squinted at Charlie, who rolled his hand in a get-on-with-it gesture. "Someone shot at me."

"What? Where are you?"

"Home. I'm fine. They missed."

"I'm on my way."

I hung up. "There. I told him. May I shower now?"

"What did he say?"

"He's coming over."

"That's it?"

"He'll have questions for you."

"You're truly not upset?"

"This moment? No. Maybe when I don't smell like duck poop I'll indulge in hysterics." Probably not.

"Shoes." Aggie pointed at my feet.

I toed off my sneakers.

She pursed her lips. "They can't be saved."

"They're only a few weeks old."

"They'll smell."

The pond smell lingered. My clothes could be washed, but the shoes were destined for the trash. I stopped at the bottom of the stairs. "Would you please make fresh coffee?"

"Of course."

Extra hot. Mr. Coffee gave me an encouraging wink. *Extra delicious.*

With that promise sustaining me, I trudged upstairs, stood beneath the shower's hot jets for five minutes, scrubbed, washed my hair, and scrubbed again. When the water cooled, I wrapped myself in a fluffy towel.

I ran a comb through my wet hair, pulled on jeans, a cotton sweater, and loafers, and stared at myself in the mirror. My eyes were too big, but my hands didn't shake. That was good.

Voices met me halfway down the stairs. Aggie. Charlie. Anarchy.

"What were you doing at the park?" Anarchy asked.

"Running."

I took a deep breath and descended the remaining steps.

Anarchy's gaze met mine, and it was as if he could see the shaking I'd hid so well. He crossed the kitchen and his arms circled me in safety.

I relaxed into his chest.

"You're not hurt?"

"Nope."

"Who did this?" he demanded.

"No idea."

Anarchy shifted his gaze from my face to Charlie. "What did the shooter look like?"

Charlie rubbed his neck and grimaced. "I didn't get a look at his face."

"What about the truck?" I asked.

"Red." Charlie frowned. "Or brown. A Ford." The frown deepened. "Or a Chevy. I'm sorry. I was so shocked, I can't remember."

"Charlie—" I accepted the mug of coffee Aggie poured for me "—what did you see?"

"Pansy got away from you, and you stopped next to the pond."

Pansy and the ducks had put on quite a show. "Why did you notice the truck?"

"A door slammed, and I noticed the driver had parked on Wornall. No one does that."

"No parking zone," Anarchy murmured.

"The guy watched while you tried coaxing Pansy out of the water. You weren't paying attention to anything but her."

True.

Charlie covered his mouth with his hand, and creases etched his forehead. "The guy pulled a gun, shot at you, saw you fall into the water, and ran back to his truck."

"Did he see you?" Anarchy asked.

"I don't think so," Charlie replied. "He focused on Ellison."

"Stocky guy?" I asked.

Charlie shook his head and held out his hands as if he needed my forgiveness. "I don't know."

"You think it was the man from the warehouse?" Anarchy asked.

"Who else?" I replied.

"What man?" Charlie demanded. "What warehouse?"

Anarchy's lips thinned. "Ongoing investigation."

Charlie scowled. "Ellison could have died."

"I'm aware." Anarchy's voice was brutally cold.

Charlie leaned against the refrigerator and crossed his arms. "What are you going to do?"

"Catch him."

Men. Egos. The testosterone in the kitchen left little room for actual air.

"Charlie, thank you for coming to my rescue."

"But you want me to leave?"

I offered him an apologetic smile. "Anarchy and I need to talk."

He nodded. Slowly. "Fine." His expression said he didn't trust Anarchy to keep me safe. "Call if you need me." He exited to the patio and cut across the back yard to the gate that linked our properties.

I settled on a stool and rested my forehead in my hands.

"More coffee?" Aggie waved Mr. Coffee's pot.

"Please."

She picked up my mug from the counter and refilled it.

"Thank you." I took a bracing sip. "How did the forklift guy know where to find me?"

He frowned. Deeply. "Your name wasn't in the paper. I made sure of it."

"Thank you for that."

Anarchy nodded and took the stool next to mine.

I rested my head on his shoulder and thought. "Is Hubb conscious?"

"Yes. Why? You don't think—"

"That Hubb shot at me? No." That was as unlikely as Mother wearing a peasant blouse and bell bottoms to play bridge at the club. "But maybe he can give you the guy's name. Did you talk to him? Did he tell you Karen was at Patriot Produce yesterday?"

Anarchy frowned. "What?"

"A woman called and insisted Karen pick up Clayton's things."

"What does that have to do with someone shooting at you?"

"Maybe nothing. But I needed to tell you about Karen. I dreaded telling you."

"The dogs need baths." Aggie escaped through the back door as if she sensed there were other things I dreaded telling him.

"What else is bothering you?"

"I talked to Grace."

"And?"

"I chickened out. She cried because no one misses Henry, and I couldn't ask her. Not when she'd been crying."

"That's it?"

I blinked. "What do you mean?"

"We're getting married. Sooner is better than later. But waiting for later is worth it. Anything else you want to tell me?"

"Mother's matchmaking."

He scowled. "You and Ardmore?"

I nodded.

"He followed you to the park."

I wrinkled my nose. "That's creepy. Maybe we went for runs at the same time."

"And maybe pigs will fly. He wants you back."

"Not happening."

"You're sure this is what you want?"

"Positive."

Anarchy had no reason for worry.

"Amber Leader," I blurted. "The receptionist at Patriot Produce. I gave her my name."

"How would she find you?"

"How many Russells are in the phone book?" I was genuinely curious.

We pulled the White Pages from its drawer and looked up Russell.

"Maybe it's not her. With so many Russells listed, they couldn't find me this quickly."

I tapped my listing—Mr. and Mrs. Henry Russell. That would change soon. Mr. and Mrs. Anarchy Jones. Did police detectives list their home addresses and phone numbers? I doubted it.

"I'll catch this guy, Ellison."

"We have no idea who he is."

"Someone at Patriot knows. You're sure you're not hurt?"

"Positive. Why?"

"I'm going to Patriot. I have more questions." Given the expression on Anarchy's face, I wouldn't want to be the person hiding the answers.

CHAPTER ELEVEN

Anarchy arrived for dinner with a bottle of wine. "It's produced in Napa, not far from where I grew up."

My breath caught—not at the wine—but at the sight of him. He wore the same plaid pants he had on when we first met.

I reached out and traced celadon threads till they met navy. "I remember these pants."

He frowned. "You do? I seldom wear them."

"I do." That I could touch his hip, that we were a couple, was still so new, I blinked with is-this-really-happening disbelief. "You had them on the morning I found Madeline's body. You offered me coffee." No wonder I fell for him.

His smile was intoxicating. "You wore a swimsuit and one of your husband's shirts."

That moment, the breeze skittering leaves across the concrete and a corpse on the pool deck, who would have thought it would lead us here?

We stared at each other for long seconds, then Anarchy said, "Something smells amazing. What's Aggie cooking?"

I took the wine from his hands. "Aggie's out with Mac."

"You cooked?" The worry in his voice might have been comical if it weren't so insulting.

"Aggie cooked. My job is taking dinner out of the oven."

He looked doubtful.

"She set a timer."

Was that relief on his face? He gathered me close. "Where's Grace?"

"She went to see *The Return of the Pink Panther* with Donna."

"The dogs?"

"Back yard."

"We're alone?"

I nodded.

He kissed me. "How did I get so lucky?"

"Mmmm. I'm the lucky one." I could spend hours kissing Anarchy.

His coffee-brown eyes searched my face. "You're sure you're okay?"

"Fine." I grabbed his hand and led him toward the kitchen where the roasting chicken scented the air with a tantalizing aroma. Early evening's soft light crept past the café curtains and filled the room with a golden aura. I fetched two wine glasses from the cabinet.

"You don't seem worried," Anarchy observed.

"About?"

"Someone shooting at you."

"Been there. Done that." And worry hadn't helped—not once.

"Are we positive it happened?"

I froze, the glasses inches from the counter. "Charlie saw the shooter."

Anarchy's closed expression said he harbored suspicions.

"Why would Charlie lie?"

"Why would someone shoot at you?"

"I saw the man at the warehouse. I can identify him."

"It's a big step from the theft of a few strawberries, if that's what he was doing, to murder."

"You honestly believe Charlie would lie about something like this?"

"He can't remember a single detail."

"He was in shock." I put the wine glasses on the counter and planted my hands on my hips. "Charlie wouldn't lie."

"Sure about that?"

"Yes."

"I talked to his real-estate agent. He only wanted one house —the one next to yours."

I opened my mouth, but no words came out. Was Charlie that delusional? Did he think moving next door would somehow win me back? And why was Anarchy investigating Charlie?

"Will you open the wine?" I needed a glass. "And please help yourself to cheese." Aggie had left us an array of cheddar, Swiss, Edam, and Gouda, along with crackers, grapes, and an unidentified jam. Up until thirty seconds ago, I'd found the cheese tray hard to resist. Now, I'd have trouble choking down a single bite.

"She thought of everything," Anarchy observed.

"She doesn't want me messing up her kitchen."

"Her kitchen?"

"The only appliance I can use properly is Mr. Coffee." And Mr. Coffee wasn't an appliance, he was a dear friend. One who'd never, ever lie to me. Or investigate a friend I swore was innocent. "About Charlie—"

"Where's the corkscrew?" asked Anarchy.

I opened a drawer, rummaged, and handed him the wine opener. "Why did you contact Charlie's realtor?"

"I don't trust Ardmore." He looked up from uncorking the wine. "Keeping you safe is a priority."

"I appreciate that, but Charlie wouldn't hurt me."

"I'm not convinced."

"And I'm not okay with you investigating Charlie."

He put the wine bottle on the counter and drew me close. "I've waited my entire life for you. Please, forgive me if I go a bit nuts when it comes to your safety."

His entire life? My annoyance dissipated like shreds of mist in the sunshine. "Talk to me first. Don't investigate people without telling me."

"Deal."

I pulled free. "How's Hubb? The day got away from me and I forgot to call Mel and ask about him."

"He'll recover. He can't remember anything prior to being poisoned and claims he's not familiar with the names of the employees on the warehouse floor."

"I believe him." It was impossible to imagine Hubb chatting with someone who actually got their hands dirty. "Who keeps the employment records?"

"Denise Bryce."

"Is someone going through her files?"

Anarchy's lips thinned.

"What?"

"We're waiting on a subpoena."

"Hubb didn't give you access?"

"His lawyer didn't."

"Who's his lawyer?"

"Tafft."

"Oh." I'd dated Hunter Tafft. "Do the doctors know what killed Denise?"

"The same poison that killed Clayton. We found it in his coffee."

Poisoned coffee? That was so wrong.

Anarchy pulled the cork from the wine, filled our glasses, and offered me one. "To us."

We clinked glasses.

"Any chance Denise and Hubb took the poison accidentally?" Even as I asked, I knew the answer.

"No."

I swirled the wine in my glass. "So Clayton dies, and you can't find anyone with a compelling motive at his office?"

"Not yet." Not till he got the files Hunter protected.

I moved on. "Karen might or might not be having an affair."

He grimaced. "Still no confirmation?"

"Nope. Did you talk to the contractor?"

"You said she was having an affair with the architect."

"That's what Jane says. But I bet Clayton drove the contractor nuts."

"Annoying someone isn't usually a motive for murder."

"What if the contractor made a few mistakes in his favor? Clayton would spot them. No question."

"I'll make a call." Anarchy eyed the cheese and added a sliver of Swiss to a cracker. "With Denise Bryce dead and Langford in the hospital, it seems likely Clayton's murder is related to Patriot."

"Produce going missing when the staff is at lunch?"

"Murder for a few crates of cabbages?"

I shuddered. "Daddy's cronies say the grocery business is tough. Maybe a competitor wants to take over."

"From the look of the place, all they need to do is wait. It will fail by itself." He stared into his wine glass. "Tell me about the Langfords."

"I've known Mel for almost twenty years. She's a bit older, but we were provisionals in the League together."

"The League?"

"The Junior League. She went away to school. Someplace in Virginia. Mary Baldwin? I think Hubb attended Hampden-Sydney. They met. They fell in love. They stayed in Virginia for five or six years."

"What brought them to Kansas City?"

"Mel's father needed a family member to take over the business."

"Do they have children?"

"A son. He attends his dad's alma mater."

"So Hubb's run the show at Patriot for nearly twenty years?"

"That sounds about right."

"Happy marriage?"

"As far as I can tell. Mel adores Hubb."

"Does he adore her?"

I hedged. "I don't know Hubb as well as I know Mel."

"That's not an answer."

"Hubb is polished and polite and charming..."

"You don't like him."

"He's not my favorite. But what do I know? I married Henry."

"Do you—"

Woof! Woof, woof, woof.

I jumped off my stool and parted the curtains. "That's Max's there's-a-problem bark."

Arooo!

"That's Pansy." I headed for the door.

"Wait."

A glance over my shoulder revealed the concern on Anarchy's face.

"What?"

"It might be a lure to get you outside."

"You just finished telling me that Charlie made up the shooter."

"If I'm wrong—"

Aroo!

"If you're wrong, we'll face him together." I opened the door and scanned the backyard. No dogs. "Max?"

Woof. The bark came from the fence line with Charlie's yard.

I ran, but Anarchy ran faster. When I caught up, he'd already crouched next to the fence, blocking my view.

"What's wrong?" How badly was Pansy hurt?

"She's stuck."

"Again?" Pansy had bad luck with fences. "How? There's no way she could force her head through the pickets."

"She's stuck under the fence." He shifted, and I saw Pansy's problem. Faced with a locked gate, she'd dug. And misjudged. Her hole wasn't deep enough, and when she'd shimmied under the fence, she'd wedged herself tight.

Her back half remained in my yard. Her front half was in Charlie's.

"What do we do?" I asked.

"I'll pull, you push."

"Or we could remove the slats," said Charlie, who'd joined us on his side of the fence.

On our side, Pansy's tail wagged.

"That could work," Anarchy allowed.

"There's a hammer in the kitchen. I'll be right back."

Pansy whined—piteously—when Charlie left.

"He's coming back," I told her.

Max, who'd settled on his haunches, rolled his eyes.

"Your girlfriend," I snapped.

His doggy expression smoothed to impassive.

I stared at Pansy's hind end. "Grace and I need to have a long talk. Pansy might be happier with Charlie."

"She let me have McCallester."

"That was different. She brought that cat home against my express wishes. I allowed Pansy to join the family." I glanced up at him. "What will we do about the cat?"

"Do?"

"McCallester and Max can't live in the same house."

Anarchy frowned. "How bad could it be?"

"Cat dangling from a chandelier bad."

"Right. I forgot."

I hadn't. The image was seared on my brain.

"Got it." Charlie loped toward us holding a hammer.

Pansy's tail thumped for her knight in shining armor, and Charlie dropped out of sight. "We'll save you, pretty girl. Don't you worry."

Her tail thumped harder.

Charlie stood. "Whose fence is this?"

"Yours," I replied.

"I could take it down."

"It's your fence. But if you do pull it down, expect Pansy to decimate your yard."

"She wouldn't do that. Would you, sugar?"

Thump, thump, thump. Pansy's tail wagged so hard the ground shook.

Using the hammer's claw, Charlie pried out the first nail. "No big plans on a Friday night?"

"A quiet night at home." I scowled at our half of the dog. "Quiet until Pansy did this."

"Any leads on who shot at Ellison?" Charlie pulled another nail.

"No description of the man or his vehicle," said Anarchy.

Charlie's jaw tightened. "Aren't you supposed to detect?"

I rested a hand on Anarchy's forearm, and his muscles relaxed beneath my touch. He drew a breath and said, "We're exploring every avenue."

Charlie pulled a board off the fence. "It's nice you can find time for a quiet dinner."

"Charlie." My voice held a warning.

Both men turned their gazes my way.

"Anarchy doesn't tell you how to do your job."

"I'm a cardiologist, Ellison. He couldn't."

"And he's a homicide detective. He's seen things that could

turn your hair white, caught vicious killers, and saved me more times than I can count."

Anarchy's lips quirked, but Charlie's eyes lit with fresh enthusiasm.

Pansy wriggled but couldn't yet maneuver to Charlie's side of the fence.

"One more, sugar." Charlie's voice softened and he crouched again. "I'll save you."

I glanced at Anarchy. Did he realize the idea I'd put in Charlie's head?

Hard to tell. Anarchy had crossed his arms. His lips formed a pencil-thin line. And his foot tapped an impatient beat.

On the other side of the fence, Charlie muttered.

"Need some help?" Anarchy asked.

"No." Charlie snapped as if Anarchy had attacked his manhood.

"Those fence nails can be tough." A smile threatened to crack Anarchy's face, and he hid his lips behind his right hand.

"I got it."

"It takes muscle."

"I got it."

"Strength."

"I said I got it."

I poked Anarchy in the ribs and whispered, "Stop it."

He dropped his hand and showed me an unrepentant smile.

Charlie cursed softly.

"Maybe it's a difficult picket. Try a different one?" I suggested.

"For the love of Pete! I've got this."

Anarchy grinned as if he'd won a lifetime supply of coffee.

I sealed my lips and glanced at Max, who watched the proceedings with poorly concealed boredom.

"Got it!" Charlie sounded triumphant. He pulled the picket from the rail, and Pansy belly-crawled to his side.

"Sorry about this, Charlie." I waved at the missing picket. "I'll call a handyman to repair the damage."

"Don't. I was serious about taking it down."

"It's your fence." I drew a resigned breath. "If you tear it down, I'll put one up."

Charlie frowned at me.

"Max and Pansy find too much trouble."

He rubbed his chin. "Without this section of fence, they could have the run of two yards. Pansy likes it on this side."

I couldn't argue that. Not when Pansy leaned against Charlie's legs with a blissful expression on her doggy face and an adoring gleam in her doggy eyes.

Anarchy lifted his wrist and peered at his watch.

"Are we keeping you, Jones?"

"Don't raze the fence. If you don't mind Pansy in your yard, leave the gate open." He lifted a warning finger. "But Ellison gave you notice—the dog is destructive. You can't hold her responsible for damages."

I was fairly certain he could, but that was a question for my lawyer who was busy hampering Anarchy's investigation. "Thank you for freeing her, Charlie. Pansy, time to go home."

Pansy didn't move.

"Pansy!"

She stared at Charlie, lost in adoration, and wagged her tail.

"Let her stay. I'll bring her home later."

I'd had it up to my eyeballs with Pansy. "Fine. Thanks, Charlie. You coming, Max?"

Max stood. Stretched. Yawned. Shook his ears.

Anarchy's arm wrapped around my waist, and with Max at our heels, we walked back to the house.

"What's that noise?" Anarchy asked.

Ding, ding, ding.

I groaned. "Oh, no."

"What?"

"The timer."

When Anarchy opened the back door, smoke billowed into the backyard. I rushed past him and pulled the chicken from the oven. The onions, potatoes, and carrots surrounding the bird were black as charcoal briquettes. So was the chicken.

I poked the carcass then glanced back at Anarchy. "Don't you laugh."

"I wouldn't dream of it."

"Should I call for pizza?"

"Hold that thought." Anarchy ventured inside and opened the refrigerator. "I'll cook. Would you prop open the back door? We can air out the kitchen."

I opened the door, and Max came in. He drew his lips away from his teeth, sneezed, and escaped upstairs.

I waved the evening paper, fanning the smoke into the yard. "You're sure about the pizza?"

"Positive. You should open the windows in the family room, get a cross-breeze going."

"Fine. But for the record—" I tapped the kitchen counter "—this is Pansy's fault."

He grinned. "Pansy didn't forget the chicken."

"Whose side are you on?"

He pulled me against his chest. "Yours. Always yours."

Brnng, brnng.

"I'd better get that. If it's Marian and I don't answer, she'll call the fire department."

"This has happened before?"

I crossed my fingers behind my back. "Never."

He answered with an I-know-you're-lying grin, and I picked up the phone. "Hello."

"Ellison, it's your mother. Is your house on fire?" News traveled fast.

"No. I burned dinner."

"Not on fire," she spoke to my father. "Ellison ruined dinner. Again. Where's Aggie?"

I assumed that question was for me. "On a date."

"Does Anarchy know you can't cook?"

"He does now."

She sighed. An opportunity lost.

"Mother, I need to air out the house."

"Fine." She hung up on me.

"Mother wants you to know I can't cook."

He grinned.

"I'm not great at dusting, vacuuming, laundry, or ironing either."

"I've been told I snore."

"By whom?"

"I have a bad relationship with lawn mowers, I'm not handy, and I prefer football to galas and balls."

"That last one is true for most men. Who told you about the snoring?"

"I don't care about clothes, always drive the speed limit, which I'm told can be annoying, and I hog the morning paper."

"The snoring? Who told you?"

He smirked as if he sensed and appreciated the jealous outrage roiling inside me. "My brother."

"Hmph." His brother? Two could play that game. "What are you making?"

"A ham and cheese omelet. Looks like Aggie left us a salad."

"Sounds delicious."

"Not as good as Aggie's chicken, but it's the company that counts."

I parted my lips and stared at him like Pansy stared at Charlie. "Do you suppose after dinner—" I shifted my gaze to the open vee of his shirt.

"Yes?"

I fluttered my lashes. "We could..."

His Adam's apple bobbed. "Yes?"

I touched my lips. "Since we're alone, maybe we could..."

"What?"

My fingers drifted to my throat.

Anarchy took a step toward me, and I retreated.

Another step and he caught me, pulled me close. "What?" His voice was whiskey rough.

I gazed up at him through my lashes, parted my lips, and said, "Plug in a couple of fans? I'd like to get rid of the smoke smell before Aggie gets home."

CHAPTER TWELVE

I descended the stairs to the kitchen. Slowly. After we'd aired out the house and devoured Anarchy's omelet, we'd finished the bottle of wine and opened a second. My head felt muzzy.

"Problem last night?" Aggie looked at me over the top of a cookbook. I couldn't see her mouth—she hid behind *Beard on Bread* (bread with facial hair?)—but I suspected a smile lurked. The orange and red flame-stitch pattern of Aggie's kaftan suggested fire.

She knew. The lingering smell of charred chicken was a dead giveaway.

"Coffee first."

Aggie poured me a mug, and I fetched the cream from the fridge.

With the heavy-handed addition of cream, the heaven in my cup turned the perfect shade.

I took three bracing sips before I admitted what happened to her chicken.

"That dog is a menace." She'd identified the true culprit

immediately. The burnt dinner was Pansy's fault, not mine. "But you could have turned off the oven before you saved her."

I scowled and drank more coffee.

"Does Dr. Ardmore still want her after last night?" Aggie shook her head at Charlie's folly. "If he's that foolish, why stand in his way?"

"Grace." I pressed my palms to my forehead. "I have to convince Grace."

"Convince me of what?" Grace had descended barefoot again.

"You're up early." Aggie's voice was as bright as morning sunshine.

"Saturday swim." The pool at the club opened on Memorial Day weekend. The following Tuesday, swim team started. Grace, who'd compete for a spot as an A swimmer, had signed up for pre-season practice. "Convince me of what?"

"Pansy got stuck under the fence." My voice was shouldn't-have-drunk-that-third-glass rough. "She dug her way next door."

Pansy, who'd curled up on the floor next to Max, thumped her tail and grinned as if last night's drama gave her joy.

"You'd really give her away?" Grace crouched next to Pansy and stroked her silky ears. "You don't want to leave us, do you?"

Pansy whined and gazed at her with we-can-still-be-friends eyes.

Grace wiped her cheeks with the back of her hand. "She's part of the family."

Aggie huffed and raised the cookbook high. I'd bet my next cup of coffee her eyes had rolled to the back of her head.

"How about a long-term loan?"

Pansy watched us as if she sensed her fate was in Grace's hands.

Grace kissed the top of Pansy's head. "Do you want to go?"

Pansy's tail thumped against the kitchen floor.

"Fine. But if he moves, she comes home."

I nodded.

"I can visit whenever I want."

"I'll ask."

"Max can too."

Max opened one eye. I suspected he'd stay home and bask in the warmth of being an only dog. Or would absence renew his doggy ardor?

"I'll talk to Charlie. How was the movie?"

"Okay." She opened the fridge and scanned its contents.

Aggie laid *Beard on Bread* on the counter. "May I fix you breakfast?"

"Not before I swim." Grace claimed a yogurt.

"How was your date, Aggie?" I frowned at Grace—would it kill her to offer Aggie a thank you?

"Mac and I went to The Prospect." She tapped a recipe in the still-open cookbook. "If I baked bread in flowerpots, would you eat it?"

Grace and I both gaped at her, but Grace spoke first. "You can bake bread?"

Aggie nodded.

Baking bread from scratch was strange and marvelous magic. "We know you make wonderful biscuits—"

"And cake." Grace licked her lips.

"And quick bread." My mouth watered at the delectable memory of Aggie's banana bread.

"But bread?" Grace frowned. "Doesn't that include yeast and kneading and proving?"

Aggie nodded. "It does."

"You can do that?" The awe in Grace's voice made me smile. It was as if Aggie had announced she had superpowers—laser vision or invisibility or incendiary speed.

"I can."

"That's so cool. Will you teach me? Please?" Grace glanced at the clock, spooned a final bite of yogurt, and headed toward the back door. "This afternoon?"

"If you'd like."

"Yes! Thanks, Aggie. Bye, Mom." She dashed out the door.

"I like bread too. But I won't ask for baking lessons."

"That's probably for the best." Aggie's brow creased. "Mac is stopping by this morning."

"Oh?" My mug was empty. How had that happened? I gave Mr. Coffee a tender pat and picked up his pot.

"He has information."

"About?"

"Patriot Produce."

I froze with the coffee pot poised above my mug. "What about Patriot?"

"I'll let him tell you."

I poured. "When will he be here?"

Aggie glanced at the clock. "Twenty minutes."

I gulped my coffee. "I'll change." Aggie was family, but that didn't mean I'd greet Mac in a peignoir.

"I'll make breakfast. What would you like?"

"Bread in a flowerpot."

"That takes time we don't have. How about scrambled eggs and bacon?"

"Sounds good." I dashed upstairs, showered, swallowed two aspirin, pulled a Lilly Pulitzer shift over my head, and grabbed a cardigan.

I returned to the kitchen and found Mac sitting at the island with his hands wrapped around a mug of coffee. He stared at Aggie, who managed two skillets and a toaster, as if he couldn't believe his luck—a sentiment I shared.

He spotted me and stood. "Good morning, Mrs. Russell."

"It's Ellison," I reminded him. "Don't stand on my account."

He didn't move a muscle.

"More coffee?" asked Aggie.

"Please."

She put a fresh mug in my hands then used tongs to flip bacon strips.

I settled on a stool next to Mac's. "Please, sit."

He relented, and together we watched Aggie cook.

"Did Aggie mention Patriot?" He stared straight ahead, as if talking were easier when he didn't look at me.

"She told me you did business with them."

Mac grimaced and massaged his neck with a hand the size of a catcher's mitt. "When I first opened the deli, they were great." He lowered his head and stared into his coffee cup's depths. "The rep stopped by regularly."

"The rep?"

"The sales guy. Ray. He told me what was freshest, what was on special."

"Special?"

"Product they needed to move fast."

I guessed the shelf life for lettuce, tomatoes, and avocados was short. "When did Ray stop coming to the deli?"

"A year ago. He found work with a new company that sells frozen food." Mac looked down his large nose. "I only use fresh. Patriot didn't replace him. That didn't bother me. I called in my orders, and they delivered."

Aggie turned off the heat beneath the eggs. "Tell her what happened when they shorted you."

"When my catering picked up—" he turned his head and smiled at me "—thank you for that." I'd told my friends about Mac's marvelous dishes, and now the demand for his Italian delicacies kept him chained to his kitchen. He took breaks only for Aggie.

"You're welcome." Mac was a fabulous chef and deserved the success.

"The first time Patriot shorted me a case of green peppers. I used the red peppers I had in the refrigerator, called, and complained. They apologized and issued a credit to my account."

"But it happened again," said Aggie.

"Almost every order," said Mac. "The produce would arrive. Usually when I was crazy busy with the lunch rush. I'd hand the driver a check then realize they'd shorted me when we put the product in the cooler. When I asked to use the credits, they couldn't find them. I'd paid for produce I never saw."

"You couldn't write the check after you inventoried the delivery?"

"Not if they delivered during peak hours." He scowled at the countertop. "Also, there's A produce and B produce."

"What's the difference?"

"Cosmetic issues or being off-spec."

"I see." Cosmetic, I understood. Off-spec? I'd take Mac's word for it.

"They shorted me, they delivered B produce and charged me for A—I can't serve my customers bruised tomatoes or wilted lettuce. They weren't reliable. They were cheating me. I found a new supplier."

I nodded. "Did you get your money back?"

Mac's wry laugh was my answer. "It wasn't just me. I talked to buddies with restaurants. Same thing happened to them."

Aggie slid plates in front of us—fluffy scrambled eggs sprinkled with fresh-cracked pepper, crisp bacon, perfectly browned toast. As good as breakfast looked, it smelled better.

"Thanks, Aggs." Mac wore the luckiest-man-on-earth expression again.

Aggie added silverware, napkins, a jam jar filled with raspberry jam, and fresh orange juice.

"Thank you." I picked up a fork and tasted the eggs. "This is amazing."

Aggie returned to her side of the island and picked up her own fork.

We ate in this-breakfast-demands-attention silence.

When half my eggs had disappeared, I asked, "Mac, when you complained, who did you talk to?"

He held up a finger, chewed, then took a quick sip of coffee. "At first I talked to a gal named Denise. I got nowhere with her, so I called the dead guy."

"Clayton Morris?"

Mac nodded. "He acted real surprised and promised he'd refund my money."

"Did he?"

"No."

"When did you talk to him?"

"Two, three weeks ago."

"More coffee?" Aggie held up the pot.

"Please." Mac and I spoke in unison.

Aggie poured, and I asked, "What else can you tell me about Patriot?"

He stared at his plate. "They were a good supplier for years. I hope they get turned around. And not just because they owe me money. There are good people who work there."

"Did the same guy deliver every time?"

"Yeah. It got to be a joke in the kitchen. He'd arrive during the lunch rush, short me, and be gone before I identified the mistake."

"What's his name?"

"Tony."

I waited for more, but Mac was busy gazing at Aggie.

"Last name?"

"Rossi."

"What did he look like?"

He frowned at me.

"Tall? Short? Black? White?"

"Medium and white."

"Anarchy has a drawing of a Patriot employee. If he brought it by, could you tell him if it's Tony?"

Mac shifted on his stool. "I guess." His lack of enthusiasm for a police visit hung like a pall. He finished his coffee and glanced at his watch. "I should get going. We're busy on Saturdays."

I stood. "I'll walk you out."

"Thank you for breakfast."

"Thank Aggie. I serve Pop-Tarts." That Milton the toaster, he looked friendly on television, but my Pop-Tarts sported black edges. Every time. "Or coffee. Nothing wrong with coffee for breakfast."

Mac, who'd just consumed an entire plate of eggs, eight strips of bacon, and three slices of toast slathered with raspberry jam, offered me a pained smile.

We walked to the front hall, and I opened the door. "Thanks for telling me about Patriot."

"You're welcome. I'd do anything for Aggie."

I should have guessed Aggie prompted Mac's revelations.

He slipped through the front door and hurried down the steps. When he reached his van, he gave me a tepid wave then drove away.

I cut across the front lawn and rang Charlie's doorbell.

He answered the door wearing plaid pajamas and a seersucker robe. His brows hovered mid-forehead as if he couldn't imagine what might bring me to his door.

"I hope I didn't wake you."

"No. Not at all. Just a lazy Saturday. The paper. Coffee." He shifted to the side and opened the door wider. "Coffee?"

I felt my across-the-street neighbor Marian Dixon's gaze bore a hole through my shoulder blades. "No, thank you. I spoke with Grace about Pansy."

"And?"

I smoothed my sweater's placket. "She agreed to a long-term loan."

Charlie tilted his head. "What does that mean?"

"Pansy's yours for as long as you live next door."

"I'm not moving." He rubbed his stubble-darkened chin. "Grace won't hold this against me, will she?"

His assumption—that he and Grace would have a relationship—troubled me. "If she gets mad at anyone, it'll be me."

"Please, thank her for me."

"I will."

"How do we do this?"

The weight of an interested gaze scratched at my neck. I glanced over my shoulder and caught Ann Stewart and her Corgi gawking at us from the sidewalk. "I'll get you a list with her vet's information, food, and preferred treats."

"Will you bring her over?"

So the neighbors could speculate? No. "How about unlatching the back gate?"

He opened the door still wider. "Are you sure you won't come in?"

Marian would snatch the receiver and phone Mother before the door closed behind me. I retreated a step. "Positive."

"Are you going to the Westbrooks' party tonight?"

"I am."

"May I escort you?"

"Anarchy is taking me."

He frowned. Deeply. Lines cut from his nose to his mouth, and the wrinkles in his forehead deepened. The twenty years that separated him from his teenage self looked more like forty. "You're serious about him?"

Charlie should harbor no illusions. I was not available. I flashed my ring. "I love him. We're getting married."

"You haven't set a date. That tells me you have doubts."

"Not a single one. We'll pick a date soon."

"Love isn't enough." He shook his head sadly, as if he regretted imparting hard-won wisdom.

"Charlie—"

"I mean it. Marriages fail. I read somewhere half of them end in divorce. Couples say 'I do' with starry-eyed hope and love in their hearts, but their dreams turn to dust. Love is grand, but building a life requires more. You and I—"

"Charlie!" If Ann and her Corgi still spied on us from the sidewalk, they were getting an earful. "I love Anarchy. I'm marrying him. End of story."

"But..." His shoulders sagged. "Why?"

"I told you. I love him."

"Because he rescued you?"

"No." Explaining love was impossible. It was the color of his eyes, the warmth of his smile, the way he followed rules. It was his low-key attitude. It was his intelligence and kindness and strength. "Anarchy's different from anyone I've ever known. He sees me."

Charlie tapped his seersucker-covered chest. "I see you."

"You see the girl you loved twenty years ago."

"That's not true."

It was one hundred percent true. Charlie didn't know me at all. "What do I care about?"

"Your daughter."

"Too easy." I crossed my arms. "What else?"

"Your dogs."

I tilted my head and waited for something insightful.

"Your art."

"Easy answers, all."

Anarchy understood the push-pull of living up to Mother's expectations. He saw the price I paid for my late husband's sins. He recognized my insecurities. He accepted I'd never fix him a decent meal. He put his needs second to Grace's.

"He's a cop. He won't fit into your world, your life." Had Mother briefed Charlie on talking points?

"He doesn't care about that. Neither do I. You should stop this."

For long seconds, Charlie's mouth opened and closed as if an argument poised on the tip of his tongue, but a sense of self-preservation kept him from voicing it.

"We can be friends." I peeked behind me. Ann hadn't moved, and she was ignoring the Corgi straining against its leash. "Nothing more."

"I'll take what I can get. For now."

"I should go."

"I'll see you tonight."

Charlie and Anarchy at the same party—didn't that sound fun? No! I waved (more of a karate chop) at Ann, who scuttled away. I watched her disappear around the corner then I cut across the lawn.

Grace pulled into the drive.

"You did it?" She climbed out of her car wearing cutoff jean shorts and a damp t-shirt. "You gave him Pansy?" Her voice carried.

"I told him she's his on a long-term loan. He'll leave the gate open. Pansy can decide."

"If he moves?"

"She comes home to us."

The smile on Grace's face was wistful. "I guess that's okay."

Charlie's comments about wedding dates still fresh in my mind, I gathered my courage and cleared my throat. "I've been meaning to ask, would you mind if Anarchy and I set a date?"

Her brows drew together. "Mind?"

"Yes." Ann and her Corgi strolled the other side of the street now. Still watching. Hopefully blocking Marian's view.

"I don't understand."

"Do you mind if we pick a date for the wedding?"

"Why are you waiting? Anarchy adores you. He'd marry you tomorrow if he could."

I felt multiple gazes—Ann's, Marian's, the Corgi's. I looked behind me. Marian's next-door neighbor, Ward Monroe, fiddled with his garden shears. He'd be more convincing if he had a hedge. The man openly stared. Who said men didn't gossip? "Your dad..." What could I say?

Grace rolled her eyes. "Anarchy and I talked about this."

"You did?" Why had no one told me? "When?"

"Before he asked you to marry him." She didn't say "duh" out loud, but it hung in the air. "He knows he can't replace Dad." She twisted her wet hair into a bun and wrapped it with a ponytail holder. "Our relationship will be different. He admits he has no parenting experience."

"And?"

"You'll be the heavy—the one who enforces the rules. He'll be the cool stepfather who gives awesome Christmas and birthday gifts."

"You don't mind?"

"As far as I'm concerned, you should marry him tomorrow. It would get Granna off your back."

"I can't put a wedding together in a day."

"Aunt Sis did."

"It took her a week."

"Only because she had to wait while Swanson's altered her suit."

"I can't get married without Aunt Sis, Karma, and Marjorie."

"Sure you can."

"Life's milestones are meant to be shared with the people we love." I couldn't get married without my family. Even if I wanted to throttle them—well, one of them.

CHAPTER THIRTEEN

I paused with my hand on the knob, drew in a deep breath, and opened the front door.

Anarchy waited on the front stoop. He wore a navy suit, a crisp white shirt, and a red and white rep tie. He looked like Steve McQueen in *The Thomas Crown Affair*. But Anarchy was better looking. And his eyes were warm and brown, my favorite color in the world.

"Wow," I murmured.

He grinned—a slow grin that curled my toes. "Back at you."

I wore a Halston dress with a bib front halter, drawstring neck, and full skirt with multiple layers of chiffon in graduated tones—from cream to butter yellow. The dress was soft and feminine and begged for twirling. I resisted. "You've been to Jack Henry." The local men's store was a favorite among bankers and lawyers and scions.

He shot his cuffs. "I didn't want to embarrass you."

He'd bought a new, conservative suit. For me. My heart melted to a puddle of goo. "I don't care what you wear. That said, you look very handsome."

His answering grin was almost shy. "Are you ready?"

"I am." I fetched my clutch and the shower gift from the bombé chest. "Let's go."

Anarchy took the gift from my hands, escorted me to his car, and opened the passenger door.

I sat, reclaimed the gift, and settled the box on my lap.

Anarchy slipped behind the wheel and slid the key into the ignition.

The ignition fired, and I cleared my throat. "I talked to Grace."

He froze with his hand on the gear shift. "Oh?"

"She said we should get married tomorrow."

"I don't think I can get a license that fast." He was serious.

"I need more than a few hours to plan."

"How long do you need?"

"Your family needs travel time."

He shook his head.

"Karma and Sis and Marjorie need travel time."

Now he nodded. "How long?"

"I'll call them in the morning."

"Two weeks."

"What?"

"We're getting married two weeks from today."

"Eeep." The sound escaped my lips.

"You do want this?"

"I do."

"Perfect. Say that two weeks from today. The rest is extraneous."

"It takes time to plan a wedding."

"I don't care about the wedding. I care about being your husband."

Two weeks?

Anarchy put the car in gear and we rolled down the drive.

"Mac came by this morning."

"Oh?"

"I tried calling you after he left."

"Peters and I spent the day interviewing Patriot employees."

"Did anyone recognize the man in the sketch?"

"No. Why did you call?"

I recounted what Mac told me.

"I'll swing by and talk to him tomorrow."

"It seems to me the murders are linked to whatever's happening at Patriot Produce."

"Agreed."

"I'd suspect Hubb, but—"

"Peters and I liked him for the murder till he almost died."

"Who else?"

"Not sure. It's why we spent the day interviewing employees."

"Did you find Amber?"

"She's missing."

"Missing? I don't enjoy looking over my shoulder." Amber gave the shooter my name. There was no other explanation.

He patted my knee. "We'll solve this. Soon. Are Ardmore and Hubb Langford acquainted?"

"I doubt it. Charlie lived in Texas for the past twenty years, and Hubb's not from Kansas City. Why do you ask?"

"Just wondering. Does Ardmore know Mel Langford?"

"Maybe. She's older. She might have attended high school with Charlie's sister. Why?"

Anarchy's hands tightened on the wheel. "We're investigating every avenue."

I closed my eyes and counted to ten. Charlie wasn't a killer. Why couldn't Anarchy see that? "Charlie has no reason to murder Hubb."

"Hmph." Anarchy pulled onto a street already lined with Mercedes, BMWs, Cadillacs, Volvos, and the odd Audi. "Should I drop you at the door?"

"No. Park. I'll walk with you." No way would I make Anarchy walk into the lion's den by himself.

He pulled to the curb, put the car in park, and leaned toward me. His lips brushed the shell of my ear. "Two weeks."

An anticipatory shiver pebbled my skin. I put aside my stop-investigating-Charlie annoyance, ignored the suddenly urgent, endlessly long list of wedding to-dos, and turned my head.

Our lips met.

The fire in Anarchy's kiss took me by surprise. His hand captured my nape and his mouth demanded more.

Tap, tap, tap.

Anarchy released me. Slowly. He scowled at the passenger window.

I sighed my disappointment.

Tap, tap, tap.

I turned my head.

Libba stood outside the car and grinned like the Cheshire Cat.

"May I kill her?" I asked.

"No." Regret laced his voice.

"You're sure?"

"Positive."

"You're the homicide detective." I opened my door.

Libba still smirked. "You two are like teenagers."

"I just rethought my maid of honor."

Libba stuck out her tongue. "No, you didn't. You adore me. Besides, better me tapping on your window than her." She pointed, and I turned my head.

Prudence strode past us, slowing only long enough to eye Libba's ensemble and mutter, "Nice dress."

Libba also wore Halston. But her dress was a metallic gold shirt dress. The collar's vee reached for her belly button. She smoothed the fabric over her hips. "Prudence, you have such a talent for making last year's fashion—" she wrinkled her nose "—current."

Prudence flashed me a glare and swished up the sidewalk, the hems of last year's jumpsuit slapping around her scrawny ankles.

"That was cruel."

Libba squinched her eyes and shook her head. "She shouldn't dish it if she can't take it."

Libba made an excellent point.

I stood.

"Great dress." Unlike Prudence, Libba meant it.

I swiveled my hips, and the chiffon swirled. "Thank you."

"Anarchy, you look dapper."

Dapper? He looked better than dapper. Delectable. Debonair. Delicious.

"Thank you, Libba." Anarchy offered her his arm. "Looks like I get to escort two beautiful women."

The three of us strolled up the Westbrooks' front walk, and Libba nodded at the gift I carried. "What did you get them?"

"A coffee press and mugs. You?"

The present in Libba's hands was smaller than mine. "A bar set."

The front door swung open, and Patty and Doyle Westbrook welcomed us to their home.

Patty nodded her approval of my dress, pretended not to notice the cut of Libba's, and waved at the large round table. "We're putting gifts there. Bars are set in the living room and the patio."

Libba air-kissed Patty's cheek, winked at Doyle, and left us in search of a martini.

"Patty, Doyle, have you met my fiancé, Anarchy Jones? Patty and Doyle are dear friends." I stretched the truth like taffy.

"So nice to meet you." Patty stared at Anarchy like a hungry teenager who'd just found a box of donuts. "Have you set a date?"

"Two weeks from tonight," Anarchy replied.

Patty blinked.

"A small family wedding," I explained the lack of invitation.

"We'd love to entertain for you."

"You're a dear to offer, but—" But what?

"The next two weeks are jam-packed." Anarchy saved me. "We'll host a reception for friends when we get back from our honeymoon. You'll celebrate with us then?"

A reception? I forced a smile.

"We'd love to toast your happiness. Where are you going for your honeymoon?"

"Italy," Anarchy replied.

We were?

"How romantic."

"We think so." Anarchy flashed her one of his melty grins, and we moved away from our host and hostess so they could welcome the next guests at the door.

"Italy?"

"Where else? Besides, we already have tickets." A murder had disrupted a planned trip to Italy. Were we tempting fate by booking a second time? "What may I get you to drink?"

"A white wine spritzer."

"Coming right up." He headed for the bar.

"Ellison." Jane Addison latched onto my arm. "Don't you look pretty."

"Thank you, Jane." I tugged on my arm, but she held firm. "What a lovely dress." She'd paired a simple navy shantung shift with marble-sized pearls and sensible pumps.

A young woman bumped into us and murmured, "Sorry."

She'd done me a favor. Jane had lost her grip on my arm. I stepped back so Jane didn't catch me a second time. "Carly?"

The woman who'd separated me from Jane turned. Carly

Westbrook had lost so much weight her cheekbones looked knife-blade sharp. "Mrs. Russell, how nice to see you."

"You too. Please, call me Ellison."

"Might as well," said Jane. "She won't be Mrs. Russell much longer."

"Oh?"

"She's getting married." Jane spoke slowly, as if Carly had difficulty with simple concepts.

"Best wishes..." Carly stared at someone over my shoulder.

I turned, and Anarchy handed me my drink. "Thank you. Anarchy, this is Carly Westbrook. Carly, this is my fiancé, Anarchy Jones."

"Nice to meet you."

"Likewise." Anarchy's eyes narrowed.

"Anarchy's a police detective," said Jane.

Carly paled. "I'd love to catch up, but I promised I'd find Dean."

"Go," I told her. "Nice seeing you."

Carly slipped into the crowd, and Jane tsked. "She's as high as a kite."

"What?"

Jane shook her head at the crying shame. "Cocaine, Ellison."

"What are you talking about?"

"The girl has a drug problem."

"She's right." Anarchy watched Carly disappear into the house. "She's on something."

Jane's nod was smug. "She's dropped twenty pounds. Did you notice her eyes? Dilated."

"I didn't notice." I didn't go to people's homes and look for signs of drug use among their family members.

"Not our problem." Jane shrugged, as if Carly's drug use didn't concern her. Who did she think she'd fool? "Have you set a date?"

"Two weeks." Anarchy held out his hand. "I don't believe I've had the pleasure. I'm Ellison's fiancé."

"I'm sorry." I took a sip of spritzer. "I thought you two knew each other."

"No." Now that Anarchy had fixed his gaze on Jane, she seemed at a loss for words.

"Jane's the best real-estate agent in town."

"You're Jane?" Anarchy hit her with an irresistible smile. "Ellison's told me all about you."

"All good, I hope."

Anarchy blinked. And lied. "Yes."

"Combining households means change. Where will you live?"

"I would never separate Ellison from her studio. We'll keep my place as a rental property."

Disappointment flashed across Jane's face.

"Jane, if you'll excuse us, Anarchy hasn't met the bride and groom." I pulled him away before she could explain why she should list his house.

"So that's Jane."

"In all her glory."

We found Genevieve and Gus on the patio, and I introduced them to Anarchy.

"I've heard so much about you." Genevieve, who'd just admitted to gossiping, flushed. "I mean, it's not every day someone marries a detective." The color on her cheeks deepened to a dark rose. "I mean—"

"She means it's nice to meet you." Gus extended his hand. "We're glad you're here."

"Thank you," Anarchy replied. "Patty and Doyle are your aunt and uncle?"

"It was so nice of them to do this." Genevieve smiled at her fiancé and her eyes sparkled like the night sky. Charlie's cynical comment about starry-eyed couples and divorce popped into my brain and refused to leave.

The men fell into a sports discussion, and I asked, "Where are you honeymooning?"

"Hawaii. I can't wait." Genevieve reached for Gus's hand. "I had no idea planning a wedding was so much work. Mom did the lion's share, but I handled the guest list and addresses. Also, I picked the bridesmaids' dresses. Those dresses." She winced. "Finding a dress that flatters six girls? Impossible."

I envisioned the dress (scraps of fabric) Libba might wear as my maid of honor, and my mouth went dry. "What about flowers?"

"Daisies. Mom had a fit, but they're my favorite flower." She shared a dreamy smile. "A year of planning, and it's three weeks away."

"You'll make a beautiful bride."

"Thank you." She glanced at my left hand where Anarchy's diamond flashed like a klieg light. "Best wishes to you too."

"Thank you." I rested my hand on Anarchy's arm. "We won't monopolize you. There are scads of people waiting to wish you well. Enjoy this time."

"We will." Another starry-eyed gaze at Gus. "We are."

Anarchy and I moved on.

"Nice couple," he observed.

"They are. What did you and Gus talk about?"

"Baseball."

Baseball? "You like baseball?" He'd already admitted to liking football, now he'd added a second sport?

"Who doesn't?"

"I'd rather watch paint dry."

"You haven't been to a game with me. You'll be a fan by the seventh inning stretch." He frowned. "Is that Mel Langford?"

I followed his gaze.

Mel, who wore a light pink sequined shirt dress, chatted with Jinx and Daisy.

"It is. I should say hello. I haven't called to ask after Hubb."

"Another drink?"

I handed him my empty glass. "Please."

Anarchy drew stares as he walked to the bar. Mine included. I tore my gaze away and joined my friends. I nodded at Jinx and Daisy. "Mel—" I kissed the air next to her cheek "—I've been a terrible friend. How's Hubb?"

"Resting comfortably. He insisted I come tonight. And you're a wonderful friend. You found him. You probably saved his life."

"I wish I'd arrived earlier. Denise might have pulled through."

A wrinkle creased Mel's forehead but disappeared in an instant. "Why did you go to the warehouse?"

"Your glasses. I'm sorry, I lost them."

She waved away my apology. "I have five pairs."

"Mel's been telling us about the fruit business," said Daisy. "Did you know bananas are picked when they're green?"

"I never thought about it."

"When I was a little girl, I loved visiting the warehouse with Daddy. I thought the building was absolutely magical."

What did she think of it now?

Anarchy joined us, handed me a spritzer, and complimented each woman.

"Have you set a date?" asked Jinx.

"Two weeks," Anarchy replied.

Daisy's eyes widened. "That's no time at all. How?"

"Just family at the wedding," I explained. "We'll host a reception later this summer."

"I hope you know how lucky you are." Daisy turned to Anarchy. Her severe expression might strike fear into an eight-year-old heart, but Anarchy was immune.

He answered her with a lazy grin and reached for my free hand. "Luckiest man on earth."

"What does Frances say about the date?" asked Jinx.

"We haven't told her." Oh, dear Lord. We'd mentioned the date to how many people? We'd told Jane Addison. Mother would learn of her daughter's wedding date from a friend. Not from her daughter. That was a problem.

Anarchy squeezed my hand as if he'd followed my thoughts to the icy inferno of Mother's anger.

Libba joined us and wrapped Mel in a hug. "So glad to see you. How's Hubb?"

"The doctors say he's lucky. He'll recover." Mel shivered in the warm late-spring air. "Are you close to an arrest, Detective Jones?"

"It's an ongoing investigation."

"I hope you catch the killer quickly. I won't rest easy till he's behind bars."

Anarchy arched a brow. "He?"

Mel nodded.

"Poison is often a woman's murder weapon."

Mel pressed her hand to her chest. "A woman?"

Was Anarchy hinting Mel was a suspect? "Darling." I squeezed his hand. Hard. "You promised not to talk shop." The worst thing Anarchy could do was use cocktail parties for informal interrogations.

"You're right. My mistake." He smiled at Mel. "My apologies."

She relaxed in the sunny warmth of his smile. "My fault. I brought it up."

"Is that Charlie Ardmore?" asked Libba.

Anarchy stiffened.

"It is," Jinx confirmed. "How did Prudence get her claws into him?"

Now I stiffened. I didn't want Charlie, but I didn't want Prudence to have him either. "Libba, go save him."

"Me? Why me?"

"You're single, and he saved you from an owl."

"Fair point." She adjusted her neckline. "Here goes."

We watched her saunter.

We watched Prudence scowl.

We watched Charlie's gaze drop. And stick.

"So much for Prudence," said Jinx. "How do you like your new neighbor?"

"He hasn't complained about me to the homeowners' association."

"Yet."

We all gaped at Daisy. She was the sweet one.

She shrugged. "Everyone complains, Ellison. Between the police cars, the fire engines, that dog, and the bodies, your neighborhood is more exciting than anyone bargained for."

"True," said Jinx. "But that petition Marian Dixon started after Max chased her cat up a macramé owl was a step too far."

"What petition?"

"Your mother put paid to the idea before it gained any steam."

"Marian Dixon started a petition? Why didn't you tell me?"

Jinx winced. "It slipped my mind."

Nothing slipped by Jinx. I exhaled. "What would Marian do with her days if she didn't spy on me?"

"Look! Libba snagged him." Jinx's obvious attempt to change the subject was a success. Our heads swiveled as Libba led her prize to the bar.

Prudence scowled at me as if I were to blame.

Since I'd sent Libba, she was right.

I gave her a tight smile, and her scowl deepened to a death glare.

Next to me, Daisy smiled brightly. "Such a lovely evening," she observed. "Patty's patio looks fabulous." Enormous terracotta planters filled with bright red geraniums dotted the patio's edge. Black wrought-iron tables and chairs encouraged conversation beneath the emerging stars. A kidney-shaped pool glittered in the glow cast by fairy lights. "The boys used my annual beds for a G.I. Joe war, and I need to replace my impatiens."

"What a shame," said Mel. If she knew Daisy's boys, she'd save her sympathy. Daisy was lucky the little hooligans hadn't salted the earth.

We observed a few seconds of silence for Daisy's dead plants.

"Will Hubb be well enough to attend the funeral on Monday?" asked Jinx.

Mel frowned. "The funeral?"

"Clayton Morris's funeral," I explained.

"Oh. Right. How stupid of me. He'll try. If the doctors say he can attend, he'll be there." Her frown deepened. "I think he'll be out for a few weeks. Such a scare."

"Who's running the company while Hubb recovers?" Jinx asked.

"I am." She glanced at the bricks beneath our feet. "This is no criticism of Hubb, but I may change a few policies and procedures. Do things the way Daddy did." If Hubb stayed gone long enough, she might save the company.

"At least two weeks."

"Well," said Daisy, "I think it's marvelous you can step in. I bet Hubb is so grateful."

Mel's forehead creased. "He's not a fan of women working." She wrung her hands. "But what choice do I have?"

Maybe Mel would untangle Patriot's snarly problems.

Daisy made a sympathetic sound in her throat. "After two murders, I'd be terrified to go to the office."

"I don't have a choice." She offered us a tired smile. "I haven't spoken with the bride and groom. Please excuse me."

"I hope I didn't offend her." Daisy pressed her fingers against her lips. "She's amazing. I could no more run my husband's business than fly to the moon on one wing."

"The company belongs to her family," said Jinx.

Daisy frowned. "Surely it belongs to Mel and Hubb now."

"No," Jinx replied. "Mel's father created a family trust. The trust owns Patriot."

"Who's the trustee?" asked Anarchy.

Jinx's eyes narrowed. "That's an excellent question."

"Look." Daisy nodded toward Libba and Charlie. "Wouldn't it be wonderful if he were the one?"

"The one?" asked Anarchy.

"Daisy wants Libba to find a husband," Jinx explained.

"She hasn't met the right man. When she does, she'll want the security of marriage."

While Jinx and Daisy debated Libba's future, I studied my friend. She stood at the pool's edge and smiled at Charlie as if she actually liked him.

"It's a perfect solution," I murmured.

"You don't mind?" Anarchy's whisper tickled my ear.

"Not in the least. Charlie's my past. You're my future."

Anarchy's arm snaked around my waist, and I leaned into him, into two weeks from tonight.

CHAPTER FOURTEEN

I awoke snuggled next to Anarchy. Cradling my head against his shoulder while his arm held me close rivaled coffee as the best way to start a day. He'd escorted me home, come in for a nightcap, and stayed (allowable because Grace spent the night at Debbie's).

I lifted my gaze from his chest to his face.

Stubble darkened his cheeks, his eyes met mine, and his lips pressed against my forehead. "Good morning."

A languid sigh rose from my toes. I was capable of languid? Who knew? "Good morning."

"That was quite a sigh."

"It was quite a night."

He grinned—a slow—languid—grin. "It could be quite a morning."

His invitation burned through me like a shot of whiskey. Dangerous. Intoxicating. "Grace will be home soon." Also, my breath could melt paint, my mascara was probably smudged like a raccoon's mask, and my hair snarled into a rat's nest.

"Thirteen days," he replied. "Sunday mornings in bed with coffee, the paper, and all the time we want."

"Sounds like heaven." I sat—reluctantly—and dragged unwilling feet to the carpet. "A quick shower, then the bathroom's yours."

A finger traced my spine. "You're sure?"

I stared at my toes. If I looked at Anarchy, I'd hop back into bed and stay there till Monday. "Yes."

Ten minutes later, I emerged from the bathroom. I'd brushed my teeth, washed off the mascara, and conditioned away the snarls. I'd also donned khakis and a camp shirt (because clothes impeded temptation).

Anarchy sat in my bed and flipped through the pages of a book from my nightstand. His chest was bare. His hair was mussed. He made my mouth go dry. "Your hair is wet."

I hadn't dried it.

"You smell like flowers."

"Just soap and shampoo."

"Come back to bed."

I took three steps before I remembered Grace. "Coffee," I croaked.

He answered with a slow smile, as if he knew I yearned—ached—to join him amongst the tangled sheets. He swung his feet to the floor, and I scurried into the hallway. There was only so much temptation I could resist.

I descended the back stairs and opened the door for Max. He raced into the back yard, on the lookout for unsuspecting squirrels.

Mr. Coffee greeted me with his usual sunny smile. *Good morning.*

"It is," I agreed, pushed Mr. Coffee's button, and took two mugs from the cabinet and the cream from the fridge.

You're glowing, Mr. Coffee observed.

"Am I?" My lips wouldn't stop smiling. "Last night was—"

"Ellison!" Mother's voice carried from the front hall.

Oh, dear Lord.

I swallowed and glanced at the back door. Could I make a clean break? She'd track me down. I sighed and called, "Kitchen."

Mother barged in wearing a Chanel suit, Ferragamo pumps, pearls, and a you-owe-me-an-explanation expression.

I pretended Mother had arrived for a morning chat and closed my fingers around the handle of Mr. Coffee's pot. "Coffee?"

"Two weeks?" she demanded.

She'd heard. I offered her a weak smile and said nothing.

"When did you plan on telling me?"

"Today. We decided last night."

"There's no reason to rush."

"There's no reason to wait."

"Grace!" Mother sounded triumphant. She'd played her trump card, would take the trick and win the game.

"Grace is delighted. She suggested we get married today."

Mother gasped. "You can't."

"We don't have a license, and I'd like Karma and Sis to be here. And Marjorie. I'll call them today."

"Have you considered marrying a police detective might be a mistake?"

"Have you considered Anarchy will be your son-in-law in less than two weeks? You should be happy for us." And if you can't be happy, pretend. "Coffee?"

She glared, and I filled both mugs. "I just made it. It's fresh."

Mother picked up the cream carton and sniffed.

"That's fresh too."

We sipped in appreciative but deafening silence. The quiet was as heavy as a sun-may-never-shine-again, bulbous-charcoal-clouds, the-threat-of-endless-cold January sky. Tombs were louder.

Anarchy didn't know we had a visitor when he descended the stairs.

He stepped into the kitchen, and Mother choked on her coffee.

"What are you doing here?" she demanded.

Anarchy's brows dipped and his jaw dropped. The poor man expected coffee, maybe a quick kiss, possibly a lingering kiss. Instead, he got Mother. He glanced my way, clearly unsure what to say.

"Anarchy spent the night."

"What?" Mother never shrieked. Never. But her "what" came darned close.

"We're getting married, Mother."

"You're not married yet. And you have a daughter. What kind of example are you setting for Grace?"

"Grace isn't here."

Mother blinked. "Our kind of people don't behave like this."

I stared at her till she flushed. My half-sister Karma was illegitimate. She was incontrovertible proof my father had behaved exactly like this.

"It's different for women," Mother snapped.

"It shouldn't be."

"Actions have consequences, Ellison. When it comes to sex —" Mother curled her lip as if the word tasted bitter on her tongue "—it's women who pay the price." She turned a scathing glare on Anarchy. "You had to advertise?"

"Advertise? Mother, what are you talking about?"

"The car parked in your driveway."

"Anarchy parked behind the house."

"There's a Corvette in your driveway."

"That's Libba's." If her car spent the night in my drive, she'd spent the night next door.

"She's here?"

"No."

"Her car is here."

"Yes."

"Where is she?"

I cut my gaze to the window over the sink and its view of the house next door.

"You let her nab Charlie?"

Anarchy crossed the kitchen, poured himself a cup of coffee, and leveled a chilly gaze at Mother.

She paid him no mind. "If you'd tried—"

"I'm in love with Anarchy. I'm marrying Anarchy."

"Have you two thought this through? Where will you live?"

"Frances."

Mother and I both turned our heads.

Anarchy leaned against the counter. He'd crossed his ankles and his hands circled the coffee mug. "Ellison and I will get married two weeks from yesterday. We'll honeymoon in Italy. We'll host a reception when we return. And I will spend the rest of my life keeping your daughter safe and happy." His tone left zero room for argument.

But Mother was Mother. "Two weeks isn't enough—"

"Two weeks. I hope you'll make peace with this, because Ellison loves you and wants you and Harrington to celebrate with us."

Mother's jaw dropped. To the floor. She'd never considered her daughter getting married without her. That, or Anarchy's standing up for me shocked her. Henry never rode a white horse into our mother-daughter battles. Henry never slayed a dragon on my behalf.

Max scratched at the back door, and I let him in.

"Where's the other one?" Mother asked.

"With Charlie."

"Why?"

"She likes him better."

"Hmph." Mother refrained from making a snide comment about how Pansy's taste was superior to mine.

I scratched behind Max's ears and gave him a biscuit.

"What remains undone?" Mother asked.

"Undone?"

"The wedding, Ellison." Did her resigned tone mean she'd waved a white flag? "What may I do?"

I didn't have a caterer, a dress, a minister, musicians, or a florist. "Nothing. I have the wedding well in hand."

"Where will this wedding take place?"

"Here. Immediate family, Libba, and Aggie." And I could argue that Libba and Aggie were family.

"I suppose I should be grateful you're not making a fuss."

"We anticipate inviting at least four hundred to the reception," said Anarchy.

We were? I glanced at his poker face. Was he needling Mother on purpose? Not a great idea. Poking a sleeping grizzly was safer.

Mother inhaled audibly and squeezed her eyes shut.

Anarchy winked at me, and I fell deeper in love.

Grace burst through the back door, spotted her grandmother, and stopped dead.

Mother opened her eyes, then narrowed them to slits. "Young lady, what are you wearing?"

"Shorts."

Ridiculously short shorts. If she wore them anyplace but the pool, we'd have words.

"You let her out in public looking like that?"

"I spent the night with a friend, then went to the pool." Grace wiped her palms against the hint of denim.

Mother sniffed, and Grace edged toward the back stairs.

I glanced at the clock on the wall. "Are you attending church?"

Mother glanced at her wristwatch and scowled. "We'll talk later." With that threat suspended in the air, she turned on her heel and marched out of the kitchen.

When we heard the front door close (not a slam—Mother

would never slam a door—but a sharp meeting of door and frame), Grace exhaled. "She's in a mood. What did you do?"

"We set a date."

Grace's smile rivaled the morning sun, and she caught me in a hug. "I'm so happy for you. Both of you. When?"

"Two weeks," Anarchy replied.

"Wow. What can I do?"

"Walk down the aisle with me."

"But—"

"Your grandfather had his chance. This isn't about giving me away; it's about creating a new family."

"It won't make Granna happy."

"Nothing about this makes Granna happy." I offered Anarchy an apologetic smile over Grace's shoulder.

Grace's arms tightened around me. "This isn't her life. It's yours."

Sometimes daughters are incredibly wise.

I SETTLED behind my desk in the family room, positioned my coffee cup just so, picked up the receiver, and dialed Aunt Sis.

"Hello." The gravel in my aunt's new husband's voice alarmed me.

"Gordon, it's Ellison. Are you all right?"

"Fine. Hoarse. We went to the World Championship Tennis Finals in Dallas, and I cheered myself hoarse when Arthur Ashe beat that upstart Swede. Never mind about me—how are you? When are you and Grace and Anarchy coming for a visit? We miss you."

"It's kind of you to invite us—"

"I hear a 'but' coming."

"Anarchy and I set a date. We're hoping you and Aunt Sis will visit us. Would you consider a trip to Kansas City?"

"For your wedding? We wouldn't miss it. Give me the date, and I'll book the tickets."

"May thirty-first."

"That's less than two weeks from now."

"I know."

He chuckled. "Is Frances having a faunching fit?"

"She's not pleased."

"I bet not. Plus, I hear you found a body."

"News travels fast."

"Martin Walls, your friend Mel's father, and I were friends all his life..." Gordon's pause carried the weight of sadness. And secrets.

I waited for more.

"His company is in trouble."

I said nothing.

"My guess is they're barely hanging on."

Would it be disloyal to Mel to agree?

"Byron Clifford is the trustee."

"He is?"

"You didn't know?"

"No." I hadn't planned on collecting information for Anarchy, but if Gordon knew the trust's details, I couldn't miss this opportunity. "Would you please explain the trust to me?"

"The trust owns the company."

"Wait."

"What?"

"May I share what you tell me with Anarchy?"

"Sure. Like I said, the company is held in trust for Mel and her children."

"Hubb runs it."

"He needed a job. Martin took him on, taught him the business, then gave him the reins."

"Why did Martin put the company in trust?"

"Martin knew produce wasn't Hubb's first choice. Martin worried Hubb would sell after he died."

I pinched the bridge of my nose. Families were complicated. Martin Walls trusted Hubb to run his company, but not own it. "What does Byron say about Hubb's leadership?"

"I haven't asked him. Truth is Byron pays more attention to the level of bourbon in his glass than his duties as trustee. Aside from collecting his fee, I doubt Patriot crosses his mind."

"So Byron wouldn't notice Hubb running Patriot into the ground?"

"You admit the company's struggling?"

"I was at their warehouse and it didn't inspire confidence."

"What does Mel say?"

"I don't think she realized how bad things were."

"Oh?"

"She seemed shocked after she visited the warehouse."

"I wouldn't want to be Hubb Langford."

"Why not?"

"Martin always said Mel had singular focus. It's too bad she wasn't a boy. She could have run the hell out of that company."

"She still could."

"If she gets the chance. Byron would have to grant his permission and Hubb would have to resign."

Or die. "Hubb Langford let his wife succeed where he failed?"

Gordon chuckled. "When pigs fly."

"I wonder..."

"What?"

I was being fanciful. If Mel Langford wanted to be rid of Hubb, she'd divorce him. Wouldn't she? "I wonder if Clayton Morris's death was an accident. Could Hubb be the target?" Did Mel want her family's company safe from further harm?

"Something to consider. Your aunt just walked in. Sis, Ellison's on the phone. She has news. Ellison, we'll talk soon."

"Ellison, what a treat to hear from you." My aunt's voice brought a smile to my face.

"Hi, Aunt Sis."

"Your mother called me."

"Did she give you the date?"

"The date?"

Mother hadn't told her. "What did Mother call you about?"

"Your ex-boyfriend."

Oh, dear Lord. "Forget about Charlie. Anarchy and I are getting married at the end of the month. We hope you and Gordon will join us."

"We wouldn't miss it. How's your mother taking this?"

"Guess."

Sis laughed.

"We're getting married in a small ceremony at the house. Just family, Libba, and Aggie."

Sis laughed harder.

We chatted about flowers and cake and small weddings for a few minutes. When we hung up, I called my sister Marjorie.

"Mother told me," she said after we'd exchanged cool pleasantries.

"About?"

"Charlie Ardmore moving in next door. She's convinced he wants you back."

"Anarchy and I set a date."

"Did you tell Mother?"

"May thirty-first."

"Does Mother know?"

"She's in denial. Can you come to the wedding?"

"It's very short notice, but we'll try. I'd like to be there when Greg becomes Mother's favorite son-in-law." Marjorie's husband manufactured condoms. While Mother appreciated the lifestyle the King Cobra afforded my sister and her family, she found the actual product crass.

"That's definitely why you should come. Not to celebrate with us. Not to toast our happiness."

"Lighten up, Ellison."

I took a deep breath. "I hope you'll come."

"Mother won't be celebrating or toasting."

"She might change her mind." Impossible things happened. Buzz Aldrin walked on the moon. An unelected president sat in the White House. I was planning a wedding in two weeks.

"You'll lose your title as favorite daughter."

"I'm not her favorite."

"Oh, please. Ever since I married Greg."

I could argue, hang up, or beg. The choice was obvious. "Please come. It won't be the same without you."

"Like I said, we'll try. I suppose you want me as your matron of honor. I'll need a new dress. What are your colors?"

"I asked Libba."

Her answering silence prickled. And stretched. "I'm your sister."

"You were matron of honor at my first wedding. It's Libba's turn."

"I suppose you'll ask Karma for your next."

"This is it."

"Everyone says that when they get married." My sister was foretelling my divorce before Anarchy and I exchanged vows?

I did not slam the receiver into the cradle. I did not invite the bird of paradise to fly up her nose. I gritted my teeth and said, "Please come."

"Make a reservation for us at The Alameda, and we'll try."

"Why don't you make sure you're coming first?"

"If it's too much trouble..."

"Marjorie, I don't know when you'll arrive or return home."

"Fine." She sighed as if making a hotel reservation was an enormous inconvenience.

"Talk soon." I rested the receiver in the cradle (gently) and looked up Karma's number.

"Hello." She answered on the second ring.

"Karma, it's Ellison."

"How are you?" Her voiced softened, warmed—as if hearing from me was the best thing that had happened to her all week.

"Fine. You?"

"Just enjoying a lazy Sunday morning."

"Anarchy and I set a date. We're getting married at the end of the month and hope you can come."

"Are you kidding? Of course I'll be there. The end of the month? That's two weeks away! Do you need help? What can I do?"

"Not a thing. We're getting married at the house. A small ceremony. Just family and a few close friends."

"Is Anarchy's family coming?"

"He's calling them today."

"I'll fly in a few days early. You may need the moral support."

"You'd do that?"

"Are you kidding? I'll rearrange my schedule as soon as I get to the office tomorrow morning. What's the name of that new hotel on the Plaza? I'll make a reservation when we hang up."

"You could stay with us." Unlike Marjorie, Karma didn't expect me to provide elaborate breakfasts, entertaining activities, and invitations to parties. Karma would sit at the kitchen counter, drink coffee, and rhapsodize over Aggie's cinnamon rolls. She'd hang out in my studio and chat or go to a movie with Grace. She'd even trade pot roast recipes with Aggie. She was the perfect guest.

"The last thing you need is a house guest."

"You're not a guest. You're family."

"Thank you." Her voice sounded thick. "And thank you for including me. Where are you registered?"

"Registered?"

"For gifts."

"No gifts. We don't need anything."

"A gift isn't about need."

"Your presence is our gift."

"Yeah, yeah, yeah." I heard her fingers drum on a table. "I know! I'll run up to Napa and find a bottle of wine you can put away for your fiftieth anniversary."

Ding, dong.

"Karma, I can't tell you how thrilled I am. But I need to hang up, there's someone at the door."

"Go. I'll call you when I've finalized my travel plans."

I hung up the phone and hurried to the front door, where Max waited. His stumpy tail wagged a mile a minute.

Libba and Pansy waited on the front stoop. Both wore ridiculous grins.

When I opened the door, Pansy trotted inside and nudged Max. The two disappeared into the kitchen, leaving me with my maid of honor.

"I hope you're not upset?"

"About?"

"Me and Charlie." That grin—it split her face. She hadn't smiled like that since—ever.

"Not remotely."

"You're sure?"

"Positive."

She exhaled, and the grin widened. "I'm so glad."

"You like him."

"I do." Her cheeks flushed. "He's…did you ever sleep together?"

The hinge in my jaw loosened. "I was in high school."

She waved away my response. "That doesn't answer my question."

"No!"

"You missed out. He's—"

"Stop!"

"What?"

"I don't want to know."

She tilted her head. "You don't?"

About Libba and Charlie? "No."

"I wonder about Anarchy."

Ew. "Don't tell me that."

"You never speculate about your friends' sex lives?"

"Never."

"You lack imagination."

"You lack boundaries."

She narrowed her eyes. "Anarchy spent the night, didn't he? You have that glow."

"What glow?"

"The glow of a woman who's had her bell rung."

Multiple times. "This is none of your business."

Libba smirked and hugged me. "I'm so happy for you. Hold tight to this. Don't let anyone interfere."

"I won't." The promise was easy, but an uneasy trickle slid down my spine.

CHAPTER FIFTEEN

Mondays were bad days for funerals. No one wanted to start the week with grief or death or a long-winded eulogy.

Rainy Mondays were even worse.

I sat alone in an uncomfortable pew in an unfamiliar church. Ninety percent of the weddings and funerals I attended were held in the same four churches—two Episcopal, two Presbyterian. This church with its plain white walls, clear rain-streaked windows, and hard pews was off for a woman who'd grown up attending an Episcopal church with soaring ceilings, dark wood-paneled walls, jewel-toned stained-glass windows, and red velvet cushions.

I shifted in the wooden pew (what was wrong with cushions?) and scanned those seated in front of me. Where was Anarchy? He was here—somewhere—to observe, not mourn.

Not that I was mourning. My heart ached for Clayton's wife and children, but my sadness extended no further.

Around me, funeral-goers brushed stray raindrops from their shoulders and spoke in hushed tones.

I peeked at my watch. Five minutes till the service, and the church wasn't half full.

Karen's friends had turned out to support her, but their husbands had picked business over a funeral. I counted eleven men. And eight of them were members of the Sunday Afternoon Literary Society. The group started during prohibition. As far as I knew, the only thing the members had ever read were Dewar's labels. Also, they hadn't met on Sundays since the Twenty-first Amendment passed. Instead they met on the first and third Tuesdays of the month for lunch (rubber chicken and three martinis). The society included preeminent lawyers, scions, and business owners. The retired members attended the funerals of deceased members en masse. I hadn't realized Clayton belonged, but there was no other explanation for the men who sat three pews in front of me.

"May I?" Jane Addison squeezed past my knees and plunked down beside me.

"Good morning," I murmured.

"Awful weather," she replied.

"We need the rain."

Banalities handled, Jane nodded and eyed the mourners in front of us. Then she twisted in the pew and studied those behind us. "Hubb Langford is here in a wheelchair."

I resisted turning. Mother had drummed into me that rubbernecking in church was simply not done. Instead I glanced out the window where lightning forked through the sky. "I'm glad he's well enough to attend."

"You found him."

"I did."

A salacious gleam danced in Jane's eyes. "Tangled up with his secretary."

"Not remotely."

Jane wrinkled her nose. "I heard—"

"Hubb's assistant died, Jane. It's a tragedy."

Her face shuttered at the implied criticism. "Doesn't mean they weren't—"

"We're at a funeral."

"Fine," she huffed. "Who killed Clayton?"

I flinched as thunder shook the windows in their frames. "Who said he was murdered?"

"Two—" she held up fingers "—almost three deaths at the same company in a week. Obviously murder."

I couldn't fault her logic. Or her counting skills.

"Who did it?" she demanded.

If I knew, I'd tell Anarchy and the case would close. "No idea."

"Karen?"

"Why would Karen kill Hubb?"

She frowned. "Mel?"

"Why would Mel kill Clayton?"

"Fine. A disgruntled employee? What does your detective say?"

"He doesn't comment on ongoing investigations." The lie came easier with repetition.

Jane crossed her arms and sighed as if she regretted pushing into my pew. Even if it weren't unconscionably rude for her to relocate, she was stuck. The organist began a hymn, and Karen and her children filed into the front pew.

We sang. We prayed. We stood. We sat. The minister gave a generic homily. We sang and prayed again. Then Karen and her children walked up the aisle.

Karen's skin seemed loose, as if she hadn't eaten since Clayton's death. Her children—both with tearstained cheeks and red eyes—flanked her. She clutched their hands hard enough for her knuckles to whiten.

"Karen looks good in black," Jane observed. "Do you suppose the architect is here?"

"The woman is burying her husband."

"Leaves her free."

"Karen adores her children. Right now she's focused on them. She'd never disrespect their father like that."

Jane pursed her lips and stared at me as if I'd said something so naïve it bordered on stupid.

When the usher excused our pew, she nearly trampled me on her way to the aisle. I'd been a gossip bust.

I let her advance a few yards before I stepped into the flow of people.

"Ellison." Elise Chandler touched my arm. "Thank you for sending the recipe."

"You're welcome. Have you tried it?"

"Not yet. But I will. Soon." She patted her eyes with a folded linen handkerchief. "Such a sad day."

"Heartbreaking," I agreed.

"Your fiancé is investigating?"

"Yes."

"So it's definitely murder?"

"Anarchy doesn't discuss his cases." Officially an effortless lie.

"Not even when you find more bodies?"

I gave her a tight smile. "Not even then."

"I heard you're marrying him at the end of the month."

"Yes."

"You've met his people?"

Where was she going with this? "I have."

"Has Frances met them?"

"Yes."

"He makes you happy?" Her tone conveyed doubt.

"He does." My voice was sharper than I intended.

Elise blinked her surprise before retreating a step. "Well, best wishes."

Ahead of us, Hubb's wheelchair sat behind the last pew. I broke away from the crowd and approached him. He was pale, a delicate shade of green—darker than leeks, lighter than celery. His skin glistened with a clammy sheen.

"Hubb, how are you?"

"Hanging in there." He offered me a weak smile. "Thanks to you."

"I'm so glad I happened along."

"Me too." He nodded toward the altar. "It's a sad day. If I'd found Clayton like you found me, we might not be here."

"How long did you work together?"

"At least a decade. He was a good man. I don't know how we'll replace him."

"Mel told me she's been going to the office. Maybe she can help."

"It's no place for a woman."

I had no response to that. "Have you thought about who might have done this?"

"I've thought of nothing else."

"And?"

He shook his head and stared at his hands. "No idea."

Did I believe him?

An enormous clap of thunder shook the church.

"Ellison." Mel joined us. Water dripped from her raincoat and dampened her hair. "How nice to see you. Darling, we should get you home. We promised the doctor."

Hubb and I glanced at the rain-lashed windows.

"We'll wait till this lets up," said Hubb.

"I pulled the car under the porte-cochere. We can't leave it there."

Again, Hubb glanced at the window. His features darkened till they matched the storm-tossed sky. "The rain is blowing."

"You won't melt. I didn't."

"May I help?" I asked.

Mel rejected my offer with a wave of her hand. "Hubb is

right about the rain. It's coming down in buckets. I'd hate for you to spoil your dress."

I wore a navy silk shirt dress. The rain would do the fabric no favors. "You're sure?"

"Positive. Please give Karen our regards."

I'd been dismissed. "Of course." I followed the stragglers through a maze of hallways to the church hall.

Tables in the room's center held plates of cookies and a coffee urn. The line to pay respects snaked the perimeter.

I spotted Anarchy in the far corner. He held a coffee cup and studied the crowd. Our gazes met, and a flush warmed my cheeks.

He grinned into his coffee cup.

Joining him in the corner would be a mistake. He was working. Everyone and their brother would ask about the investigation as soon as we parted. I swallowed a sigh and weighed the line's length against my need to visit the powder room.

The powder room won.

I retreated to the hallway and stopped a woman carrying a tray of cookies. "Would you please tell me where I can find the ladies' room?"

"We're a bit of a warren. You're in the new section of the building. The ladies' room is in the older section. Take a right, then a left, then a right."

"Thank you." I ventured down the hallway and turned right. A new hallway stretched perpendicular. I turned left, and the noise from the reception faded. My heels tapped against the tiled floors. Echoed.

I turned right and found a janitor's closet. The woman with the cookies hadn't said which right. Maybe I needed to walk farther. I backtracked, took a right, walked, and located a ladies' room. The smell was musty. The plumbing was ancient. And, when I washed my hands at a porcelain sink surrounded by pink Formica, I used powdered soap from a chrome dispenser. I took a moment and touched up my lipstick, then stepped into the hall.

I stared at the white walls. Did I turn left or right? I guessed left. I couldn't be the first person to become confused in the church's hallways. Why didn't they have signs?

I gripped my handbag (navy blue alligator) and kept walking. I was hopelessly turned around. Left or right? The church was big, but if I kept going, I'd run into someone. Eventually.

I turned right. Had I walked this hallway before? White walls, the low hum of fluorescent bulbs, closed doors. Each hallway looked the same.

I paused and heard footsteps. "Hello?"

The footsteps stopped.

"Hello?"

No answer. But the footsteps resumed. Heavy footsteps. A man.

Ice crystals formed around my heart. My hands clenched, and my mouth went dry. Was the forklift driver here for Clayton's funeral? Was he the man who'd shot at me at the park? Was he following me now?

The footsteps grew louder. Closer.

I bent and slipped off my pumps—if I heard the stranger's heavy tread, he heard my heels tap on the tile floor. Barefoot, I ran.

The menace-laden thud of the stranger's steps sped up.

Left or right?

I dashed right. Was I running in a circle? I rounded a corner, paused, and strained to hear my pursuer over the blood rushing in my ears.

Voices. Two women chatted down the hallway and around a corner.

I drew breath deep into my lungs and sprinted toward them. I rounded the corner and slammed into someone.

She fell backward, grabbed my arms, and pulled me with her to the floor.

We crashed in a tangle of arms, legs, and sharp elbows.

I struggled to free myself. "I'm so very sorry."

"Sure you are."

I lifted my gaze from the paste broach on the woman's dress, and my limbs shuddered. I'd knocked Prudence flat? Of all the people to crash into—she'd claim a chronic injury and sue me.

"Get off."

I scrambled away from her, retrieved my dropped shoes and handbag, and stood.

"What were you doing?" She eyed my bare feet.

"Someone was following me."

Her eyes narrowed. "Sure they were. There's a run in my stockings."

I glanced over my shoulder. "We should probably get back to the reception."

Kate Bristol, the woman with whom Prudence was chatting, wore a worried expression. "Following you?"

I nodded so hard my neck hurt—although the pain in the neck could be Prudence related. "Which way is the reception?" There was safety in numbers.

Kate pointed to the left.

"We should go."

"She's being dramatic," said Prudence. "No one followed her."

"Right, Prudence. I decided to run barefoot through the halls for fun."

Prudence drew her lips back from her horsey teeth and snarled at me.

I slipped on my shoes, straightened my dress, and smoothed my hair. "The left, you say?"

Kate nodded.

I hurried toward the reception, ducked inside, and searched

for Anarchy. The crowd hadn't thinned—no one wanted to brave the storm—and I couldn't spot him.

He found me. "What's wrong? What happened?"

I looked into his coffee-colored eyes and felt a golf ball block my throat.

"Ellison?"

"Someone followed me. Chased me."

His brows drew together and his lips thinned. "Stay here."

Stay here? I wanted to argue. He couldn't tell me what to do. But before I could point out his high-handedness, he stepped into the hallway.

I leaned against the nearest wall. The line to offer condolences was short. I could speak to Karen. Should speak to Karen. Except pushing away from the wall was too hard. The adrenaline draining from my system left my legs weak and shaking. Also, if I went anywhere, it would be after Anarchy. Stay here?

Someone touched my arm. I jumped. High. When I landed, I leaned over and gasped for breath.

"What's wrong?" asked Jinx. "You look as if you've seen a ghost."

"A man followed me from the ladies' room."

Prudence passed through the doorway and scowled at me. "She knocked me down."

Jinx shrugged. "Who could blame her?"

Prudence flushed an unbecoming shade of three-days-old salmon.

"I'm sorry, Prudence. Bumping into you was an accident. I hope you're not—"

Bang!

A nearby woman shrieked, then giggled.

"Just the thunder," said the man standing next to her.

Was he kidding?

I pushed away from the wall.

Jinx's grip on my arm tightened. "Where are you going?"

"That was a gunshot."

"My question stands."

"Anarchy's out there." I nodded toward the hall.

"If people are shooting, I'm certain he'd want you here where it's safe."

"What if he's the one who got shot?" The idea twisted my stomach into intricate knots. I slipped into the hallway and called, "Anarchy?"

Was that a moan?

I tiptoed toward a turn in the hallway. White walls stretched ahead of me. Was that—I squinted at the floor—blood?

I ran.

Around a second corner, I found Anarchy in a growing pool of crimson. "Jinx!"

Her head appeared at the hallway's end.

"Call an ambulance. Now!" Trusting she'd do as I asked, I knelt next to Anarchy.

His shirt was drenched in blood.

"Anarchy!"

He didn't answer.

"Anarchy!" My voice rose an octave.

He didn't respond. Didn't move.

Horror opened its maw and swallowed me whole.

No. No, no, no.

Where had the bullet entered? My fingers fumbled with the buttons of his sodden shirt, and tears raced down my cheeks.

A man pushed me aside. "I'm a doctor."

I ceded my spot near Anarchy's chest as the man ripped through the cloth hiding Anarchy's wound.

I knelt near his ankles and pressed my hand against his leg. He wouldn't leave this life if he sensed me near him. A pretty lie. "Save him. Please."

The doctor didn't look up from whatever he was doing to Anarchy's chest. "I'll try."

An arm settled around my shoulders, and someone forced a handkerchief into my free hand.

I spared a quick glance. Jinx. "This can't be the end," I told her. Anarchy and I were poised at the starting line—coffee in bed, lazy Sundays, I'll-wash-you-dry, honey-how-was-your-day kisses, better-now-I'm-with-you kisses, growing old together. Now that future drowned in a flood of crimson.

How could I continue without him?

"Ellison." Jinx used a voice saved for wounded animals.

"He can't die."

"The ambulance is on its way."

The doctor's sleeves were stained red to his elbows.

Could a person lose so much blood and live?

Anarchy couldn't die. Could. Not. He'd finally found what he wanted—who he wanted. The solemn, serious man I'd met at a crime scene had changed. He laughed. He teased. He flirted. He kissed me till I was breathless.

In my chest, my heart shattered, and the white walls, the red blood, and the navy of Anarchy's suit faded to gray. I felt the weight of too many stares. "The ambulance?" I croaked.

"On its way," Jinx promised.

I willed life into my fingertips, imagined its spark passing from my hand to Anarchy's leg. From there, the current traveled to his heart and tethered him to the world. To me.

The hallway blurred behind a veil of tears, and I prayed. I bargained with God. I denied the bleak future promised by the lake of Anarchy's blood.

"Ellison." Jinx pulled on my arm. "Let go."

Let go? Was she mad?

"The EMTs..."

I looked up at men wearing grave expressions. "Fine. But I'm riding in the ambulance."

If Anarchy died, I didn't want him to be with strangers.

CHAPTER SIXTEEN

The EMTs wheeled Anarchy through the pouring rain. Their running footsteps splashed on the wet pavement. I ran behind them and climbed into the ambulance.

"You can't..." began the younger of the two. If a twenty-three-year-old boy thought he'd keep me away, he had another think coming.

"Let her," said his older partner.

Did that mean Anarchy wouldn't make it to the hospital and he wanted me to have these last few minutes?

"You'll stay out of our way?" the older man demanded.

I nodded and huddled into the corner.

"Who is he?" he asked.

"My fiancé."

"His name?" The EMT spoke with the patience of a man who regularly received ridiculous answers to simple questions.

"Anarchy Jones."

His brows lifted. "Seriously?"

"Yes. He's a detective."

"A private detective?"

"A homicide detective. A cop."

The man's lips thinned, and he nodded at his young coworker who applied pressure to Anarchy's chest. "You hear that?"

"Got it."

"What happened?"

"I don't know." My head sank to my hands. "Someone shot him." Someone who'd followed me. This was my fault. Guilt and grief arm-wrestled for supremacy. Grief won, but guilt was a poor loser and would demand a rematch.

"Hell of a thing," said the older man. "Getting shot at a funeral."

A hot finger poked at my grief.

"Makes you wonder what the world is coming to," he continued.

The finger poked a second time, and I welcomed its heat. Rage's fire felt better than sadness's biting cold. I closed my eyes and imagined pulling a trigger, ending the man who'd shot Anarchy.

A part of me recognized revenge wouldn't heal Anarchy. But the image—a gun in my hand and a fallen body at my feet—kept me from falling to pieces.

We reached the hospital, and a crowd of people clad in scrubs swarmed around us. They took Anarchy from me.

Drenched, furious, miserable, and hobbled by guilt, I followed them inside.

"Mrs. Russell, are you hurt?" One of the ER nurses recognized me. I was a frequent visitor.

"No. My fiancé…" I searched the hall for Anarchy, but they'd whisked him away. He was gone. My face crumpled.

She offered me a sympathetic smile and took hold of my arm. "We'll take good care of him. I promise. You look as if you should sit down." She led me through the swinging doors to the waiting room and a row of chairs. "You sit here. Is there anyone I can call?"

"Detective Peters." I gave her his phone number. Detective Peters didn't like me. I wasn't sure he liked Anarchy. But he wouldn't stand by and let a cop get shot—not without tearing up the city to find the shooter.

"I'll call him right away."

She left me, and I sat and gazed at the older man sitting across from me. His hands were folded in his lap and his lips moved silently. Praying? Why was he here? His wife? Had they enjoyed decades of happiness together?

Prayer was a good idea. I clasped my hands together and begged God. *Please, please don't take him. Not today. Please grant us a long, happy life together. Please give me the strength to get through this and—*

"Coffee?" The receptionist pressed a Styrofoam cup into my chilled hands. "The nurse had me call Detective Peters. He's on his way." She glanced at the floor and a deep pink stained her cheeks. "I also called your mother."

Mother? Having Mother with me would be the cherry on top of this terrible day. Her *I warned you* echoed through my brain. She'd told me over and over again that as a cop's wife, I'd spend the rest of my life worrying. I'd happily worry if it meant Anarchy lived through this. And having Mother here? My shoulders stiffened with a realization. If strings needed pulling, having Mother here to pull them was a brilliant idea. One I should have come up with myself.

A man and his very pregnant wife burst through the doors and the receptionist hurried back to her desk. Seconds later, an orderly appeared with a wheelchair and whisked the woman to the obstetrics ward. The man scrawled his signature on three forms and ran after her.

I glanced at my watch. I'd give the doctors five more minutes before I demanded an update. I sipped my coffee (not fresh and needed cream) and counted the seconds.

At the one-hundred-forty-third second, a doctor emerged from behind the doors. His expression was grim.

Seeing his face, my hands shook and I spilled the remainder of my coffee. Worse, a horrible part of me hoped he'd come to talk to the old man. I closed my eyes.

"Mrs. Russell?"

I forced my eyes open and accidentally crushed the empty cup in my hands. If he told me—

"We've taken your fiancé to surgery."

He wasn't dead. I exhaled a breath I hadn't realized I was holding.

"We'll do our best for him."

That didn't sound good. There were questions I should ask. Important questions. But I couldn't speak.

"You can wait here or in the surgical waiting room."

What had the bullet hit? What was the prognosis? How long would he be in surgery? Who was operating? Good questions that went unasked because my voice had disappeared.

"May we get you fresh coffee?"

"No," I murmured. "I've had enough."

He left me, and I stood. I'd be better off—closer to Anarchy—in the surgical waiting room.

Detective Peters exploded through the emergency room doors. He spotted me and charged over. "What happened?"

The receptionist looked up from her paperwork and frowned at the man disrupting her waiting room. Detective Peters, in his rumpled wet raincoat, didn't look like a cop. If anything, he looked like an escaped lunatic.

"Someone shot him," I whispered.

"Who?" he demanded.

I shook my head.

"Where is he?"

"Surgery."

"How bad?"

I covered my face with my hands and my shoulders shook.

"Tell me what happened." Peters' voice was gentle. Almost kind. Usually he treated me like gum on the bottom of his shoe.

The kindness nearly destroyed me. I took a breath, ignored the ache in my jaw and lump in my throat, and said, "We were at Clayton Morris's funeral."

"And?"

"Someone followed me. I told Anarchy about it and he ventured into the hallway."

"Did you see the shooter?"

"No." I lowered my head to my hands. My stomach churned, and the coffee I'd drunk threatened a reappearance. "I feel sick."

The receptionist appeared with a wastebasket. "What can I get you?"

The man who shot Anarchy in handcuffs, please.

"She'll have a glass of water." Peters lowered himself into the chair next to mine. "You feel guilty?"

Yes! And horrified. And scared out of my mind. Unfortunately the rage that made an appearance in the ambulance had ebbed and left a terrifying emptiness in its wake. I gritted my teeth and stared at my knees.

"I can't tell you how to feel, but I can say the man who pulled the trigger is to blame. Not you."

"Thank you," I whispered.

He grunted. "Where was he shot?"

My lips trembled. "His chest."

Peters did the most extraordinary thing. He patted my knee. "Keep the faith. It ain't over till it's over."

Comfort by cliché actually worked. I felt marginally better.

Mother breezed through the emergency room doors, spotted me, and frowned. "What happened to you?"

"To me? Nothing."

"You're soaked."

"It's raining." And strictly speaking I was damp, not soaking. I'd dried a bit since arriving.

"You look like something the cat dragged in. Go clean up."

I opened my mouth to argue, but she held up her hand. "You'll feel better with your hair combed. Straighten your appearance, and I'll check on Anarchy."

I nodded—mainly because Mother, who was the chairman of the hospital board, could gather information not available to the rest of us.

She marched to the receptionist's desk, and I retreated to the ladies' room.

The woman in the mirror was bedraggled and pale and her eyes were five times too big for her face. There was nothing I could do about the blood stains on my dress, but I washed Anarchy's blood from my hands, wiped away smudged mascara, took a comb from my handbag, and started on the rat's nest atop my head. When I finished combing, I braced my hands on the sink and moaned.

I might have stayed there forever, but there existed the real possibility that Mother had news. I returned to the waiting room where Mother gave me an approving nod. "Much better."

"Anarchy?"

Her gaze slid left. "Still in surgery."

"The prognosis?"

"They don't know till after the surgery." She was telling me he might die.

A chasm of grief opened at my feet.

"Don't give up on him," said Peters. "He's a fighter."

Unable to speak, I flashed him a grateful smile. The world was upside down when I looked to Peters for comfort.

"We're to go to the surgical waiting room. A nurse will bring us updates every thirty minutes."

Both Mother and Peters being kind? That could mean only one thing—Anarchy was dying.

"Can I get you coffee?" asked Peters.

My lower lip trembled.

"She doesn't need coffee," said Mother. "She needs to pull herself together."

Mother's disapproval was as familiar as a favorite sweater or Mr. Coffee's sunny gingham face. Bracing like a brisk walk or a stiff scotch. Her attitude (no-strong-emotion-in-public) helped. My chin firmed.

Mother led the way. Her sensible pumps tapped a steady rhythm, and the set of her shoulders said she'd stand for no more weepy nonsense.

Peters walked next to me as if he expected me to collapse.

Watching the determined swing of Mother's skirt, I pushed aside fear and grief and latched onto rage. Anarchy would be fine, and we'd catch the person who shot him, and they'd rot in jail for the rest of eternity.

"Frances." A woman in the pink version of a doctor's coat welcomed us to the waiting room. "Is Harrington—"

"Good afternoon, Sandra. It's not Harrington. Ellison's fiancé was shot in the line of duty."

Sandra blinked. "In the line of duty?"

"He's a homicide detective," Mother's voice was flat, daring Sandra to pass judgment.

"Oh." Sandra's reply was faint. "I see. May I get you coffee?"

"Nothing for me," Mother replied. "Ellison?"

"Please."

Sandra nodded and shifted a who-in-the-world-are-you gaze to Peters. "Anything for you, sir?"

"No, thank you."

We sat.

"Awful woman," Mother whispered. "Her husband's a doctor here."

"What's so bad about her?" asked Peters.

"Doctors' wives." Mother shook her head.

"What about 'em?"

"They've done well for themselves." What Mother meant but didn't say was that Sandra had married up.

Sandra returned with my coffee.

"Thank you." Gratitude colored my voice.

We sat in silence. I had no small talk in me, Mother wasn't interested in speaking to Peters, and Peters was too busy scowling at an innocuous painting of a garden to spare any words.

When a nurse in scrubs and a surgical cap entered the waiting room, I leapt from my chair. She offered me a sympathetic grimace. "The bullet hit his aorta."

I sagged into my chair.

"It was a low-caliber bullet, and it appears the aortic wall contained the hemorrhage. He has a decent chance for recovery."

Would it be odd if I kissed her? "Thank you."

"How much longer in surgery?" asked Peters.

"Another two hours," the nurse replied.

I latched onto that. Two hours. I could make it two hours. Then Anarchy would be out of surgery, he'd be fine.

Peters stood. "What else can you tell us?"

"Nothing now."

"I need to call the station."

The nurse pointed. "There's a payphone down the hall."

Peters grunted his thanks and left us.

"Such a delightful man," said Mother. "One wonders where he developed his sparkling vocabulary."

"Stop it," I snapped. "He's worried too." I was standing up for Peters? What next? Pigs flying?

Mother nodded at the nurse. "Thank you for the update."

"My pleasure, Mrs. Walford. Someone will be out again soon."

When the nurse disappeared behind the swinging doors that

led to the operating rooms, Mother turned to me. "This is what you're signing up for—a lifetime of worry."

Really? "You want to discuss that now?"

"It's for your own good."

Mother's words were gasoline on the fire of my rage. Rather than whack her with my handbag (so tempting), I took a deep breath. "I need to draw."

She frowned. "What?"

"I. Need. To. Draw." That or I could scream. Loudly. Till my voice broke. I knew which she'd prefer.

"If sketching will help…"

"It will." I waved at Sandra, and she trotted over to us.

"More coffee?"

"No, thank you. May I please have a few pieces of paper and a pencil?"

She blinked. "I'll see what I can find."

Mother and I watched her cross the waiting room and rummage in a desk. She returned with ten sheets of copy paper and a number two pencil.

"Thank you." I grabbed a stack of magazines as a base and sketched a face.

Mother looked at the harsh lines. "Are you drawing Anarchy?"

"No." I slashed cheekbones, gouged at eyes, and nearly ripped the paper drawing a hard, unforgiving mouth.

"Who is that?"

"Someone I saw at Patriot."

Mother's eyes narrowed. "Is that who shot Anarchy?"

"Maybe."

"Give it to Detective Peters."

"I already did."

"Then why are you drawing such an unpleasant face?"

"Because I need to draw." I used art to process emotion, and I had a zillion emotions to process.

She clucked her disapproval. "You should try drawing something pleasant." She pointed at the innocuous painting. "Like a garden."

"I'm not in a garden mood."

"That face is disturbing."

"Fine." I folded the paper in half and stuffed it in my handbag.

"Draw Anarchy," she suggested.

Not the worst idea. I sketched his lean face, the twinkle in his eyes, the softness in his mouth when we were alone.

Peters returned, glanced at my drawing, and lowered himself into the chair next to mine. "I spoke with the captain. No stone unturned, Ellison. We'll catch this guy."

"Thank you." I couldn't say more.

Mother stood and paced.

Peters glanced at his watch. "Another fifteen minutes till they update us again."

"I should call home."

"Go," said Peters. "If the nurse comes early, I'll make sure she stays till you can talk to her."

A nice Peters, a kind Peters—I blinked away surprise. And fresh tears. I couldn't speak, so I nodded, hurried down the hall, inserted a dime into the payphone, and dialed.

"Russell residence."

"Aggie, it's me." My voice creaked and cracked and broke.

"What's wrong?"

I breathed through my mouth, ignored the sharp ache in my jaw and the sharper pain in my heart.

"You're scaring me," she said.

"Anarchy was shot. I'm at the hospital."

"How bad?"

"Bad." I could say no more.

"I'll bring Grace as soon as she gets home from school."

I pressed my hand against my lips. "Thank you."

I endured the next two hours by sketching my anger and fear. When Mother tsked her disapproval of the harsh lines on the paper, I pretended not to hear her.

When the nurse appeared with updates, I listened carefully, prayed silently, and thanked her profusely.

When Peters checked in with the station then returned to his seat, I let a question burn in my eyes. *Had they caught the shooter?*

Each time, he scowled and shook his head.

When my father arrived and pulled me into an encompassing hug, I nearly shattered. Instead, I gulped air into my lungs, wiped my eyes, and stayed strong.

When Grace raced into the waiting room and wrapped her arms around me, I swallowed my tears. "He has a good chance." Did my smile look as brittle as hers?

"He'll be fine. I know it."

How could I argue? "I'm sure you're right." The alternative was unthinkable.

"Has anyone called his family?" asked Mother.

"We're his family."

"His parents," she clarified.

"The captain called them," said Peters.

"And?" Mother lifted her left brow.

Peters grunted. "He called them."

"Are they coming?" she demanded. When he shrugged, she turned on me. "You should have called, Ellison."

She was right. I swallowed a sigh. Celeste was in California, and Anarchy would be out of surgery long before she could get here. If I'd remembered her, I'd have waited till we had actual news before I called.

Daddy patted her arm. "Let it go, Frannie."

Mother huffed. "I'm just—"

"Let it go."

Mother swallowed whatever scold she'd planned.

A doctor pushed through the swinging doors and

approached us. I searched his face and found only fatigue.

"Mrs. Russell?"

"That's me." I stuck my hand up like a child in grade school.

He nodded. "Detective Peters?"

Peters grunted.

"The two of you are listed as next of kin."

I gripped the chair's arms so hard my fingers hurt. "Is he…"

"He's stable and in recovery."

I eased my grip and reached for Peters' hand. "And? What's the prognosis?"

"He's not out of the woods. We'll keep him in intensive care and monitor his vitals."

"Will he recover fully?" asked Mother.

I knew what she was thinking—I shouldn't marry a man limited by injury. I scowled at her.

"There's no reason he shouldn't make a full recovery."

Ha! Take that, Mother. Floating in a sea of grief and worry, I latched onto that—a full recovery—like a life ring. I missed whatever he said next, but the people around me nodded.

"When can I see him?" I blurted.

"Now. Then I'm sending you home."

Home? No. I had to stay with him. "But—"

"Take it or leave it."

"I'll take it." I followed the doctor into the recovery room where nurses flitted around Anarchy's bed.

"Give Mrs. Russell a moment, please."

The nurses scattered, and I took Anarchy's hand.

"Don't you dare leave me," I whispered. "We have a whole lifetime in front of us." I smoothed a lock of damp hair from his forehead and willed him to open his eyes or smile or squeeze my hand.

He did none of those things.

I sat beside him—held his hand—till the nurses made me leave.

CHAPTER SEVENTEEN

"That's Stan Klemp." Mel Langford sat next to me on her living room couch. She wore a Lilly kaftan (chartreuse with Kelly green and hot pink butterflies) that clashed with the harvest gold velvet of her couch.

I wore a pair of jeans, worn penny loafers, and a twin set. I was presentable (not even Mother would complain) on the outside. Inside? I struggled to maintain my composure. My gaze caught on the spot where Mel's finger touched the drawing. "Who?"

"Stan Klemp. I recognize him from the company Christmas party. Hubb." Mel beckoned to her husband. "Come look."

Using the arms of a flame-stitch wingback chair, Hubb (who'd dressed for bed in a seersucker robe over plaid pajamas with leather slippers) pushed himself to standing and shuffled over to the couch where we sat.

He stared at my drawing and his eyes narrowed to slits. "I don't think so."

"It is," Mel insisted. "I recognize him."

Hubb rubbed his chin. "I don't see a resemblance."

"I know your employees better than you do." Mel's voice was light, but I heard censure.

Hubb heard it too. He scowled.

"I attend the company picnic in June and the Christmas party each December," she told me. "My dad treated his employees like family." It was there again—thinly veiled criticism.

Hubb's scowl deepened.

They could work on their issues later. For now, I wanted a name. "Stan Klemp?"

Mel tapped the drawing with the tip of her frosted fingernail. "I'm positive that's him."

"If you say so." Hubb's doubt was obvious.

"Do you have an address for him?"

Mel frowned. "Not here, but I'm sure there's one on file at the office. Why are you interested in Stan?"

"He may be behind the attempt on Hubb's life." He might be the man who shot Anarchy.

"Good gracious." Mel sat back on the couch and clasped her hands. "Why would Stan do such a thing?" Her eyes sought her husband.

Hubb held out his hand. "May I please see the sketch?"

I picked up the drawing from the coffee table and gave it to him.

He took his time studying the face. "If it is Stan, and I'm not sure it is, we let him go in January."

"You fired him?" Mel sounded surprised.

Hubb nodded.

"You never said." She clasped her hands in her lap. "Why?"

"We caught him stealing."

"Darling, the man is obviously holding a grudge. We need to share everything with the police. He's murdered two people. Nearly killed you."

Hubb retreated to his chair. "Ellison, where did you come by that picture?"

"I drew it."

"You?"

"I saw this man driving a forklift at Patriot the day I found you."

Hubb paled.

Mel gasped. "I told you, Hubb. I told you a company-wide lunch hour was a bad idea. The warehouse stood empty, and Stan helped himself to whatever he wanted. He poisoned something. Clayton ate or drank it. So did Denise. So did you. We need that address immediately."

"The police can stop by in the morning," I said.

Mel shook her head. "No. I won't feel safe till Stan is caught. I'll go now."

"Now?" Hubb frowned. "It will be dark soon, and I don't want you in that neighborhood alone at night."

Mel waved aside his concerns. "I'll be fine. Besides—" her gaze shifted my way "—Ellison will go with me."

If it meant catching Stan a second faster, I'd go in a heartbeat. "Of course."

Mel stood.

"This is a bad idea," said Hubb.

"I can't spend another night staring at the ceiling, fretting over who wants you dead."

Hubb scowled at his wife.

I didn't have the energy for their marital spat. "Mel, may I please use your phone?"

"Of course." She smoothed her skirt. "There's one in the family room."

I left her with her how dare you tell me what I can and can't do attitude,, Hubb with his I'm your husband attitude, and their ire in the living room, and found a more casual room where a burnt sienna couch faced off with two avocado green chairs. A green rotary dial phone squatted on the table next to the sofa.

I sat, lifted the receiver, and dialed home.

Aggie answered. "Russell residence."

"Aggie, it's me. Any word from the hospital?"

"No."

No news was good news. "Maybe I should call them."

"How long since you last checked in?"

I glanced at my watch. "Thirty minutes." Thirty infinite minutes.

"I'd give it another hour before you call again."

"You're right." I shouldn't pester the hospital. Should. Not. Not even when my heart demanded I park myself outside Anarchy's room. "Mel Langford and I are headed to Patriot Produce."

"Tonight?"

"Mel recognized the man in my drawing. We'll pick up his address and phone number, then I'll come home." I'd stop by the hospital on my way.

"It can't wait till morning?"

I pictured Anarchy in a hospital bed. Pale. Not yet out of danger. "It cannot."

She sighed. "What should I tell Grace? She's worried about you."

"Tell her I'll be home within the hour." We hung up, and I found Mel just outside the family room door. "I'm ready."

"You told your housekeeper where you're going."

She'd eavesdropped?

"I did."

She frowned. "Why?"

"In case I don't come back."

She rolled her eyes. "The neighborhood's not that dangerous."

"There's a killer loose." And trouble made a habit of finding me.

"Fair point." She scooped a handbag off the back of a chair. "Shall we?"

I found my car keys in my purse. "I'll follow you."

"You don't want to drive together?"

"I'm going to the hospital when we're done."

"Fine."

Mel drove a blue Mercedes sedan. She observed the speed limit, and I followed her down the trafficway, onto the boulevard, and into Patriot's parking lot.

The warehouse loomed above us. Its eastern windows absorbed the coming night. Black holes that warned me away. I got out of my car and shivered in the warm breeze.

"This won't take but a minute," Mel promised. "I know exactly where to find the personnel files."

I nodded, and we entered the dark building.

She stopped just inside the door to the warehouse floor and flipped a switch. Light chased away the gloom. Mel surveyed the warehouse floor and sighed.

"Everything okay?"

"I shouldn't complain, but..." She rubbed her hand over her eyes.

"But?"

"I feel disloyal saying this, but my father would spin in his grave if he knew Patriot looked like this."

I gave a sympathetic cluck.

"Dad took such pride in this place." She frowned. "Patriot has never held Hubb's heart. He hasn't managed the company well." She glanced at the floor that needed a broom, a mop, and a liberal application of Clorox bleach. "Employees stealing? Then sneaking in during the lunch hour? That never happened when my dad was alive." Mel pursed her lips. "I should spend more time here. This is my father's legacy."

It was too bad Martin didn't give Mel the reins. She cared about the business, and under her leadership the warehouse would be spotless. As it was—I shuddered to think I'd eaten fruit or vegetables that came from this building.

"My housekeeper's friend was a longtime customer."

"Was?"

"Problems with his orders, problems with billing, problems with customer service."

"I hate hearing that."

"I'm sorry. I thought you'd want to know."

"Oh, I do. I just wish things were different."

"You'd run Patriot?"

"In a New York minute." Her face fell. "But if I took over, what would Hubb do? Men take so much of their identities from their work. I couldn't be the wife who reclaimed her family's company because her husband failed."

I glanced around the cavernous warehouse with its dim lights and faint smell of rot. "You care about this place."

"I do."

"You may need to step in."

"I know." Her glum expression was at odds with her bright kaftan. She straightened her shoulders. "That's tomorrow's problem. Tonight, we need an address. This way." She lifted her hem, climbed the stairs, and led me to an office.

Inside, filing cabinets lined the walls—open filing cabinets. The light from the warehouse revealed their contents, spilled onto the floor in after-a-tornado chaos.

Mel gasped. "What happened?"

"I think we should go." A creepy-crawly sensation trickled the length of my spine, and I shivered.

"Go? No. We need to call the police." She crossed the room, located the phone in the mess on the floor, dropped the receiver into the cradle, waited a few seconds, then picked it up.

A shadow crossed her face. "The line is dead."

"We should leave. Now." The creepy-crawly sensation had me grasping my keys and looking over my shoulder.

"Maybe you're right," she allowed.

The warehouse lights went out.

I stood frozen and blind for long seconds, then Mel screamed.

My heart tried to escape my chest. Finding no exit, it raced a million miles an hour. "What happened? Are you hurt?"

"I thought I felt something."

"Felt something?" Dread tickled my spine.

"On my foot," Mel explained.

"Like what?"

"Like a rat."

"A rat?" I squeaked.

"There are traps throughout the warehouse, but it's impossible to keep them out. And once they get it in, they multiply."

"A rat?" My voice approached a pitch best heard by dogs.

"I'm sorry if I startled you." She sounded blasé.

How could she sound blasé about rats? They were vermin with terrifying teeth and tails like naked snakes. I forced air into my lungs. "What about the lights?"

"What about them?"

"They went out."

"That happens."

"The lights go out by themselves?"

"Old wiring. Dad joked the warehouse was haunted."

Great. Just great. A dark, rat-infested, ghost-infested warehouse with faulty wiring. I searched for the light switch on the wall, found it, and flipped it. Nothing happened. "Can we go? Please?"

"Hold on."

The sound of a drawer opening reached me.

"What are you doing?" I asked.

"Looking for a flashlight."

"Good idea. Did you find one?"

"No."

I swallowed a not-helpful sarcastic retort.

"We'll be fine," said Mel. "Just go slow when you descend the stairs."

Go slow? I'd inch down those stairs. "Fine."

"Where are you?" she asked.

"By the door."

"Keep talking. I'll find you."

Talking? About what? My fiancé who still hadn't opened his eyes? Her husband who nearly died? "I really hate rats. Did you know their teeth never stop growing? Also, they have collapsible skeletons."

"What does that mean?"

"They can squeeze through a hole the size of a quarter."

"Really?"

I shuddered. "I wouldn't lie about rats. They can jump three feet in the air."

"How do you know this stuff?"

"Henry insisted I face my fears."

"Did it work?"

"I haven't fainted. Yet."

A hand circled my wrist, and I jumped.

"Looks like you have three-foot vertical leap too."

"Rats, Mel. I'm fixated on the rats."

"Forget the rats, Ellison. We go down the stairs, out the door, and you can go to the hospital."

"What about you?"

"I'm calling the police."

Much as I wanted to, I couldn't leave her. "The phone is dead."

"I'll drive to the liquor store down the street. They have a payphone. Come on." She tugged on my wrist "Let's go."

We stopped at the top of the stairs, and my free hand groped for the rail.

"You go first," she said.

"Me?" I had a vision of a hand planted between my shoulder blades and a strong shove. "I think you should lead the way."

"Fine."

Molasses in January moved faster than I did, but I reached the bottom. "Mel?"

She didn't answer.

"Mel?" I squeaked. "Where are you?"

Silence was the only response. Silence and the scurry of little feet.

"Mel!" Which way to the exit? Holding my hands in front of me, I walked—tiptoed—in the direction I hoped to find the door. How could a building be so dark? The hands in front of my face were invisible in the gloom. "Mel?"

No one answered. On the upside, no feet scurried.

I hobbled forward and bumped into a stack of crates. Crates that shouldn't be in front of me. Great. I was turned around, lost in the dark, and there were rats. Just the thought of one of those creatures jumping at me froze my feet to the floor.

I took a moment—took a deep breath—and straightened my shoulders. I'd come here for an address, to help catch the man who'd shot Anarchy. I was brave.

Or not. I swallowed a whimper.

"Ellison?" Mel hadn't fallen and broken her neck. Stan Klemp hadn't abducted her. She hadn't left me.

Gratitude expanded my chest. "I'm here."

"Be careful not to trip in the dark. It's pitch black in here. I tried the mechanical room. The lights won't come on, but I found a flashlight."

I spotted a gleam in the darkness. "If you stay still, I can follow the beam."

"Fine."

I put rats out of my mind. At least, I tried. I also swore never to darken Patriot's door again. I hurried toward the light.

"This was a wasted trip." Mel's voice bounced around the warehouse. If not for the flashlight's beam, I'd never find her.

I didn't answer—not right away. My focus remained on rats. What if I stepped on a rat? What if one leapt on me from atop a crate? I'd never recover. "Do you think Stan Klemp tossed that office?"

"Who else?"

Thinking about Stan was one hundred percent better than thinking about rats. "Why destroy the whole office?"

"He didn't know we'd identified him. Maybe he made that mess to hide the theft of his personnel file." Mel made a good point, and she stood only twenty feet away—even if the acoustics in the warehouse made her sound as if she waited on the other side. "It's so heartbreaking. For Clayton and his family. For Denise and hers."

I stubbed my toe on a crate and swallowed a curse.

"What's taking you so long?"

The beam shifted so its light illuminated the floor.

"Keep the flashlight steady."

"I am."

"Can you lift the beam?"

The light lifted from a pool on the floor, and a shaft cut through the darkness. I blinked when a second beam blinded me.

A second beam?

Oh. Dear. Lord.

Stan was here. In the warehouse. With us.

I ducked behind the nearest crate.

"Mel?" I scrambled away from the light.

"Where are you? What are you doing?"

The other beam had to be Stan's. Who else would lurk in the dark? "We're not alone."

Mel fell silent.

I crouched behind a crate and slapped my hands over my mouth when an animal scurried over my foot.

A rat.

A rat!

Screaming wouldn't help, and it would give away my hiding spot. I swallowed the cry.

Mel had said something about traps. They needed more. Or poison.

The thought stopped me. What about poison? How simple would it be to slip rat poison into someone's coffee? If we made it out of the warehouse, I'd ask Mel if they used poison for rodent control.

For now, I listened.

Someone approached. The tread was too heavy for the sandals Mel wore beneath her kaftan.

I stood and braced my hands on crates that smelled like dirt. Potatoes?

The steps drew closer, and I pushed hard.

Two crates fell, and I ran. "Run, Mel!"

Hopefully we found the exit before the swearing man dug free from the mountain of potatoes.

I ran, too scared of the man behind me to worry about rats.

For the moment.

If I got out of this warehouse, I'd rethink my stance on cats.

"Ellison, where are you?"

No idea. The stacked crates and the darkness made sight or determining my location impossible. I breathed deep. "I smell strawberries."

"Keep going."

I ventured five steps. "Oranges."

"Perfect. Keep walking. Straight."

I did as Mel instructed.

"What do you smell now?"

"Apples."

"Turn left."

I turned.

"Do you see the exit sign?"

"I do." Those four letters lit in a dull red were lovelier than springtime. I ran toward them. When I reached the door, Mel grabbed my arm.

I jumped.

"There's that three-foot leap again."

"You startled me."

"I'm sorry. Let's get out of here." We escaped Patriot's darkness and hurried to the parking lot.

I unlocked my car door. "You're not staying?" Waiting here for the police was dangerous. "I saw a second flashlight in the warehouse."

"No, I'm not staying. I'll go to Ponak's or the liquor store and use their phone to call the police. When I see the squad cars, I'll come back."

A good plan. "I can stay with you."

"It's sweet of you to offer but I'm fine. And I'll be around other people till the police arrive."

"You're sure?" It felt wrong to leave her.

"Positive. Go."

"Be careful." I slid behind the wheel, inserted the key in the ignition, and started the car. As I pulled out of the lot, I saw Mel's headlights illuminate the warehouse's brick walls. Only then did I remember my question. I should have asked her about rat poison.

My hands gripped the wheel, and the adrenaline powering my escape drained away. My throat was dry, and when I relaxed my fingers, they shook like aspen leaves.

Stan Klemp was the killer.

He poisoned Clayton, Denise, and Hubb. He shot Anarchy. It made sense. Hubb fired him, and an angry Stan snuck into Patriot when no one was there and stole produce. Had Clayton caught him in the act? No. If Clayton discovered Stan stealing, Stan wouldn't wait for poison. He'd shoot. Stan poisoned the executives because he lost his job? That made more sense. What about Denise? Had her death been an accident? What about me? I'd seen him. I could identify him. That's why he shot at me in the park, why he stalked me at Clayton's funeral.

I drove to the hospital. I needed to share my theory with Anarchy. He might not hear me, wouldn't respond, but I'd feel better if I told him (saw him), and maybe I'd spot the flaw in my reasoning.

Because, despite the sense my theory made, there was a hole in my logic. I knew it, but I couldn't see it. And the last thing I wanted was to offer Peters a flawed theory.

CHAPTER EIGHTEEN

Beeps and monitors and tubes reminded me of the horrifying extent of Anarchy's injuries. For one selfish instant, I closed my eyes and pretended this awful day hadn't happened—that Anarchy and I were at home, curled up on the couch with drinks in our hands and the TV tuned to a cop show where bullets always missed the hero.

I opened my eyes to a raw-oatmeal-colored treatment room and the man I loved in a hospital bed. I dragged the chair so close to his bed that the metal frame dug into my knee. I welcomed the physical pain and claimed his hand. "Is this how you feel when I end up in the hospital? If so, I'm sorry." Grief and terror and anger made for a potent emotional cocktail. "You look better," I told him. Was his color better? "Not so pale."

I squeezed his fingers gently. "I wish you'd wake up. There's so much I need to tell you."

I gave him a few seconds to open his eyes, then swallowed my disappointment. "That's okay. Concentrate on healing. I went to Patriot with Mel. Stan Klemp was there. At least I think it was him. I pushed a stack of crates onto a man. Before I could get a look at his face, Mel and I ran."

Anarchy didn't respond, and I rested my head against our clasped hands.

"They have rats at Patriot." An unexpected shudder shook me. "Nasty creatures. Those tails. Those eyes." I pushed down a wave of revulsion. "I bet they have rat poison. Stan could have poisoned Clayton, Hubb, and Denise. He stole from Patriot, and Hubb fired him, back in January." Tears wet our hands. "Are you sure you won't wake up?"

Anarchy didn't move.

I lifted my head and stared at the tubes leading to his other arm. "Stan as the killer makes sense, but..." I exhaled. "But I'm not convinced. You have gut feelings. Now I do too."

I squeezed his hand and felt a small answering pressure. "Anarchy?" Hope made me squeak. "Can you hear me? Can you open your eyes?"

Had I imagined that pressure? I wanted so badly for him to open his eyes, to smile, to stay with me. Forever. "Anarchy?" I squeezed tighter.

His fingers didn't respond. His eyes didn't open. His lips didn't curve into a smile. The bright hope that spread its petals within my heart shrank to a tight bud.

This was the worry Mother warned against. This was more than worry. This was a tearing pain that shredded my heart, tightened my stomach, and swelled my jaw with an unending ache.

"Did you squeeze my hand?" I whispered. "Can you do it again? Please?"

Nothing.

"Please wake up. I can't imagine life without you. I was alone for so long—I was married, but I was alone." Tears pricked my eyes. "Then you came along."

"You can't go in there." An outraged voice carried from the hall.

Two seconds later, Celeste burst into Anarchy's room.

She looked first at her son. Then she shifted her gaze to me and curled her upper lip.

I stood. "Good evening, Celeste."

"How is he?" Worry lined her face.

"Stable."

"I got here as soon as I could." She clutched a light blue Samsonite suitcase with one hand and smoothed a peasant tunic over a pair of baggy linen pants with the other.

"I'm glad you're here."

Her eyes narrowed. "Are you?"

"I am." I was. Sort of. "Is Professor Jones with you?" I'd not yet met Anarchy's father.

Her face shuttered. "It's the end of the semester. He's very busy."

If Grace were in the hospital, nothing on earth—not distance, not final exams, not natural disasters—would keep me from her. I'd never liked Anarchy's description of his father. Now I seethed. "I see."

Celeste's lips thinned, and the lines in her face deepened. "What do the doctors say?"

The nurse who'd followed Celeste into Anarchy's room wore a no-nonsense frown. "That he shouldn't be disturbed. The patient needs his rest. You should go."

"I just got here," Celeste objected.

"Please," I said. "Can you give Mrs. Jones a moment with her son?"

The nurse sniffed. "One minute. That's all. And you—" she pointed at me "—have to leave."

I leaned over and brushed a kiss across Anarchy's forehead. "I'll be back." Reluctantly I let go of his hand and walked toward the door.

"Ellison." Anarchy's hoarse voice was the sweetest sound I'd ever heard. I spun to face him.

He stared at me with coffee-brown eyes, and the tightness

banding my chest eased. We had a future. Tears welled in my eyes.

"I'll get the doctor." The nurse disappeared into the corridor.

I raced to Anarchy's bedside and reclaimed his hand. "You're awake."

"I came all this way because your captain—" Celeste cut her eyes at me as if I were responsible for feeding her lies "—said your condition was critical."

"Someone shot him in the chest," I replied. It didn't get more critical than that.

Celeste sniffed.

"Water," Anarchy croaked.

I glanced around the room but found no ugly plastic water pitcher. Also, on consideration, I wasn't giving him a drop till the doctor saw him.

"There's a glass in the bathroom. I'll fill it for you, dear." Celeste dropped her suitcase.

"Celeste."

She paused in the doorway to the lavatory. "What?"

"The doctor should see him first."

"Don't be ridiculous. My son is thirsty."

"I really think—"

"When I want your opinion, I'll ask for it."

Celeste was tired and worried—at least that's what I told myself as I swallowed a biting reply.

"Ellison is right," Anarchy croaked. "I'll wait."

Celeste ignored us both, stepped into the bathroom, and turned on the tap.

As she filled the glass, I kissed Anarchy's cheek. "I was so worried."

His face was still too pale, and his eyes lacked their usual sparkle, but he smiled. "You're not getting rid of me that easily."

A second kiss. "Glad to hear it."

Celeste appeared with the water glass. She held it out as if she expected him to take it.

"When did you get here?" Anarchy asked.

"I just arrived." She held the glass closer, and Anarchy shook his head slowly from side to side.

She frowned and gave a put-upon sigh. "Do you still have that cat?"

"I do."

"Then I can't stay at your apartment." She spared me a quick slit-eyed glance. "I'm allergic."

She'd soon be family. I had to make the offer but prayed she'd opt for a hotel. "You can stay with me, Celeste."

"With you?" Her gaze dropped to the ring on my left hand as she considered. "If it's no trouble…"

It was endless trouble. "No trouble at all."

A man with a stethoscope draped around his neck entered the room. He spotted the glass Celeste still held out to Anarchy. "Let's wait on that, shall we?" His gaze shifted to me. "If you'd excuse us?"

"Of course," I replied. "Celeste?"

She didn't budge.

I gave Anarchy another kiss, picked up her suitcase, and stepped out of the room.

Celeste followed a moment later. "I didn't have the chance to talk to my son."

"When the doctor is done—"

"What happened?"

"To Anarchy? He was shot."

"I know that," she snapped. "What were the circumstances?"

I rested against the wall and tilted my head toward the ceiling. "I'll let Anarchy tell you."

She huffed. "What are you doing?"

"Waiting."

"For what?"

"To speak to the doctor."

"Why would he tell you anything?"

I kept my voice mild. "I'm Anarchy's fiancée."

"I'm his mother."

There was no arguing her point. I offered a tight smile in reply. Explaining Mother's role at the hospital would earn me nothing but a diatribe about special treatment.

Five endless minutes later, the doctor emerged. His gaze shifted between me and Celeste, and he made his choice. "A word, Mrs. Russell?"

"Of course." I followed him toward the nurses' station and ignored the heat of Celeste's glare between my shoulder blades.

I held tight to the counter's edge. The fear and anger that sustained me had drained and my knees wobbled.

"Are you all right?" The doctor's voice was kind.

I eyed his badge—Dr. Porter. "I'll be okay. Just tired and a bit overwhelmed."

He searched my face and gave a quick jerk of his chin. "Your fiancé is lucky to be alive. We'll keep him a few days, but when we release him, he'll still need bed rest."

"Not a problem."

"He should take things slow."

I nodded.

"I say this because he strikes me as the kind of man who'd get up from his hospital bed and return to work."

Anarchy was exactly that kind of man. "I'll make sure he follows your orders." I could be as implacable as Mother when the occasion called for it.

We glanced toward Anarchy's room.

Celeste had disappeared. Presumably, she'd returned to her son's bedside.

"How long will he be on bed rest?"

Dr. Porter rubbed his chin. "I'd like a week, but I suspect we'll be lucky to get four days."

"Thank you for all you've done."

"He's a strong man with a lot to live for. He told me you're marrying in two weeks."

"We can do that?"

He smiled his approval, and I almost hugged him.

The drive home with Celeste in the passenger seat and her suitcase jammed into the trunk was all I expected and more.

"You should postpone the wedding," she said. "There's no hurry."

I tightened my grip on the steering wheel.

"It's not as if you're pregnant. You're not pregnant, are you?"

"No."

"You're not getting any younger."

Oh, dear Lord.

"Anarchy and I have decided not to have children."

"No grandchildren?"

Not from my womb.

She pursed her lips. "Anarchy agreed to that?"

"He did."

"He's giving up a lot to marry you."

"His choice." Not hers. Thank heavens.

"What about me? What if I want grandchildren?"

My grip tightened till my knuckles cracked. "You have other children. Talk to them."

"You're wrong for him."

I pulled into the drive and put the car in park. "Take that up with Anarchy."

"I will."

I opened the car door and forced a smile. "Shall we?"

Celeste stared at me. "If you'll let me use your phone, I'll call a taxi."

"You're not staying?"

"I just told you my opinions about you and my son."

"You did," I agreed. I amped up the sweetness in my smile. "I love Anarchy, and Anarchy loves you. You're welcome in my—our—home."

Her mouth opened, but no words came out.

"Celeste, it's late. Come in, have a bite to eat, rest. If you want to move to a hotel tomorrow, I'll drive you myself."

She stared at me as if I'd sprouted horns.

I levered myself out of the car. "I'll get your suitcase."

The front door opened, and Grace ran down the stairs. "You're late. I worried."

I hugged her. "I'm sorry. I stopped by the hospital. Anarchy woke up. He'll recover."

Grace's smile reached her ears.

"Anarchy's mother is in the car," I whispered.

She stiffened. "Why?"

"She's staying with us."

"Seriously?"

"Shh. We're taking the high road."

"If you say so."

We led Celeste inside where Max greeted her with a nose to her crotch.

I didn't scold him (maybe I'd taken the low road after all). "Is Aggie here?"

"She and Mac had theater tickets."

"Dinner?"

"She left a salad in the fridge."

"Is salad okay, Celeste?"

Celeste, who was engaged trying to remove Max from her nether regions, didn't reply.

"Max." I kept my voice mild. "No."

He ignored me, and I hid a smile behind my hand.

Grace's brows lifted—usually I scolded Max for accosting guests. "Are you hungry? I'm starved."

Moments later we gathered around the breakfast room

table. A bowl of tossed salad topped with grilled chicken sat in the center.

Without asking if she'd prefer iced tea or something stronger, I poured chilled water into Celeste's glass. “Grace took your suitcase upstairs to the blue room.”

“Thank you.” She sipped her water. "It’s kind of you to let me stay.”

“You’re Anarchy’s mother.”

We ate Aggie's salad and made stilted conversation. When dinner (finally) ended, I sent Celeste to the family room. While she watched television, I loaded the dishwasher. Grace claimed homework and escaped to her room. I was only a little jealous.

The counters gleamed. The floor was spotless. I’d even wiped down the front of the refrigerator and the unused oven. I gave Mr. Coffee a fond pat.

She’s a handful.

And then some. “I’m taking the high road,” I whispered.

Good for you.

“The high road sucks.”

He chuckled, and I folded the tea towel and dragged myself to the den, where Celeste watched a program on PBS and held an open book on her lap.

“May I get you anything? Coffee?”

“No, thank you.”

I edged toward the door. “Well then, I’m headed to bed.”

Celeste glanced at her watch. and I remembered she was on West Coast time. It might be half past eight here (it felt like two in the morning), but for her it was barely dinner time.

“I’m exhausted. I'll see you in the morning.”

Max and I retreated to my bedroom, and I called the hospital.

The operator refused to connect me to Anarchy's room, so I settled for the nurses' station. "This is Ellison Russell. I’m calling to check on my fiancé, Detective Jones.”

"He continues to improve."

Wonderful news. "May I please speak with him?"

"He's resting, Mrs. Russell. We can't disturb him."

"Of course. I understand."

"He'll move to a general ward in the morning."

"Thank you." I'd feel more grateful if she'd let me speak with him. I hung up the receiver and got ready for bed. Sleep came easy.

Grrr.

I opened my left eye and found the clock face in the dark. Five minutes past midnight. I closed my eye.

Grrr.

"What, Max?" It had been a stressful day. I needed to sleep, not doggie stress in the middle of the night.

Grrr. Max paced in front of the closed door to the hallway.

I sighed, swung my feet to the floor, pulled on a robe, and after a few seconds' consideration, fetched the gun I kept in the nightstand.

"If you're growling at Celeste, and I point a gun at her, I'll never hear the end of it."

It was too dark to see clearly, but I was fairly certain Max rolled his eyes.

We stepped into the hallway and I peeked into Grace's room. She slept, and I didn't disturb her. Instead, I eased her door closed and whispered to Max, "Lead the way."

We descended the front stairs, and in the porch light filtering through the windows, I noticed a ridge of hair standing straight on Max's back. Maybe there really was something amiss.

That or Celeste was watching the late show.

We tiptoed through the dark house.

"Celeste?" I whispered.

No answer.

I should have checked her bedroom before I came downstairs.

Grrr.

Max's growl raised the hair on my neck.

I followed him to the family room where blue static played on the television. Its light revealed a body on the floor.

My heart stopped. In. Its. Tracks. How would I explain this to Anarchy?

I stumbled forward, tripped over my feet, and knelt next to her. "Celeste!"

Grrr.

Max's growl told me Celeste hadn't tripped on the coffee table. I gripped the gun hidden in the folds of my robe.

"Stand up. Slow." A man—Stan—stepped out of the darkness gathered in the corner.

So I could give him an easier target? Not likely.

I didn't move. "You shot Anarchy."

"The guy at the church? He saw my face."

I'd seen his face.

"Stand up."

"What did you do to her?" My free hand hovered above Celeste's unmoving shoulder.

"I came up behind her and hit her on the head." He thrust his gun at me. "Get up."

I shifted and aimed the gun still hidden in my robe. "How did you get in here?"

"I'm good with locks."

That was it. I'd resisted installing an alarm, but I was tired of bad guys wandering into my house. I'd call in the morning. "You should put down your gun."

His answering laugh carried a sneer. "Yeah?"

"You're not a good shot. You missed me at the park. The man you shot—Anarchy—will live."

He took a step closer to me and the sneer settled on his features. "This close, I won't miss."

"You really should go."

He lifted his gun, and I shot him.

His face registered surprise, and he fell backward.

I struggled to my feet and kicked the gun he'd dropped far from his outstretched hand. I didn't think he'd be moving again soon, but leaving a gun a few inches from a killer's hand was plain stupid. Then I picked up the phone and called the operator. "I shot an intruder in my house. Please send the police and an ambulance."

"Mom!" A pale-faced Grace stared at me from the room's entrance.

"I'm okay, Grace." She flipped on the lights, and I blinked in the sudden brightness.

"Who is that?" She pointed at Stan.

With the receiver still clutched in my hand, I replied, "He broke in."

"Is Celeste okay?"

"He said he hit her on the head. Are you sending an ambulance?" I spoke into the phone.

"Your address?"

I gave it to her.

"Help is on the way."

"Thank you." I hung up.

"Who is he?" Grace demanded.

"He shot Anarchy."

"You shot him."

"I did."

"Is he dead?"

"I don't think so."

"Then shoot him again." Celeste's voice was weak but vehement. She pushed herself to her knees and scowled at Stan.

"I can't."

"Sure you can. Pull the trigger."

I'd shot a man with a gun pointed at me. Self-defense. To shoot an unconscious intruder was murder. "No."

"He shot my son."

"And he'll go to jail for it. I won't shoot him again." But I wouldn't mind kicking him a time or two.

I heard sirens in the distance. "Grace?"

She tore her gaze from the blood pooling beneath Stan. "What?"

"Would you please call your grandparents?" Better they hear of this from Grace than the neighbors. "Tell them not to come."

There'd been plenty of shootings at my house. Mother's presence seldom enhanced the experience.

"On it."

"Celeste, how badly are you hurt?" Her color was poor; a trickle of blood stained her hairline.

She pushed herself to sitting, leaned against the couch, and sighed. "I'll live."

Not what I asked, but I wasn't about to split hairs.

Ding, dong.

"If you're all right, I'll let the police in."

She stared at me. "You're very calm."

"This isn't my first rodeo."

She lifted her brows. "One thing's for certain."

"Oh?"

"My son will never be bored."

CHAPTER NINETEEN

The neighbors gathered at the bottom of the driveway. Seersucker robes for the men, floral house dresses pulled over nightgowns for the women. They all wore matching here-we-go-again expressions.

I waved.

"There's an intruder, ma'am?" The uniformed police officer on my stoop couldn't be more than five or six years older than Grace, and he seemed overwhelmed.

I offered him an encouraging smile. "I shot him."

He blinked.

Maybe smiling when I told the police I'd shot a man wasn't the best idea. "He pointed a gun at me."

"Where did you get a gun?" The police officer stepped into the foyer.

"My nightstand." I closed the door behind him.

He rubbed a hand across his eyes. "How did you know an intruder was in the house?"

"Max told me."

"Max?"

Max stared at the young police officer with a vaguely

concerned expression on his long face.

"My dog," I explained.

"Your dog told you there was an intruder?"

"Exactly."

The officer fingered his gun.

"He didn't say, *Ellison, there's a killer in the family room*. He growled."

Now the officer frowned. "A killer?"

"Stan Klemp. He shot Detective Jones."

Ding, dong.

"May I?" I asked.

The officer nodded, and I opened the door to Peters. "Oh good, you're here."

Peters scowled. "What happened?"

"Mrs. Russell says her dog told her there was a killer in the house and she shot him. The intruder, not the dog."

"I'd never shoot Max."

Peters looked as if he'd like to shoot us both.

"I shot Stan Klemp."

Peters' brows lifted and his mustache twitched.

"He broke in and assaulted Anarchy's mother."

"She's here? Now?"

I nodded. "You've met her?

"Once." Peters' expression said he'd never speak ill of his partner's mother, but he was sorely tempted.

I understood completely.

"Where is she?"

"The family room," I replied.

"Would you please make coffee?" Did Peters want coffee, or did he want me out of the way? Did it matter?

"Of course."

I went to the kitchen, punched Mr. Coffee's buttons, then returned to the front door and let in more police officers and a pair of EMTs pushing gurneys.

I led them to the family room where Celeste rested on the sofa and Stan sprawled on the floor. I needed new carpet—I made a note to call in the morning. Or, given the frequent bloodshed in my family room, maybe I should have the hardwoods refinished and buy area rugs. A nice Ushak—

"Ellison?"

I shifted my gaze from the ruined carpet to Peters. "Yes?"

He frowned. "You okay?"

"Fine."

He grunted and stood. "Klemp's dead."

"Dead?" I grabbed the door frame. "How is that possible?"

"You shot him," said Celeste. Not helpful.

"Come on." Peters took my arm. "Let's get you some coffee."

I nodded but didn't release the frame. It was the only thing holding me upright. "I didn't mean to kill him."

"Good riddance," said Celeste.

Peters tightened his grip on my elbow, led me to the kitchen, and installed me on a stool. "Do you take cream?"

"Yes." My voice was faint.

He poured me a cup, added cream, and waited while I took a restorative sip. "What happened?"

"Max woke me. I came downstairs and found Celeste on the floor. Klemp stepped out of the shadows, admitted he shot Anarchy, and aimed his gun at me."

"You brought your gun downstairs with you?"

Given the frequency Max's growls meant intruders, I'd be a fool not to. "Of course."

He grunted.

The coffee worked its magic, and I glanced around the kitchen. "Where's Grace?"

"I'm here, Mom." She'd taken a few minutes to dress.

Tap, tap.

We shifted our gazes to the back door.

"Stay put." Peters' hand hovered near his holster. "I'll get it."

He yanked open the door.

"Ellison?" Charlie stood on the other side. "Are you okay?"

"Fine. Sorry for the hullabaloo."

He waved away my apology. "The Realtor warned me."

"She did?"

Charlie rubbed the back of his hand across his chin and ignored my question. "What happened?"

"Police investigation." Peters closed the door, but Charlie wedged his foot in.

"What happened?" he insisted.

"The man who shot at me in the park broke in."

"Dear God. Are you hurt?"

"She shot him." Was that pride in Peters' voice? "He's dead. You need to leave."

"But—"

"I'm fine, Charlie."

"You heard the lady." Peters succeeded in closing the door.

Tap, tap.

"She'll call you later," Peters shouted. He was not a subtle man. "Ellison, drink more coffee. You look pale."

I stared into my cup as doubts assailed me.

"Don't you feel guilty about shooting Klemp. He killed two people. Almost killed Hubb Langford." Peters rubbed his chest. "Almost killed Jones."

"I—"

Grace draped an arm around my shoulders. "Detective Peters is right. He was a horrible man, and he might have killed you."

"I know, honey." So much death over stolen strawberries.

"I don't want to go to the hospital." Celeste's voice carried.

I glanced over my shoulder. "I should probably—"

"You sit," said Peters. "I'll handle it." He disappeared into the family room.

"Is it me, or is he behaving differently?" asked Grace.

"It's not you." Peters had seemed almost human lately.

"It's almost as if he likes us."

"That's crazy talk," I argued. But Grace made an excellent point. Peters was still his rumpled cigar-smoking sneering self, but his attitude toward us had changed.

He re-entered the kitchen with Celeste on his arm and a familiar scowl on his face.

"I don't need to go to the hospital," Celeste insisted.

"You had a head injury that knocked you unconscious. A doctor should check you out." First Peters was kind, now he was reasonable.

She pursed her lips and glared at us.

"Anarchy wouldn't forgive us if anything happened to you while he's hospitalized. I'll follow you," I offered. "When they're done shining lights in your eyes, I'll bring you home."

"Fine." Celeste made it sound as if she'd granted us an enormous favor.

A cowed EMT led her toward the front door, and Celeste looked over her shoulder. "You'll follow?"

"I'll change clothes and be right behind you."

Celeste allowed the EMT to lead her away, and I turned to Peters. "How long will you be here?"

He rubbed his chin and glanced at his watch. "Why?"

"Because I have to go to the hospital, and I don't want Grace left alone."

"Mom." She coupled my name with an epic eyeroll.

"Takes hours to clear a homicide scene. I'll be here till you get back." He grimaced. "We need your formal statement, but it can wait till morning."

"Thank you. Help yourself to coffee."

I drove to the hospital with my mind on the man I'd shot.

Did Stan have help for his lunchtime raids on Patriot's warehouse? Amber? Had she given him my name?

I pulled into the hospital lot without noticing how I got

there. The car knew the way.

Stan had poisoned Clayton, Denise, and Hubb, but shot at me and Anarchy. Why?

I leaned my head against the steering wheel and groaned. Stan didn't seem like a poisoner. In my mind, poisoners were wily and subtle. Stan seemed like a shooter—blunt, quick, violent.

If I was right, and Stan hadn't poisoned the people at Patriot, who had?

Were the theft and murders separate issues?

Unable to decide, I hauled myself out of the car and pushed through the doors to the emergency room waiting area.

"Good evening, Mrs. Russell," said the receptionist. She knew my name. Recognized me. And she didn't look remotely familiar. If ever there was a sign I visited too often, that was it.

"I'm here for Mrs. Jones."

She nodded. "Doctor is seeing her now."

"Thank you." I sat down to wait.

"You've been here often lately."

"Just one of those weeks." I glanced around the empty waiting room. "Slow night?"

She shrugged. "You caught us at a lull."

"How much longer for Mrs. Jones?"

She glanced at her watch. "Thirty minutes."

Plenty of time to peek in on Anarchy. I stood. "I'll be back in a few minutes."

She nodded, her attention drawn to a pregnant couple waddling through the doors.

I hurried down the hall, taking lefts and rights as if the hospital's blueprints were etched on my brain. When I reached intensive care, I slowed, peered around a corner, and assessed the activity at the nurses' station.

Empty.

I raced past the abandoned station and dashed into Anarchy's room.

The dim light from the monitors revealed his face. He slept. Peacefully. I took the chair next to his bed and claimed his hand.

His eyes flew open. "Ellison?"

"Shh. I'm not supposed to be here."

He grinned. "Rule breaker."

"We can't all follow the rules. You'd be out of a job."

"I'm glad you're here." His gaze scanned the dark room and he frowned. "What time is it? Why are you here so late?"

"Stan broke into my house."

The monitor's beeps nearly deafened me.

"I'm fine. Grace is fine."

"I sense a 'but.'"

"Stan hit your mom on the head. The doctors are checking her out now. "

"What happened?"

"I shot him." I swallowed. "He's dead."

Anarchy's fingers tightened around mine—their warmth melted the ice around my heart. "You okay?" he asked.

No. "I will be. Peters is at the house with Grace. He's been..." I searched for a word.

"Nicer," Anarchy suggested.

"That's one way to describe it."

"He doesn't want to break in a new partner."

I nodded—there was no replacing Anarchy. "Why did a poisoner start shooting people?" I voiced the question that had bothered me since the moment I'd found Stan in my house.

"I don't know."

I squared my shoulders. "What if Clayton or Hubb discovered the theft and someone else poisoned them?"

Anarchy frowned. "Like who?"

"Amber. Maybe she had a relationship with Stan. They could be in on it together."

"Did you mention your theory to Peters?"

"No."

"You should. He'll find her." A frown creased his brow. "I'd help, but I'm useless right now."

"Your job is to heal quickly."

"Oh?"

"Wedding. Or have you forgotten?"

"I didn't forget. If I had a license, I'd call the hospital chaplain and ask him to marry us right now."

I shook my head. "Tempting as that is, my family would never forgive us."

"Does that mean Frances would give you the silent treatment for months?"

"Maybe a year."

"And you don't see that as a positive?"

I leaned forward and kissed his cheek. "Speaking of mothers, I should check on yours."

He tightened his hold on my hand. "Wait."

I waited.

"I love you."

I kissed him a second time. "Love you too. Now hurry up and get better."

~

Tap, tap.

I opened an eye and scowled at the door.

Despite the warning inherent in my expression, it opened. Aggie stuck her head into my room. "Your mother called."

Imagine that.

"Also, Karen Morris is here."

"Karen?"

"Yes."

"Here?"

"Yes."

"Now?" I groaned. "If you'll offer her coffee, I'll be down in ten minutes."

Aggie stepped into my room, held out a mug of heaven, and said, "I already offered her fresh coffee. And she's happy to wait."

I took a long sip, then swung my feet to the floor. "Ten minutes."

A quick trip to the bathroom included a toothbrush, a hairbrush, and a quick swipe with a blush brush. Then I threw on a pair of khaki slacks and a camp shirt and headed downstairs.

Karen sat in the living room where Max monitored her cookie consumption.

"I'm sorry to keep you waiting."

She rose from the couch, and Max hoovered the crumbs that fell from her lap.

We hugged.

"I'm sorry about what happened at Clayton's service," I said.

"Not your fault."

We separated, and Karen stared with wet eyes at the cookie in her hands. "The man who shot your fiancé—did he murder Clayton?"

"Maybe. His name was Stan Klemp."

Karen didn't react. The name meant nothing to her.

"He's dead."

Her face crumpled, and she sagged. "Dead?"

Maybe she did know him.

"I need to know why," she whispered. "Why did he kill Clayton?" She put the cookie on her plate. "The children want answers. I want answers."

"Stan worked for Patriot and was fired for stealing."

She took a fresh cookie from the platter. "Why kill Clayton?"

"Maybe he wanted revenge," I suggested.

"Clayton didn't fire him."

"Did Clayton take his coffee black?"

She blinked, and her head moved from side to side. "With sugar. Wait. That's not right. With sweetener. He gained a few pounds and switched to the sugar-free stuff."

"Stan may have poisoned something in the break room."

"Like the sweetener?"

"Maybe."

"It can't be the sweetener." The cookie crumbled in her fingers. "Hubb drinks his coffee black."

"Don't even think it." I spoke to Max, who eyed the crumbs on Karen's plate with an open mouth and avaricious gleam in his eyes. Would she let him lick?

He settled onto his haunches and sighed.

Karen glanced at the crumbs. "The cookies are very good."

"Just think, if I had Aggie years ago, you could have halved your baking."

"I love baking. It was a pleasure to help you." She frowned. "If it's not the sweetener, what else could it be?"

"No idea."

Without a cookie to keep them busy, Karen's fingers laced together, and a single tear ran down her cheek. "I'm a terrible friend. Your fiancé was shot, and I didn't even ask about him."

"The doctors say he'll recover."

"Thank heavens." She leaned forward and helped herself to a fresh cookie.

Max tracked its progress. He drooled.

Karen chewed.

I thought about Stan Klemp. "You're sure Clayton never mentioned Stan?" Theft seemed like something he'd mention.

Karen closed her eyes. Considering my question, or savoring Aggie's cookie? "Mostly he talked about profit and loss and the percentage of product lost to spoilage."

"Ellison?" Mother's voice carried from the front hall.

Karen stiffened.

"In the living room," I called.

She stormed in. "What happened here last—" She spotted Karen. "Good morning."

"Mother, you remember Karen?"

"Of course."

Karen stood, and Max sucked up the fallen crumbs. "How nice to see you, Mrs. Walford."

"I'm so sorry for your loss."

"Thank you." Karen brushed a crumb from her shirt. "Ellison, I'll let you visit with your mother."

"You're welcome to stay." I'd only downed one cup of coffee—I was nowhere near ready to deal with Mother by myself.

"I should go." Karen edged toward the door. "If I think of anything, I'll let you know. Also, please tell your housekeeper her cookies are marvelous. I want the recipe."

"Of course. I'll walk you to the door."

"No, no. I'll see myself out." She left me with Mother.

"How's Anarchy?"

I blinked my surprise. I'd expected a lecture on shooting intruders or dead bodies or both. "He'll recover."

"Wonderful news." She pursed her lips, and I waited for the zinger. "How close are you and Karen?"

"We're friends."

"And Mel Langford?"

"Closer friends."

Mother frowned. "There's something rotten with that company."

"How do you know?"

"Byron Clifford had too many last night and told your father."

"What's wrong? What problems?"

Mother's sour expression told me everything. Daddy had been vague. He'd offered no details. "Your father wouldn't break Byron's confidence." She sighed.

"What do you suppose it is?"

"Something unsavory. I don't want you included in the gossip." In her own way, Mother looked out for me.

"Any guesses as to what Byron told Daddy?"

"No, but it's bad enough your father made me promise to come see you in person."

"Would he tell me?"

She directed a death glare at me. Why would Daddy tell me something he'd withheld from his wife?

I was better at keeping secrets. I didn't say that out loud. I'd already reached my daily quota for near-death experiences.

"Distance yourself from those women."

"That doesn't seem fair. Their husbands ran Patriot, not them."

"Don't be naïve, Ellison. When this horrible secret leaks, they'll be tainted by the scandal."

"Thank you for your concern."

Deep lines cut into her forehead. "You're not taking my advice."

"Where would I be if my friends abandoned me when scandal touched me?" I thought of the women who'd stood by me despite the bodies.

Mother's expression turned vinegary. "What happened here last night?"

"A man named Stan Klemp broke into the house, attacked Celeste—"

"Celeste is here?"

"Celeste is in the hospital. The doctors are keeping her for observation."

Mother gave a relieved sigh. Because Celeste wasn't in residence or because her injuries weren't severe?

"He attacked Celeste, and I shot him."

She wrinkled her nose as if she'd smelled rotting vegetables. "This is related to Patriot, isn't it?"

"Probably. Stan Klemp shot Anarchy."

"Did he kill Clayton?"

"I don't think so."

"Why not?"

"Because he didn't strike me as the kind of man with the patience for poison."

"Then who?"

"There's a woman who works at Patriot. In all likelihood, she gave Stan my address. It's possible she killed Clayton."

"The police are looking for her?"

"They are." Maybe.

"She knows where you live?"

"Anyone with a phone book and a bit of patience can figure out where I live."

"Are you safe? Anarchy can't protect you."

"I can protect myself."

"Don't be ridiculous." Mother's faith in me defied words.

"I appreciate your concern, but we'll be fine."

Brnng, brnng.

Hopefully Aggie would interrupt with an urgent message.

Brnng, brnng.

"Don't make light of this, Ellison."

Brnng, brnng.

"It's not just your safety at risk. What about Grace?"

"Mrs. Walford?" Aggie spoke from the room's entrance. "I'm sorry to interrupt, but Mr. Walford is on the line."

Mother looked at her watch, frowned, then swept out of the living room to take her call in Henry's study.

I claimed a cookie.

"More coffee?" asked Aggie.

"Please."

I nibbled the edge of the cookie and thought. Hard. What had Byron Clifford told Daddy? What kind of trouble at Patriot? More than a former employee stealing product? What was big enough to justify murder?

CHAPTER TWENTY

I held open the front door and hoped my smile hid my feelings. I'd rather move back to Mother's than welcome Celeste into my home a second time.

She pressed her fingers to her temples and sighed dramatically.

"How are you feeling?" I asked.

"Head injuries are so tricky. I should rest." She walked to the stairs. "Please bring me some tea. You do have tea?"

"I'm sure we do."

"Herbal. Chamomile would be nice."

If we had tea, it was a box of Lipton hiding behind a jar of crunchy peanut butter in the pantry. Grace ate only creamy—and that jar had a second birthday coming. "I'll see what I can do."

She nodded, then winced as if the tiniest movement pained her.

"Will you be well enough to join us for dinner?"

"Who is *us*?"

"Grace and me."

She gave another dramatic sigh. "I still say Anarchy should

come home. I'd take better care of him than the hospital. I wouldn't let him work."

Anarchy had insisted on reviewing case files. "Peters gave him one file," I replied.

"Peters. Is that the man in the rumpled raincoat?"

"Anarchy's partner."

Celeste sniffed and climbed the stairs. "Remember, chamomile."

If she weren't Anarchy's mother, I'd serve her coffee. I walked into the kitchen where Aggie's formation of a meatloaf had claimed Max's full attention. "Do we have herbal tea?"

She paused with hands covered in meatloaf mix. "We do."

"Celeste would like a cup. If you'll tell me where it is, I'll make it."

"The pantry, behind the peanut butter." She waited till I was halfway out of the kitchen and added, "Your mother called. She and your father are coming for dinner."

"Celeste is here." Celeste had monologued about vaginas at our last family dinner. I clutched the door to the pantry. "Did you tell Mother about Celeste?"

"I mentioned that." She frowned. "I also mentioned I was making meatloaf."

Aggie's meatloaf was Daddy's favorite.

"Does Celeste eat meat?" I couldn't remember.

"I'm also serving Brussel sprouts, baked potatoes, and a salad. Think of it as a dry run for the wedding."

I groaned, found a box of Celestial Seasonings Sleepytime on the shelf behind the peanut butter (who knew?), and hid it behind my back. If Mr. Coffee saw me with decaffeinated tea, he'd worry.

Aggie covered the meatloaf with her special sauce, and I put a kettle on to boil.

"She wanted chamomile, but this will have to do."

"Tell her I bought it at a health food store."

"Cup and saucer or mug?" If I used good china, Celeste would accuse me of putting on airs. If used a mug, she'd think I'd put in no effort. I couldn't win.

"Mug."

I filled an earthenware pot with the heated water, dropped a few tea bags on a plate, and took a pottery mug from the cabinet. I put everything on a tray, carried it to the blue room, and knocked on the door.

A loud snore answered me.

I turned on my heel and took the tray back to the kitchen.

"She insists on chamomile?"

"She's asleep."

Aggie slid the meatloaf into the oven. "Maybe you should lie down for an hour."

"I have too much on my mind." No way could I rest.

Ding, dong.

"I'll get it."

The possibility of raw meat gone, Max followed me to the front door.

I pulled on the handle and Libba breezed in. "How are you?"

"Fine."

She searched my face. "And Anarchy?"

"Still in the hospital."

"And?"

"He'll be fine."

She exhaled. "That's wonderful news."

"It is." I glanced out the door. Libba's car was not in my driveway. "Charlie told you about last night?"

"Stop smirking," she replied.

"I'm not smirking."

"Yes, you are."

"Why don't the two of you come for dinner? Aggie made meatloaf."

Her eyes narrowed with suspicion. "Who else is coming?"

I scratched behind Max's ears and tried to look innocent.

"Answer the question."

"Mother and Daddy."

She recoiled.

"And Celeste."

"Have you lost your ever-loving mind?"

"Say you'll come. Please."

"I can't."

"Some friend you are."

"I can't. I promised to take dinner to Mel and Hubb."

"You? Dinner?"

"I'm picking it up from the club." Libba was the rare woman with her own membership. It didn't mean she could play golf during men's tee times. Didn't mean she was allowed in the men's grill.

"Have you ever wondered what would happen if women got equal treatment?"

"What do you mean?"

"Take Mel for example. Her father gave Hubb the reins to the family company. I can't help but think Mel would have done a better..."

"What?"

I held up a finger. "I had a thought."

"You?"

"It happens. Would you say Karen and Clayton were happy?"

"As far as I know."

"What about Mel and Hubb?"

"You can't think Mel is involved. She adores Hubb."

"I need to talk to Anarchy."

"Now?"

"Now. Please tell Aggie I went to the hospital." I grabbed my handbag from its spot atop the bombé chest, hopped into my car, and raced down the drive.

The hospital corridors blurred as I hurried to Anarchy's

room. He'd tell me my theory was crazy, Peters would find Amber, and this whole mess would go away.

Or I was right.

"Oomph."

"I apologize," I said to the man I'd bumped in my hurry to get to Anarchy.

He turned.

"Hubb." I blinked. "What are you doing here?"

"Waiting on Mel." He nodded toward a hospital room. "She's visiting Byron Clifford."

"Byron's in the hospital?"

"Heart attack."

"That seems impossible. He had drinks with my father just the other night. How is he?"

"Ellison!" Mel stepped out of Byron's room. "What a surprise. You're here to visit Byron?"

"Anarchy."

"Of course. So awful what happened."

"He's recovering."

"Good news."

"How's Byron?"

"The doctors are still running tests. He and my father were the best of friends." She patted under her eyes. "He helps Hubb run Patriot."

Hubb opened his mouth as if he meant to dispute Byron's role, but remained quiet.

"Is that so?" I asked.

Mel nodded. "I don't know where we'd be without him."

Was that grinding sound Hubb's teeth?

I smiled at Hubb. "Mel tells me she's spent time at the office so you can rest."

The grinding sound was definitely Hubb's teeth.

"I'm enjoying it," said Mel. Rats, rotting strawberries, theft, falling crates—she was welcome to it. "We won't keep you." She rested her hand on Hubb's arm. "Libba's bringing dinner. So kind of her. Hubb's useless in the kitchen, and I've been at the office most of the day."

For an instant, annoyance flashed across his face.

I swallowed. "Did you hear the man who shot Anarchy broke into my house?"

Mel gasped and pressed her hands to her cheeks. "Ellison, no!"

Hubb's eyes widened. "What happened?"

"I shot him."

Mel sagged. "Is he dead?"

"Yes."

"Did he admit his crimes?" she asked. "He killed Clayton and Denise, almost killed Hubb."

"He said he didn't do it, claimed someone framed him." Would they see through my lie? I shifted my gaze to the end of the corridor and Anarchy's room.

"Framed him?" asked Mel.

"He didn't know anything about the poison." I took a step backward.

Mel covered her mouth with her palm. "If he's telling the truth, there's still a killer at Patriot."

"He was lying. The man shot a cop." The certainty in Hubb's voice smoothed the worry lines from Mel's forehead.

"You're probably right." I took another step. "If you'll excuse me?"

"Of course," said Mel. "Please give your fiancé our regards."

I nodded, hurried down the hall, and pretended I didn't feel the combined weight of their stares on my back.

Anarchy lifted his gaze from a bed covered in papers.

"Peters told me he gave you one file."

"This is one file."

"It's enormous and the doctor said to rest."

He grinned and cleared papers from the bed's edge.

"Why are you smiling?"

"I like it when you fuss at me."

I'd flown over here with a theory to share. The opposite of restful. "Get used to it."

"I'm surprised to see you." He patted the cleared spot on the bed.

"I missed you." Not a lie.

"Missed you too. But…"

"But?"

"You haven't been gone long. Something's bothering you."

I sat. "Am I so easy to read?"

"Tell me what's worrying you."

"I don't think Stan killed Clayton or Denise."

He didn't laugh or roll his eyes or dismiss my theory. "Then who?"

I glanced at the closed door. "Hubb Langford."

"He's a victim."

I waggled my hand. "The other victims are dead."

"What's his motive?"

I glanced at my hands folded in my lap. "He and Mel don't own Patriot, a trust does."

"So?"

"If they divorced, the company and Hubb's job would go to Mel."

"They seem like a happy couple."

"She seems happy. I'm not so sure about Hubb."

He ceded my point with a slight nod. "Why kill Clayton?"

"I think Hubb stole from Patriot, and Clayton discovered the theft."

Anarchy rubbed his jaw. "What about Stan Klemp?"

"He helped Hubb steal, but he didn't poison anyone."

"Hubb's behind the poison? You're suggesting Langford poisoned himself."

"Did you find the source of the poison?" I asked.

Anarchy glanced at a sheet of paper. "There's a kitchenette for the executives. We found poison in the artificial sweetener."

"Aha!"

"What?"

"Hubb Langford drinks his coffee black."

The door behind me opened, and Anarchy stiffened.

I glanced over my shoulder. Hubb and Mel stood in the doorway.

Hubb looked pale.

Mel looked green. "Is it true?"

"Of course not," Hubb snapped.

"Have a forensic accountant go through Patriot's books," I suggested.

"Shut up, Ellison. You've done enough damage."

"You gave Stan my address." Stan had attacked Celeste. Suppose Grace had decided to watch the late show? "How could you?"

Hubb bared his teeth.

"You lied when you said you didn't recognize him."

"Shut up."

"You'd lose everything in a divorce, so you decided to steal."

"Hubb?" Mel's voice quavered.

"She's lying."

I was telling the absolute truth. "You've been to Patriot, Mel. You saw how he's run the place. Unhappy customers. Theft. Rats." A chill trickled down my spine.

"She's right," Mel murmured. "Daddy's company is in disarray."

"Daddy's company. I'm so sick of your father, I could die. He didn't trust me to run things my way. He had that drunk Byron peering over my shoulder. This is his fault."

"You're blaming my father for your failings?"

"Your father was an ass."

Mel gasped as if Hubb had slapped her. "He gave you a chance."

"And made me thank him for it every day for the rest of his miserable life."

Mel shifted her gaze to me. "A forensic accountant, you say? Do you know one?"

"I do," said Anarchy.

Hubb's face was a study in fury. "They won't find anything."

"Clayton did." My voice was small, but Hubb heard me.

He sneered. "You can't prove a thing."

"The circumstantial evidence is strong," said Anarchy.

"My lawyer will argue Klemp is the killer."

And Stan couldn't testify, because I'd killed him.

"Come on, Mel. We're leaving."

Tears welled in Mel's eyes, and she shook her head. "I'm not going anywhere with you."

"Don't be ridiculous. You can't believe this wild speculation."

"Just go."

Hubb disappeared through the door, and I stood and went to Mel. "What can I do?"

She stepped away from my outstretched hands. "You've done enough." She shook her head. "That's not fair. Byron warned me. Talk to him. He may have the proof you need." Mel turned on her heel and marched out of the room.

"That went well."

"You knew they were outside?"

"I knew they might be." I returned to Anarchy's bedside. "What happens now?"

"The boring part. Peters and I put together the case, convince a prosecutor, see it through."

I reclaimed my seat and took his hand in mine. "What if he runs?"

"We'll catch him. For years, I cared more about justice than anything."

"Now you don't?"

"No. I still care. But I care about you more. And we have a wedding to plan."

MOTHER GAPED at me across the dinner table. "You're serious? Hubb Langford is responsible?"

I nodded.

"I don't understand." She shook her head as if a murderer among her social set was beyond her comprehension. By now, one would think she'd be accustomed.

"Clayton discovered the theft, and Hubb killed him," I replied.

"Yes, yes." She waved away Clayton's murder. "But you're saying Hubb poisoned himself."

"Who'd suspect him of murder if he was also a victim?"

"And the secretary?"

"Maybe Denise knew Hubb stole. Maybe she was additional cover for the murder. Only Hubb knows."

Daddy paused with a bite of Aggie's meatloaf halfway to his mouth. "I never liked him."

Celeste pushed a Brussel sprout around her plate. "I blame the patriarchy. If that woman's father had trusted her to lead the company, her husband wouldn't have killed people."

Daddy stared.

Celeste pointed the tines of her fork at him. "You don't understand. You don't have a vagina."

Libba sprayed wine from her nose, and Charlie shifted in his chair. "What happens next with the case?"

I offered him a grateful smile. "The police will file charges."

"From what Byron told me, if they can't convict Hubb for murder, they'll get him for theft." Daddy chewed his meatloaf.

"Byron should have put down the bourbon bottle and kept better tabs on Hubb," said Mother.

For once, we agreed.

"Did you see Byron when you went to the hospital?" Mother eyed a Brussel sprout with distaste. "What's wrong with asparagus?"

"Nothing. And, no, I didn't see Byron. Just Anarchy."

Her lips curled. "Such a shame you'll have to postpone the wedding."

Celeste nodded hard enough to give herself whiplash. "A shame."

"We're not postponing anything."

"But Anarchy's still in the hospital," Mother replied.

"He'll be out in a few days."

"Your honeymoon." Mother put down her fork and clasped her hands. "He won't be well enough to travel."

The whole table pretended a delayed honeymoon was Mother's real objection to a wedding in less than two weeks.

I smiled sweetly. "We'll go later in the summer."

Daddy rested his hand on Mother's. "She's sure about this, Frances. So is he. It's time to wish them well."

Mother's pursed lips said she'd rather discuss vaginas with Celeste, but she gave me a regal nod. "Promise me you'll avoid finding more bodies before the wedding."

We all knew how that would go. But I promised—practiced. "I do."

ALSO BY JULIE MULHERN

The Country Club Murders

The Deep End

Guaranteed to Bleed

Clouds in My Coffee

Send in the Clowns

Watching the Detectives

Cold as Ice

Shadow Dancing

Back Stabbers

Telephone Line

Stayin' Alive

Killer Queen

Night Moves

Lyin' Eyes

The Poppy Fields Adventures

Fields' Guide to Abduction

Fields' Guide to Assassins

Fields' Guide to Voodoo

Fields' Guide to Fog

Fields' Guide to Pharaohs

Fields' Guide to Dirty Money

Fields' Guide to Smuggling

The Bayou Series

Bayou Moon

Bayou Nights

CPSIA information can be obtained
at www.ICGtesting.com
Printed in the USA
LVHW052330180723
752727LV00010B/354